C000145851

# Oxymoron Murders

# & Other Short Stories of the Unexpected

By
Jay Myers

*The Oxymoron Murders*
*& Other Short Stories of the Unexpected*

Text Copyright
© 2022 Jay Myers
All rights reserved

e-book: September 2022
Paperback: September 2022

*Published on the day of my father's 100th birthday!*

\* \* \*

Fiction by Jay Myers
*Twenty Million Leagues Above the Sea*
*The Colour Conspiracy*
*I Shot the Sheriff*

\* \* \*

Facebook: @JayMyersFiction
Instagram: @jay_myers_novels

To Sam & Mildred Myers
Always remembered
Always loved


For Elaine


And to . . .
*Midas, Buddy & Dakota*

In Memory of:

*Dave Mitchinson*

Colleague, Friend, Gentle Soul

"It is an oxymoron. Call it a literary paradox if you have a mind to. Henrietta's account of the crime is a contradiction of events. Meaning is muddled, confused – simply absurd. And yet . . . I shall prove otherwise!"

Detective Roule
(The Oxymoron Murders)

# Contents

Frank pulled out a chair from the table – a gesture of welcome. The visitor moved uneasily as if her joints had become inflexible, and sat down. Frank closed the door and took a seat on the opposite side of the table.

"Have you never seen a snow woman before?"

# North
# of
# 58

The flight from Winnipeg to Churchill was the last to land before the big storm roared into town.

Frank Hathaway made the same trip every year, catching the first flight out of Winnipeg for his week-long vacation, north of the 58$^{th}$ parallel, about 870km south of the Arctic Circle.

Nothing else mattered to him except the power and splendour of nature itself, harsh though it could be at this time of year. When winter storms bully and bluster. When snow reshapes the landscape. Blinding white, tranquil and bitter cold.

Spending a week in northern Manitoba in February on the western shore of Hudson Bay, 1,000km from home, was not everyone's picture of a dream holiday. In Frank's case, it had become an idyllic refuge from his daily routine.

Only a single paved road connected the airport with the town of Churchill and its 13 residential streets.

The drove of polar bears – as many as 1,000 – had long since made their annual migration northward towards the capes and headlands of Hudson Bay, where the hard-set, freshwater winter ice offered the perfect overland route to hunt seals throughout the winter.

Gone, too, for the season, were 58,000 beluga whales and more than 200 species of birds. There would be no pacific loons or harlequin ducks, willow ptarmigans, ringed-billed gulls or horned larks.

Also on the missing list for the harsh winter were short-billed dowitcher shorebirds, snow buntings, red-throated loons, northern waterthrush wood warblers and long-tailed jaegers.

Only the dazzling Northern Lights remained on stage for the frigid winter months to entertain those who were interested in witnessing such a stunning spectacle – weather permitting.

\* \* \*

Frank Hathaway was a kind, yet unremarkable man of average height, weight and intelligence. He owned *Hathaway's Hardware* with three store locations. He was also happily married to Helen and had two teenage boys and a six-year-old black Labrador named Yardley.

This year marked Frank's tenth trip to Churchill, population 899. The nearest city was Thompson on the Burntwood River, about 400km southwest, population 13,678.

It was also Frank's fiftieth birthday. To mark this landmark occasion, Frank had managed to purchase – with the blessing of his family – a small log cabin northeast of the town of Churchill.

The cabin was a small, sturdy old building standing proudly within a stone's throw of Hudson Bay itself, well distanced from virtually all human activity – from the retail outlets at *Bayport Plaza* and the *Duke of Marlborough School* to the *Churchill Volunteer Fire Department* and the *Iceberg Inn*, two miles southeast of the Churchill River, where Frank had reserved the same room for the past nine seasons.

Frank called his newly acquired patch of real estate *Hathaway's House* where, for one week in the calendar year, he would have the freedom to think or dream, or do nothing at all if he so wished and not utter a word to another living soul. He aspired to feel like a free spirit and allow nature to wrap its arms around him as it wished.

Frank's family and closest friends had no idea what compelled him to spend part of his precious vacation time, year after year, in such a harsh place at this time of year, secluded from the rest of the world. For his part, Frank was also unable to satisfy their puzzlement with a reasonable explanation.

He loved the exhilaration of the North and had never tired of the unique experience, unlike his family who had no passion for winter and all its white, cold and icy baggage.

Frank enjoyed playing tennis and golf in the summer, and had always shunned winter sports his entire life.

Skiing, skating or ice fishing had never tempted him. Nor had he ever contemplated the prospect of hunting in any season.

This was different.

As the aircraft made its choppy descent towards Churchill Airport, Frank couldn't see any familiar landmarks. The howling winter storm had begun.

"Ladies and gentlemen, this is the captain speaking. We will shortly be landing in Churchill. Please make sure your seatbelts are fastened and your seat is in the upright position. I do apologise for the bumpy ride. As you can see from the swirling snow, we seem to be at the mercy of a sub-arctic weather system, which is not unusual for this time of year. We hope you have a pleasant day and make sure you keep warm."

Frank came well prepared with flannel shirt jackets, elephant corduroy trousers, alpaca socks, snow mitts and goggles and, for the first time now that he owned his own cabin, a pair of egg-shaped gawky-looking snowshoes.

He also had one other piece of winter apparel: a Russian Cossack trapper hat made of muskrat fur with long, generous ear flaps and a wide front brim. It could be fastened under the chin to cover the ears and lower jaw, providing protection from the penetrating bite of the Arctic cold.

The hat cost $200 and was a birthday gift from his wife and two sons. Frank wore it with immense pride as he walked through the aircraft to disembark.

Frank didn't care about the weather. A snow blizzard at this time of year was not unusual. Frank had seen plenty of them living in Winnipeg. Though, even he would have to admit that this storm was different.

Frank had always been fortunate when he travelled. He managed to secure a ride in the last taxi leaving Churchill Airport. Driving conditions were near to impossible. Frank didn't care.

The taxi took him as far as the driver dared. The road had come to an abrupt end. The drifting snow had made certain that no vehicle would travel any further. Frank paid the driver, said, *'thank you'*, took his suitcase and walked the rest of the way to his cabin – *Hathaway's House*.

It took him more than twenty minutes or so he reckoned, and he whistled the whole time, improvising tune after tune despite the harsh conditions.

Stacked in front of the cabin door and protected from the drifting snow by a substantial roof overhang were a handful of cardboard boxes filled with food and drink, and a collection of assorted supplies including a large snow shovel.

During his previous visits to Churchill, Frank had befriended a number of local residents, all of whom promised to provide him with essential provisions for his week's visit including propane for heat, light and cooking. Although Frank kept offering to pay, his wishes fell on deaf ears.

"Hello . . . Helen? It's Frank. I'm in the cabin."

"Your voice is faint, dear. The connection isn't very good, I'm afraid."

"It's snowing here . . . a lot . . . I mean, there's a big storm on its way."

"Sorry dear, your voice is breaking up. It's snowing here too – hello? Frank? Can you hear me?"

"Yes, just barely. There's this storm –"

"What's that noise in the background?"

"The wind. That's why – hello?"

"I can hardly hear you, dear."

"How are the boys –? Hello? Helen? Are you still there? Hello?"

"Call me later. Enjoy the –"

"I love you, Helen . . . Helen?"

Frank replaced the battery in his cell phone – he always carried a spare. The signal was dead.

Although it was fast approaching noon, daylight had been choked by the onslaught of snow. The terrain had become distorted and unrecognisable. The skyline separating ground and sky had vanished. The snow was beating down at all angles, driven by the high-pitched screaming wind.

Frank turned on his VHF radio – he sold such things in his hardware store and had borrowed one for the trip – and managed to receive the local weather forecast. The newscaster's voice was noticeably woeful:

*'More than 80 centimetres of snow are predicted, with winds gusting to nearly 110 kilometres per hour and temperatures as low as minus forty-five degrees centigrade . . .'*

Frank thought it could be a record for this time of year. He smiled at the prospect, then lost the radio signal.

* * *

The storm raged for three days and as many nights. The following morning, the snow had drifted up to the cabin windows. Frank donned his snowshoes and skittered across the glistening ocean of whiteness.

He embraced the bitter, freezer-like air wrapped around his partially exposed face and was pleased that he had taken a pair of snow goggles.

The sky was a silky, deep blue and the sun glittered sharply against the densely packed tonnage of snow.

Frank marvelled at the sight.

It was raw and brutal.

The morning was calm and serene, as if nothing of any consequence had ever fallen from the sky. Frank was at once overcome with nature's potent hand. Never before had he seen such windswept desolation and brilliant whiteness – boundless layers of snow dunes as if shaped by a master stonemason.

Smooth and exquisite.

Only the sharp-edged profile of Frank's snowshoes spoiled the flawless glaze of the terrain, for not a single impression of man or animal could be detected in the snow.

Along this vast white plain, there were no familiar landmarks and no sign of human life save for a small, solitary cabin known as *Hathaway's House* owned by a kind, yet unremarkable man from Winnipeg, whose name was Frank Hathaway.

By all accounts, there was nothing of interest to be

seen. Except for . . . well, perhaps Frank had been mistaken. Yet, there appeared to be something – an object – in the distance standing upright, serene and immobile.

Frank embraced the new day with vigour and a sense of adventure like any young schoolboy. Surely, he knew at once what awaited him in the distance – it could only be a snowman, he thought.

He circled the finely sculpted figure, observing it from all angles. It was much more intricate and well proportioned than he had first anticipated for it was, without question, a life-size *snow woman*. Here! In the middle of nowhere.

Carefully arranged white spruce branches shaped her bountiful hair and also accounted for her slender and delicate hands and fingers. Three gemstones adorned her face: brown jasper for her eyes, pink agate for her nose and light blue quartz – one of the rarest colours – for her mouth.

For a fleeting moment, Frank thought that she too had regarded him with an equal measure of fascination. He laughed away such whimsical thoughts, blaming it on the weather and the play of light against her finely crafted face.

He took off his snow mitts and tried to take a picture of the *snow woman* on his phone. His fingers were too cold. He fumbled trying to complete the task. Then he tried to call his wife. The speed-dial key was easier to manipulate. The line was busy. He would call her later.

As he walked back to the cabin, he turned around repeatedly to stare at the lady of snow, contemplating who had built her and when, for her construction could not have been a simple task.

Was it one person had done the job and where did he or she come from? There were no footprints or other evidence of activity around the site that Frank could identify, unless such marks had been erased by the gusting wind.

Where did the snow builders locate such fine-looking white spruce branches, for there were no trees to be seen in any direction?

Where would such colourful gemstones have been collected to adorn the lady's face? More importantly, how could such a thing remain upright after such a storm?

Back at the cabin Frank tried to contact his wife. Her number was still busy. There was a fault on the line, he thought.

Frank spent his time listening to the radio when he could, reading, cooking and exploring the lay of the land. In just a matter of days, he had mastered the knack of walking in his cumbersome snowshoes and thought he might buy a pair for his wife and two sons.

He left the cabin three times every day for short to medium-length outings, never losing sight of the cabin's roofline against the sky.

On one occasion, he even managed to take a picture of himself standing on the surface of Hudson Bay itself, revelling in his own isolation.

He danced in sprawling elliptical circles on the snow-packed ice until he was too dizzy to continue and fell to his knees a happy man.

\* \* \*

Frank was certainly not short of food or the ability to prepare a tasty meal for himself. To mark the midway point of his holiday, he roasted a whole chicken served with a heap of mashed potatoes topped with gravy, a fusion of tinned corn and tinned peas, a single raw carrot cut into long thin strips and a chunky stick of French bread.

On the table in pride of place were three, tall and slender, dark green bottles each labelled *vin rouge*. Evidently homemade, Frank concluded – a gift from one of the local residents.

*Who shall I thank?* He wondered.

Halfway through his dinner and having already consumed the first bottle of wine, Frank heard a thump on his door. At first, he ignored it until a second, third and fourth muffled blow prompted his immediate attention.

*Who could be visiting me at this time of night and in such weather? It could be the winemaker,* he thought.

Here on the vast Hudson Bay-Arctic Lowlands, the cabin's pale goldenrod light was a powerful beacon, a singular point of interest to anyone who might have seen it.

When Frank opened the door to his cabin, he gasped. He was unable to speak until his brain had a chance to process the impossible.

"I saw your light through the window. May I come in?"

Frank backpedalled.

"I thought you might like company tonight."

Frank was bewildered. He looked long and hard at the visitor . . . baffled . . . mystified. Words failed him.

"I dare not stay too long. You understand."

Frank understood only too well, then blinked twice and nodded.

"But . . . you are –"

"Yes, I know who I am," said the visitor.

Frank pulled out a chair from the table – a gesture of welcome. The visitor moved uneasily as if her joints had become inflexible, and sat down. Frank closed the door and took a seat on the opposite side of the table.

"Have you never seen a *snow woman* before?"

"Not *talking* and *sitting* at my table! How is this possible? Why are you here? How –"

"I was curious to see you. We are both alike – alone in the snow," she said. "I like people. I live near your cabin."

Frank was flushed, animated in spirit and in voice.

The *snow woman's* facial expressions were subtle, yet real. The gemstones that made up her eyes, nose and mouth twitched as she spoke. Her voice was delicate and sweet.

A single gemstone of light blue quartz fell from the corner of her lips, bounced off the empty wine bottle and came to rest, miraculously, in Frank's hand. He walked over to her, returned the piece of quartz to its rightful place and touched her shoulder with his fingers. She flinched. He withdrew his hand quickly, for the snow was beginning to melt.

"I'm sorry," said Frank.

"For what?"

"For making your arm drip. I think I should open the door. I wouldn't want you to feel uncomfortable."

"You are so kind."

Frank put on his coat and opened the door to the inhospitable, frigid night air, but he refused to wear his hat or snow mitts out of respect for his guest.

"Can I offer you something to eat? I have more than enough chicken and vegetables. Coffee . . . tea – no, I don't suppose that's a good idea, is it?"

"Hot food does not agree with me."

"Will you have a glass of wine? It's been in the fridge all day."

She nodded.

"I only have red. It's very pleasant, if you have a mind to try it."

She nodded again. Frank was convinced that she had smiled at him. He poured some wine into a small glass and placed it in her stylish, yet delicate fingers made of white spruce branches. Frank watched in disbelief as the *snow woman* prodded the rim of the glass deep into her snowy mouth until the wine had disappeared.

The wine's effect took hold immediately. The *snow woman's* face had become suffused with colour as if she had been swabbed with a fresh layer of cerise-coloured snow.

"I think the wine suits you," said Frank. "It's nice to see a bit of colour in your face. You look happier."

His cheeks too had also turned a vivid reddish pink, not from the wine . . . from the biting cold air streaming in through the front door. Still, he refused to wear his hat and snow mitts. He opened the second bottle of wine and poured another glass for himself.

"Would you like more wine?" Frank asked, always the perfect gentleman.

"No . . . no. One glass is fine."

"How is it possible that you can speak and move? I must know," asked Frank.

"How do you speak and go from place to place? Can *you* explain it? Asked the *snow woman*."

Frank thought for a minute and said: "No, I can't. I've never thought about it before."

"Then why do you ask me?"

"Because you are made of snow!"

"There is much more to ice and snow than you might think," said the *snow woman*. "I feel pain and joy too. Worry distorts my body – it's not a pretty sight. There is always someone who wants to kick and throw things at you, or worse . . . put their fist through your stomach and laugh at your miserable misfortune. People are cruel. They torment you for the fun of it. When I cry, ice crystals prevent me from seeing clearly. When I laugh, my nose falls off and my mouth goes crooked. There are decent people as well, who appreciate what I am, for they feel sorry for me, mend the wounds and restore my dignity. I am fortunate. I have good friends who look after me each winter. Listen to my heart. Then you will understand."

Frank took the *snow woman* at her word and pressed the side of his face gently on her breast and held this awkward pose without flinching.

He heard a steady beat of sorts, a repetitive pattern like a sigh-and-hiss. To Frank, it was a resilient life force, real and believable without question.

He stepped away sharply as if suddenly embarrassed by his intrusive position and finished the second bottle of wine by pouring another glass for himself. He sat down and rubbed the side of his face. His ear and cheek were wet and frozen.

"I am not as accustomed to the weather as you are. My name is Frank. What is yours, if you have one?"

"I have been called *Nutaryuk* by those who created me. It is a name from the Inuit language and means *fresh snow*."

"Who made you?"

"I did not yet have eyes to see who had shaped the snow."

"And the branches for your hair, and the gemstones for your face?" asked Frank. "How is it possible that such things can be found in these conditions?"

"My happy friends collect charms for me during the summer and save them for me. They visit with me every winter and bring their precious trinkets to make me look pretty."

"You are pretty – the prettiest *snow woman* I have ever met. I must know everything about you. You move and talk and understand me. How is it possible?"

Frank attempted to take a picture of her on his phone, but his fingers were too stiff for the job. *Nutaryuk* did not answer. She looked away from Frank as if bullied and badgered by his questions, and remained sitting in her chair, as tranquil and still as she had been when

14

Frank first saw her in the snow.

Frank stood up sharply. His body trembled. Anger and frustration washed over his face.

"Tell me, I must know!" Frank pleaded with her. "What's it like to be a snowman – woman . . . *snow person*? To be made of snow and yet know everything? Are there others who share your secret? Am I the only one you have talked to? I won't tell anyone. I promise. Tell me what gives you life!"

Frank was groggy, unsure of his footing, unable to hold his head up, and in this single act of frustration, he knocked over the third bottle of wine with a resounding bang.

Dizzy with too much drink, Frank lost his balance, collapsed in his chair, slumped forward and passed out. Tufts of crystallized snow blew into the cabin through the open door and had settled on his head.

* * *

The shrill ring of his phone was a jolt out of the blue. It jarred him awake. By the time Frank had the presence of mind to take action, the phone had gone silent.

Frank was alone and cold to the bone.

He had slept throughout the night.

On the chair where *Nutaryuk* had sat was a small clump of white spruce branches and two gemstones of brown jasper, and on the floor beneath her chair was a handful of translucent slush.

Frank grabbed his boots, hat and mitts, and ran from the cabin, leaving behind his snowshoes, goggles and

15

phone. It was snowing once again.

A thick and heavy deluge.

A second storm.

Relentless squalls.

*"Snow woman! Snow woman!"* he called out.

Frank had forgotten her name.

"I should have written it down," he berated himself out loud. "Come back! Please. I'm sorry. I want to take your picture to show my family and friends. Where are you? I can't see you. You must come back."

Frank trundled onwards, still feeling the effects of too much wine, struggling to advance in the deep snow.

He never looked back and soon lost sight of the cabin's position.

Visibility was zero.

*"Snow woman! Snow woman!"*

"Where are you? I want to be your special friend. I must know –"

His voice trailed off.

The cold was searing.

Frank Hathaway's aspiration to feel like a free spirit and allow nature to wrap its arms around him had taken on a new intensity, a dangerous reality.

"I remember your name now," shouted Frank – a prisoner of the storm.

*"Nutaryuk!"*

"It's me, Frank Hathaway. Where have you gone?"

The emptiness . . . the stillness . . . had unexpectedly become oppressive. Frank had no idea where he was or how far he had strayed from his cabin. It could be one hundred yards or one thousand, and in any direction.

He had been caught in the beast's lair, swallowed by the jaws of the storm, devoured by the snow. Dire though the situation was, it made no difference.

Finding *Nutaryuk* was all that mattered.

So, he carried on the best he could . . . walking, stumbling and falling in the deep snow, calling out the *snow woman's* name, and looking for her footsteps imprinted into the snow.

*She'll pass this way*, thought Frank. *I bet she knows where I am. It can only be a matter of time. She knows the way. She can see better. We'll go back to the cabin together.*

He stopped and waited.

Time was running out for Frank. He called the *snow woman's* name repeatedly. *Nutaryuk* was nowhere to be seen. Frank Hathaway was lost.

Despite the thick padding and insulation of his snow boots, Frank could no longer feel his toes. His feet were rigid, frozen to the bone. So too were his arms and legs. His voice was weak, and he could no longer blink, for he had also left his snow goggle behind.

\* \* \*

On the last day of Frank's vacation week, a group of outdoor enthusiasts – snow shovels and hockey sticks to hand – approached Frank's cabin. The second storm had cleared. Once again, the sky was a rich and vibrant blue.

It was evident that the cabin door had been left open as drifts of snow covered much of the table and floor.

The occupant was nowhere to be seen. Leftover food covered with shiny crystals of ice, a pair of snowshoes and a cell phone stained with frozen red wine were the only points of interest other than two gemstones of brown jasper and a smattering of white spruce branches on a chair.

The group carried on to the verge of Hudson Bay where they planned to clear a small area for a game of hockey.

Further out on the ice-frozen bay, was a snowman.

"Hey! Look at this, guys!"

"Some snowman, eh?"

"Strange place to build one, way out here."

"Good job though."

"Yeah. The proportions are pretty accurate, too."

"I like the way his arms are raised like he's trying to wave, and his head is turned to one side as if he's looking for someone in the distance."

"Maybe he's got a female friend. You know, a snow lady."

"Very funny."

"Feel this. I think someone has put a hat on his head. It's got flaps too. Decent quality I'd say. Probably leather. Hard as rock. I think it's real . . . or was."

"I'm surprised he hasn't collapsed by now. The legs are the first to go, especially with the weight of all that snow."

"Most of his body has turned to ice. It's pretty solid. He's not going to fall over any time soon, and he won't be melting any time soon. You can bet on that."

"We'll have to play around him."

"Or use him for target practice. How many shots do you think it would take to knock his head off?"

"I've got a better idea. He can be the referee."

"All he needs is a whistle."

"As long as he keeps his mouth shut and doesn't send anybody to the penalty box."

Everyone laughed.

\* \* \*

In the days and weeks that followed, numerous search parties from Winnipeg and Churchill tried their best to learn what had happened to Frank. The only evidence they found was an empty cabin.

When springtime came round and the ice and snow had melted, the beluga whales, loons, ducks and a host of wildlife also returned home for another season.

Frank Hathway never found his way back to the cabin or called his wife again.

Frank Hathaway would not be going home.

Henry was emboldened by the storm. The explosive cracks of thunder and ghoulish-looking fissures of lightning only added to his inner rage at the world and his exclusion from it.

# The
# Brewster
# Boy

He was killed by a bolt of lightning. By all rights, it was his own fault.

Henry Brewster used to cycle through *Crescent Park* in all weathers. To the locals, it was known as the 'rec', where children and dogs played.

Henry enjoyed flinging sticks and stones at squirrels and birds, and anything else that lived amongst the trees and bushes. He didn't care and stopped at nothing to inflict pain and discomfort on those who were free and happy.

Henry Brewster was a bully.

He was fifteen years old.

Polly Locks lived across the street in *The Crow's Nest*, a family-owned pub run by her parents for the past decade. Every afternoon at about four o'clock, Polly sat and waited at her bedroom window for Henry and his tricycle to appear.

Numerous times – nearly always as the story goes – she would shout and scream through the opened window, not to scare the bully away, but to warn the *others* of imminent danger, especially those innocent creatures who lived in the 'rec'.

On countless occasions, she would grab her mother's long wooden spoon – the one with the deep, over-sized bowl – and run across the road waving her weapon high over her head and launch a mock attack, threatening to smash the bully's trike, or at least leave a lasting mark.

The fact that she was the same age and taller than Henry Brewster was of no consequence. Henry was not the sort to be intimidated.

At first, her reckless actions scared the children and dogs, and adults she knew by name. People soon caught on to her intent and applauded her brazen behaviour.

Henry returned Polly's carefree jousting without fear and rattled his fist in retaliation.

"Stay away from my bike Polly Locks. One day, little girl, you'll be sorry."

Henry was the only one in his neighbourhood who had always been unable to ride a two-wheeled bicycle and, for this alone, he had been browbeaten day in and day out. He suffered from mild dyspraxia and found it impossible to manage the coordination and balance necessary to ride one.

So, in its place, his parents had given him an adult tricycle, and against all odds Henry mastered the trike remarkably well.

Despite this major success, he could not change the

way others continued to treat him. He was unliked and excluded.

He never broke free from the tormenting behaviour and soon turned into a bully-boy himself.

Henry was emboldened by the storm. The explosive cracks of thunder and ghoulish-looking fissures of lightning only added to his inner rage at the world and his exclusion from it.

Henry Brewster enjoyed the challenge of fighting nature itself. It made him wild.

Polly was troubled by Henry's hurtful deeds, and never understood what drove him to despair. She regretted her own less-than-kind behaviour for not having taken the time to help him in and outside of school.

Polly saw the tragedy play out from her bedroom window.

She screamed when she saw the bolt of lightning that would end Henry Brewster's life. It looked like a giant sequoia that had fallen through time and space from another galaxy and couldn't be stopped. It glinted silver, white and blue, and was wicked. The thwack of thunder that followed only seconds later shook the entire house.

The leading edge of the lightning bolt struck the top of Henry's head and emerged through his shoes, irradiating his entire body like a special effect in a macabre horror film.

Henry bounded from his seat several times and not once did he call out or fall to the ground. Then it started to rain – a swirling, lashing deluge that seemed to overwhelm Henry and his tricycle, obscuring them both from view.

Henry Brewster's untimely death was a sad day for the school and the entire community.

No one ever forgot it.

Especially Polly Locks.

* * *

Richard Hollister was addicted to collecting second-hand junk – items of every description – discarded and donated to recycling centres.

Every weekend, he travelled round his home county hoping to find bargains, from vintage tools and wooden storage boxes to landscape paintings and golf clubs. It was entertaining and unpredictable.

His wife had her own interests and hobbies – designing and making quilts, in particular – so she was only too pleased that her husband was pursuing an enjoyable and time-consuming pastime of his own.

One fine Sunday morning and quite by chance, he happened upon a recycling mecca of significant scope and size, more than ninety miles from home. It was called *Returned to Life* and was bursting with all manner of noteworthy finds.

One item captured his attention. It was an adult tricycle, the only one of its kind that he could see. It was set apart from the large collection of other bicycles and occupied a unique display area bordered on all sides by a white picket fence.

He opened the gate to examine it in more detail. It

looked more like a prized trophy on display than a rusty old piece of junk that had been discarded by its owner.

The trike was positioned in the centre of a wooden podium. This too, thought Hollister, had been specially constructed.

Much of the once-polished green metallic paint had been bleached and sucked dry of pigment over time by the sun. A succession of ugly black curls was etched along the entire length of the seat pole. A handful of spokes were either misaligned or missing altogether, and all had a degree of rust.

The leather saddle was uneven and brittle along its edge and badly charred in various places where the rider sat – clear evidence of neglect and exposure to the elements. While the rear wheel guards were scratched and dented, the tyres looked fair and rideable assuming the gearing mechanism and brakes were up to the task.

This was the last relic that Richard Hollister had planned on buying. He had never thought of owning a tricycle before, much less riding one simply for the fun of it. He warmed to the novelty and imagined all kinds of refinements: racing stripes, mirrors, flags, horns, buzzers and bells, and a new colour. Anything except green.

The cost of getting this tricycle back on the road, Richard thought, could be more than the cost of owning it, and the investment would be justified if he could buy it at the right price.

"How much for the trike?" shouted Hollister to a young lad who was adding a more derelict bicycles to the groaning heap of metal and rubber that had seen better days.

The lad stopped what he was doing and walked over to the trike and remained outside the enclosure. He sucked on his bottom lip and stared through the white picket fence.

Richard Hollister was sitting on the tricycle like a victorious jockey waiting in the winner's enclosure for his trophy.

"How much?"

"You mean, you want to buy it?"

"Has someone else beaten me to it?"

"No."

"Does it belong to you? I do apologise."

"No. It's not mine."

"Good morning," said a middle-aged woman who suddenly appeared. She was fidgety and nervous, and squinted at Hollister through a pair of thick-framed bifocals. She too, stayed outside of the enclosure.

"Can I help you? I'm one of the managers. We are all volunteers, you know. I look after the place on Sundays."

"I'd like to buy it – the trike, I mean. Tell me, why is it separated from all the other bikes? Do you know anything about it?"

The young lad stared at the woman. Both were at a loss for words as if they had just been caught with stolen merchandise.

"Do you live around here?" the woman asked.

"No. About a hundred miles south. I'm out for a ride in the country. I like to buy and collect old and odd things that I find interesting. It's a hobby of mine. I trust we can agree on a price."

"Are you certain that you want it? You would be the twelfth person to buy it. Some have kept it for a day, some for a week and some for an entire month. Each one has returned it to us, claiming it was . . . shall I say, *unsuitable*.

"Is there something wrong with it? Is it broken? I am happy to restore it."

"I don't think you would be happy with it. You see, it belonged to the Brewster boy."

"Sorry. I'm not familiar with the name."

"Henry Brewster. He lived in the village not far from here. Died eleven months ago. Struck by lightning! He was in *Crescent Park* during the storm. Riding his trike! The story was in the local newspaper. Nobody knows what he was doing there. Silly boy. His parents were devasted. They're still in a bad way. A real tragedy if you ask me."

"Ahhhh, I see. I didn't know anything about it. I am sorry to hear the story. That would explain the marks I saw on the trike. Tell me, why is it on display?"

"It's been sitting here all these months, exactly as you see it. Henry's parents didn't want to keep the trike after Henry died, so they gave it to us. It's become part of the family around here, so to speak. People come from miles around just to see it up close and touch it. They like to stand next to it and have their photograph taken. People do the strangest things. So, we decided to build a special place to display it. Henry Brewster loved his trike. We are eager for the community to know that we care."

"Let me buy it. I'll give you a fair price. Honest. It is a sad story, I admit. Let me bring the trike back to life."

"Well, if you truly want to have it, I think it would be acceptable. Why don't you take it home? Try it out, and if you want to keep it, then we can agree on a price. If you also find it unsuitable, just bring it back and we'll put it back on display."

"That's kind of you," said Hollister and gave the woman his contact details. "Very kind indeed."

He had bought something unique, and although no final price had been agreed, Hollister was prepared to pay whatever was required.

Hollister and the young lad thought it best to lift the trike onto the car's roof. They spent more than thirty minutes securing it in place with heavy-duty twine, using much more than was required.

They stood back and admired their handiwork, well proud of their accomplishment. Although it looked dangerous and illegal – far from being roadworthy – no one seemed bothered about it.

"Good luck," said the woman as Hollister began to drive away.

"Don't worry, I'll get it back on the road where it belongs," he said. "I'll come back in a few days and pay you, too!"

"I hope Henry likes you!"

Hollister stopped the car and stuck his head out the window.

"What do you mean?"

"I forgot to tell you."

"What?"

"Don't you know? The trike is haunted!"

He dismissed the woman's parting commentary with a fleeting wave of his hand – a well-meaning gesture of thanks and goodbye – and thought no more about what she had said.

Richard Hollister was a happy man on this fine Sunday and couldn't wait to show his wife what he had found. To say that his journey home was uneventful would not be entirely accurate. He never mentioned it to anyone.

* * *

On a long, desolate stretch of road, Hollister hears an odd series of noises originating from the engine . . . thumping, clinking, tapping. He can't be sure. There is a pattern, a rhythm to the unwanted jangle. Repetitive, annoying . . . and worrying. He knows nothing about cars and dreads the thought of breaking down, today of all days.

Instinctively, he checks his mobile. Only twenty percent charge remaining. He remembers and spits out the words: *'damn . . . I forgot to charge it this morning'*.

He is ambushed by a surge of adrenalin. The muscles in his neck and scalp contract. His breathing and heart rate swell.

Then it occurs to him. The clatter is coming from the car's roof! Not the engine. Hollister slows down, cutting his speed in half. *The twine has come undone*, he thinks to himself. He had never tied anything to the roof of his car before – ever.

29

The racket stops. Hollister feels better, happier, more relaxed. *Drive slowly*, he tells himself. *Be safe.*

He looks pensively in his wing mirror, then opens his window. *Excellent. No police. I could lose my license. Just relax. You'll be home in forty minutes.*

Then it happens.

The trike comes lose. The wheels start turning.

Spinning with pace. Deliberate and blatant.

Not to lurch and pitch over the side. Nor plunge and tumble backwards.

But forward like a movie stunt. Along the top of the car. Down the front windscreen.

Perfectly balanced and straight.

The trike's three wheels hit the road with uncanny tempo and precision.

Hollister's car catches up in an instant. The trike's front wheel swerves to avoid a stone.

Hollister sees it as clear and well-defined as if looking through a magnifying glass.

One of the trike's back wheels, however, rolls over the same stone as if by design. The result is predictable.

The stone is propelled backwards, up into the air at a steep angle.

The windscreen is cracked exactly in line with the driver's eyes. The driver's vision is blurred.

It's too late.

The car collides into the back of the trike, pushing it sideways. The trike slews towards the verge and finally comes to rest against a tree.

Hollister's foot digs into the brake pedal. The car skids. He manages to steer it into a layby and brings his vehicle to a halt. He runs back to see if the trike has survived the impact.

Remarkably, Hollister can find no serious faults. A small number of dings and scrapes, of course, yet no serious damage to the frame or wheels. He reaches for the handlebars calmly and, with a gentle touch, guides the trike back to the car.

Unable to lift the trike back onto the top of the car single-handedly, Hollister folds the rear seats down and stuffs the trike into the boot, pushing it in as far as it will go. He retrieves a lengthy piece of twine from the road, lowers the tailgate and ties it tightly to the trike.

*All-in-all, it does look less obtrusive and more secure than it did before. This must be my lucky day*, thought Hollister.

\* \* \*

Having paid for the trike in full, Hollister spent all his time on the trike, thinking, planning and making list of accessories, including front and rear lights; horns and bells; a rear wire basket; new pedals and handlebar grips with a mirror on each side; a new saddle; and three new, pristine wheels.

He also invested heavily to repair, refurbish and replace, as necessary, every moving part, nut and bolt, to create the best trike anyone had ever seen. Yet, this was not enough.

There was one more finishing touch as important as anything else. The bike would need to be re-painted.

*Shiny, gloss black will do nicely*, he decided. *It will*

*sparkle in the sunlight.*

It took three weeks to complete the entire restoration. Hollister was delighted with the result. He unveiled his pride and joy the following Sunday at a family BBQ and seized the opportunity to entertain his guests with what hew had learned about Henry Brewster and how he had come to own the boy's trike.

Friends, neighbours and children – those who were big enough to reach the pedals – all enjoyed a ride on the trike that fine Sunday.

"Make it short, now," said Hollister. "Let the others have a turn. Five minutes each at the most. Please be careful. And don't scratch the paint! Please!"

\* \* \*

The demonstration rides are over.

The trike is left unattended.

Hollister's driveway is uneven.

The trike wobbles from side to side.

The wind picks up.

The front wheel catches on a downward slope.

The trike starts to roll.

Down the driveway.

Towards the road.

The trike veers to the left, along the pavement.

Hollister can't believe his eyes.

He chases after it to save it from clear destruction.

He stops in disbelief, and despairs.

Jackson, the loveable Yorkshire Terrier who lives next door is being pursued by the riderless trike.

Alternate blasts of the trike's horns and bells ring in Hollister's ears.

*'That damn Brewster boy!'* bewails Hollister.

Jackson is making a race of it, but the trike is making up ground, closing the distance between the hunter and the hunted. Jackson looks behind him, bewildered, scared, his energy sapping quickly.

Jackson changes tactics and direction.

He runs across the street.

Cars whizz by from all directions.

The trike's pace is unyielding.

Hollister screams Jackson's name.

Jackson ignores Hollister's cries.

The trike stops abruptly at the kerb.

Jackson is clear and safe.

He ducks under a hedge on the other side of the road and is lost from sight.

Hollister approaches the trike with due care. He stands behind it and waits patiently, trying to catch his breath and come to terms with what had just happened.

* * *

Hollister found an old chain and padlock and secured the trike in his garage before retiring for the night.

The next morning, when he removed the lock and chain, he was puzzled by the marks he saw on the rear frame and seat stem where the chain had been used to secure the trike. Mysterious abrasions were clear to see. The metal and paint were scored and scraped in a few places as if the chain itself had been pulled or dragged

33

relentlessly to sever the shackle.

Convinced that this was not the work of intruders and could not have been done by those who had taken the trike for a brief ride the previous day, Hollister came to a wild and distressing conclusion. Henry Brewster was not dead at all!

Hollister's wife dismissed her husband's alarming premise with unreserved scepticism. Nevertheless, she was pragmatic about it.

"If you think the trike is haunted, dear, then give it back. The last thing we need is a ghost in the garage."

Hollister knew she didn't believe a word of it.

"There's no point keeping something if you're not happy with it. Someone else will appreciate the time and money you've invested. It *is* a beautiful trike."

Hollister had already made up his mind.

Unwilling to transport the trike on top of the car or stuffed inside the boot, Hollister notified the recycling centre that he was sending it back by a local transport company. Hollister took his responsibility seriously and was eager to be there in person when the trike arrived.

"Is this the same trike, Mr Hollister?" asked the manager, who had been waiting for him. "I can't believe what you have done! You have undoubtedly spent a great deal of time and money on Henry's trike. He would have appreciated it. Are sure about this . . . returning it, I mean?"

"Yes. I did enjoy having it, although I must admit, I didn't have too much time to ride. Like the others who have owned it, I'm afraid to say that I too have found it *unsuitable*. I am happy to donate it. No need to refund my money."

"That's very kind of you Mr Hollister. I understand how you feel. One day, the trike will find a new home, especially now that it has been completely restored and is roadworthy once again. You have done a remarkable job!"

And with that, Richard Hollister left *Returned to Life* and drove home. Henry Brewster's trike was returned to its rightful place on the podium inside the white picket fence.

On the morning of the third day, it was gone!

The trike had been taken – stolen – not that anyone was surprised to see such a coveted item go missing.

The crime was committed on the first anniversary of Henry Brewster's death.

And another storm was brewing.

* * *

A sphere of light plays along the wall.

It bounds in slow motion from side to side across the entire width of the room like a tennis ball.

The clock face sparkles.

It shows three minutes before midnight.

Shadows weld to the walls once again.

Polly Locks is asleep.

Rain tumbles from the sky. It is inconspicuous at first as if children are tap dancing in soft leather shoes.

Swiftly, the weight of the storm's barrage slaps every surface like soldiers marching to the front line.

Loud and intrusive.

The sphere of light returns for another show.

Distant thunder growls.

Then, booming cracks of thunder.

Frequent and vicious.

Lightning bolts play in Polly's room, smearing the oak floor with a glaze of while light like a fresh coat of lacquer.

Hard-edged shadows peel away.

Shapes are distorted against the storm's intrusion.

Polly is startled from her short-lived slumber.

She stumbles to the window.

Her breath is sucked out of her.

Shock waves knock her dizzy.

She sees a globe of light from *Crescent Park*.

Dazzling and hurtful, aimed squarely at her window.

A car headlight?

She squints through the storm's layers of menace.

Lightning. Thunder. Wind and rain.

The storm's wrath hurtles on.

The orb of light approaches.

It flashes off and on . . . with purpose and intent.

Polly struggles to identify –

She screams.

She knows!

Both arms shield her face.

Horns and bells whistle in her ears.

Shrill, dark and ugly.

Polly's eyes strain to their limit.

The light comes for her.

Tears well up.

No time to fetch the long wooden spoon – the one with the deep, over-sized bowl.

"Stay away from my bike, Polly Locks." The voice is soft and clear.

"What? Who's there?"

Polly spins full circle, expecting to see the speaker lurking in a dark corner behind her.

She is alone in the room.

"I'm outside, Polly."

It was Henry's voice.

"Do you want to play in the rain?"

Her face presses firmly against the window.

The glass is cold.

She paints a picture with her breath.

Fear rises in her throat.

She feels sick.

It's light from Henry Brewster's tricycle.

Dazzling, garish and blinding.

"What does Nevis Rue truly mean?
It's a very strange name."

"Not really, it's quite simple. If you haven't
worked it out by morning, I'll tell you.
It's a puzzle, more than anything else.
You'll get a kick out of it."

# The
# Competition

Kelly Rideout had become a media celebrity. Had it not been for the competition, none of this would have happened.

Kelly worked for *The Daily Encounter* in London along with more than 7,000 other journalists in more than twenty-five countries. It was the most popular and widely read newspaper in the world.

When she joined at the age of 18, Miss Rideout was the youngest columnist in the history of the newspaper. She wrote about everything, from creative and culinary arts – films, theatre, art, music and food – to travel destinations tucked away in forgotten nooks and crannies around the globe.

Five years later, she was given a new assignment. She won it and, in an instant, had become the envy of those who knew her by sight or by name.

A new hotel was being built. Ordinarily, this would not have attracted any more notice than a restaurant, cinema or department store.

This was different.

The hotel was called *Nevis Rue*. Unnamed sources said it was going to be the most imposing, majestic and luxurious hotel ever built . . . the ultimate go-to-place for the world's super rich and famous.

Other than those who had designed and built *Nevis Rue* – they were sworn to secrecy at the highest level – no one else knew anything more about it, including the people at the influential newspaper itself.

There were no pictures of *Nevis Rue* and no specifics about its architectural design, interior décor, rooms, food, facilities or cost of construction. Not a single fact about the physical nature of the hotel was known or could be learned, not by the *Encounter* or any other media organisation, and unquestionably not from the lips of any celebrity.

There was, however, one promotional teaser – trite and predictable though it was – that soon found its way into the public domain.

Nevis Rue . . .
A palace of awe-inspiring splendour
Accommodation without compare
Surroundings that defy language
For all those who dare!

More intriguing was the possible location, for that too had remained a mystery. Rumours percolated rapidly. Social media was abuzz with constant chatter.

Everyone knew and no one knew.

*Nevis Rue* had ignited the public's imagination. Deny human beings exactly what they want to know, and they stir up a frenzy to find out all there is to learn. It didn't take long for rumours to spread.

Of the 'possible' locations making the rounds on social media, various locations topped the unofficial shortlist:

Khartoum where the White Nile and
Blue Nile rivers meet

Lake Hövsgöl, Mongolia,
near the Russian border

Mato Grosso, west-central Brazil,
in the Amazon rainforest

Tropic of Capricorn, Alice Springs,
in the Australian Outback

Somewhere in the Pacific Ocean,
10 miles off the coast of Hawaii

Not wanting to miss out on a golden opportunity to sell more newspapers, *The Daily Encounter* came up with a clever idea. The paper would launch a competition amongst all its employees – from reporters and editors to artists and accountants. Every department and every post within the organisation would be eligible to enter. One person's staff number would be selected at random by computer.

The prize?

One week at the *Nevis Rue* hotel, all expenses paid by the paper.

There was one stipulation set out in the terms and conditions of the competition. The winner would be required to write a series of detailed stories complete with pictures, including video, about his or her experiences during their stay at *Nevis Rue*.

The plan was to publish a different story each day for a month in the paper, with simultaneous broadcasts allied to the paper's social media channels.

Not everyone employed by the paper could write for print and online audiences. That was to be expected. There was a big pool of talented journalists who could polish even the roughest prose and transform it into the style required.

The paper thought it was a reasonable trade-off for a free luxury holiday.

\* \* \*

"Hey, Kelly. What are you doing here?"

"Hi Jim. I work for the paper, remember?"

"I know. It's just that I've never seen you in the office before – in person. You're always travelling somewhere-or-other, dashing off to the cinema, an off-the-wall art exhibition or eating in a fancy restaurant from London to Cape Cod. I read all your columns.

Nice work, Kelly."

"Thanks, Jim. That's what I do for a living. I can't very well eat *chevreffes* or *poulet fafa* at my desk, or turn the lights off in my office and watch the latest film releases, can I?"

"No, I guess not. You're lucky."

"Sometimes, I think you're the lucky one, Jim."

"How so?"

"I'm always travelling. Don't get me wrong, I do love the lifestyle. Sometimes it would be nice to live a normal life with normal working hours. Like you. I'd like to find the right guy, settle down, have kids."

"Don't look at me, Kelly. I'd give anything to have *your* life. There's nothing special about me."

"Come on, Jim! You're the Production Manager for *The Daily Encounter*. You work in this wonderful building every day of your life – except for most weekends. You have a routine, a home life."

"I'd prefer your routine, Kelly, to be honest. I'm sure I could learn to adapt to your schedule. Besides, I do love travelling. Speaking of which, I assume you know all about the competition?"

"Who doesn't? I've received three reminders about it already. I think the winner is going to be announced at the close of play tomorrow. Everyone who works for the paper is automatically entered."

"I would like to win very much. My wife and the kids could sure use a holiday."

"Sorry, Jim, I don't mean to burst your bubble. There is only *one* prize winner from the paper. It's not the winner-and-his-family sort of thing. It's always about money. You know, the cost of sending someone to *Nevis Rue*. The airfare alone could be a fortune, not to mention the hotel charges, unless the paper is getting a deal."

"Newspapers always get deals. More likely, a freebee. That's the nature of the game."

"You ought to read the fine print to be certain or wait until you win first before promising anything to your wife or kids."

"Even so, I'm not sure my wife would let me go on holiday by myself."

"Of course, she would. It's only for a week. She knows how hard you work. Although –"

"I'm listening."

"Even if you did win, Jim, you'd still have to work. You'd have to interview all kinds of people at the hotel, sample the restaurants, bars and nightclubs, explore the grounds and surrounding countryside . . . get a feel for the place – the whole package. And write stories for the paper as well. Don't forget that part of the prize."

"When do I start?"

They laughed.

"I'm not the world's best writer, Kelly. If I win, I'll pay you to fix my grammar and spelling and add all the appropriate adjectives."

"Happy to help, Jim."

"Any idea where the hotel might be?"

"It could be a cruise ship, sailing around the world – you know, a hotel on wheels or in this case, rudders. That might explain of the hype. I'd bet on it.

"The name sounds French or Spanish. I've been to

Hawaii before, and I'm not interested in the Australian Outback or being stuck in the Amazon rainforest. I think I'd like to visit Khartoum. I fancy a dip in the Nile. Very exotic if you ask me. Lots to see and do."

"You never know, Jim. Maybe they've built the hotel in the middle of Disney World!"

"Been there three times! As long as they don't send me to the North Pole. Give me a beach with soft, white sand, sunshine and a blue sky and I'll go anywhere."

"Sorry, Jim, I'd love to stay and chat with you, but I have to rush off to a meeting with the publisher. You know how it is? It happens all the time when I come into the office."

"No worries."

"Good luck, Jim."

"You too, Kelly."

\* \* \*

"Sorry I'm late," Mr Prosper."

"Not at all. Nice to see you, Kelly. Come in."

"I was chatting with Jim Gamble. Haven't seen him for a while."

"How is Jim? Nice guy."

"He's fine. We were talking about the competition."

"Very timely subject these days. That's exactly what I wanted to talk to you about."

"Happy to interview the winner, if that's what you have in mind."

"Well, not exactly."

"Happy to ghost-write the stories and edit his or her

45

phone video imagery, if that works. I'll even do it for free."

Mr Prosper picked up an envelope from his desk and waved it in the air.

"As the publisher of the *Encounter*, I wanted to tell you in advance, face-to-face, that you have won the competition."

"Me? Oh my God. I won the competition? That's insane. I mean, that's wonderful! Does anybody else know about this?"

"Not at the moment. You and I are the only ones. You can't tell anybody else just yet until the paper makes it official tomorrow. And I do mean NO ONE, Kelly. You do understand?"

"Yes sir, of course I do. This is fantastic. I can hardly believe it You'll get the best stories I've ever written, Mr Prosper. You can count on me to deliver."

Behind Kelly's smile was a trickle of doubt. Did she win the competition in a fair and just way, or had she been selected, *given* the prize on a silver platter by the *Encounter* so it could publish what the paper considered to be the best stories possible?

Kelly didn't ask. She didn't want to know. *It's none of my business*, she thought. She just said, *'thank you'* and waited for further details about the prize.

Mr Prosper stood up and gave Kelly the envelope.

"Bedtime reading. All the documentation is inside. Best to look it over in the privacy and in the comfort of your own home. Please don't lose it. Above all else, do not share the details with colleagues, friends or family. Not yet. Is that understood?"

"Yes. Completely."

"If your preference is not to accept the prize, then that too will be perfectly acceptable. Don't forget. This is a competition. There are no obligations."

"I'm sure I'll love it. When do I leave?"

"Forty-eight hours."

"That sounds a bit urgent."

"Yes, I know. The people who own *Nevis Rue* have offered us an exclusive. They've been following our competition and thought it would a clever idea to do advance publicity."

"What do you mean?"

"The opening has been delayed by two weeks, so the competition winner – YOU – can stay at the hotel before it opens officially and report on it. That's why I wanted to tell you in advance. It's all hush-hush at the moment. They want you to visit straight away. You would become the first person in the world to stay at *Nevis Rue*. It would be a stunning publicity coup for the newspaper, not to mention a once-in-a-lifetime experience for you, Kelly."

"Well then, count me in. I'm sure I'll love it. Yes! I'll do it. I'll go. I accept the prize. Why wouldn't I?"

"Are you sure, Kelly?"

"Absolutely!"

Mr Prosper gave Kelly a small, red canvas bag with all kinds of zips, straps and pockets.

"Here . . . you'd better take this as well. Brand new camera equipment. It comes with the prize. It's yours Kelly. Keep it as a souvenir. Don't forget to take hundreds – no, make that thousands of stills and video.

I've seen your work. It's superb! The hotel has a special media suite with the latest IT equipment so that you can file your stories. So, Kelly Rideout, are you absolutely sure you're up for the challenge?"

"I'm your girl, Mr Prosper."

"Excellent! Still, have a look at the paperwork. If you have any questions, call me. My private number is inside the envelope."

"Tell me, Mr Prosper, where is *Nevis Rue*? Do I need to take a bikini or my snow skis?

\* \* \*

"Good evening, you must be Kelly Rideout from *The Daily Encounter*."

"I am indeed."

"My name is T J Hornbeam. I'm the Manger here at *Nevis Rue*."

"Congratulations. It's wonderful to meet you."

"You too. How was the trip?"

"Very comfortable. I slept the entire journey."

"I'm sure you will enjoy your stay here."

"I am looking forward to it, I can tell you."

"The main express elevator is still being installed. It will be fully operational first thing in the morning, so I'm afraid you'll have to take the stairs. It shouldn't be too strenuous. Leave your luggage here and my team will bring it up to your room. We have given you the penthouse suite for your entire stay."

"That is very kind of you."

"Not at all. Tomorrow, I have planned a busy day for

you, so try to rest if you can. Are you hungry? Would you like a plate of food sent up to your room?"

"No, I'm fine, thanks."

"Right, then. My assistant, Vivian Stride – oh, here she comes now – will accompany you.

Kelly was thankful that she had made the trip. It was a welcome break from her life. She had been meaning to take some well-earned time off and a trip to *Nevis Rue* provided the perfect solution.

Well, almost. She was still required to write stories and take pictures.

This was different!

"Tell me, Ms Stride –"

"Vivian, please . . ."

"What does *Nevis Rue* truly mean? It's a very strange name."

"Not really, it's quite simple. If you haven't worked it out by morning, I'll tell you. It's a puzzle, more than anything else. You'll get a kick out of it."

"I am also intrigued by the architecture. I couldn't see too much when I arrived. Is the hotel, in fact, built like a pyramid?"

"Pretty much, although it has a domed top instead of a pointed apex, as well as bullnosed – or rounded – edges along each of the four sides. From a distance it looks like a monster traffic cone. With the wind and dust we get here, it seems to provide ample protection, so needn't worry about the weather conditions."

"It looks overpowering when you get up close."

"You'll get a better look at the hotel tomorrow. The hotel is 91 metres high on seven levels, the same height as the *Tower of Babel*. It's a bit of trivial nonsense in my opinion. You know how architects think. They live in their own special world, and I mean that in a positive way. You'll be meeting with the architect tomorrow. She's quite proud of what she has achieved and will answer any question you might care to ask."

From what Kelly could determined, it appeared as though most, if not the entire, hotel was constructed of semi-transparent, metre-square blocks made of dark, yellowish-brown ochre-coloured glass.

"I'd call it butterscotch," said Vivian Stride. "The glass is made from the soil. Stronger than concrete, too. And dirt cheap! Pardon the pun. The architect will explain how it was done and what this process means for the construction of future buildings."

"Fascinating."

"We have arranged a 'ride-and-walk' excursion for tomorrow afternoon so you can see for yourself what the terrain looks like up close and personal. We also have a custom-made expedition suit for you."

"Unbelievable! Can't wait for tomorrow!"

Kelly was already thinking about her first story and the astonishing imagery waiting to be captured.

\* \* \*

Kelly Rideout's penthouse suite was striking. It was spacious with an inordinately high, vaulted ceiling She had never seen anything like it. The room was oval, and it too was made of semi-transparent glass blocks. She looked out of her window. It was too dark to see the landscape, so she set her alarm for an early start.

The first light of day revealed a vast butterscotch-coloured plain bedecked with canyons, volcanoes and dry lake beds as if a team of landscape gardeners had placed everything meticulously by hand according to a grand design.

The most dazzling sight was the *Nevis Rue* crater, dropping 800 metres to the floor below ribbed with bizarre, circular configurations as if had once been stirred with a stick in ever-decreasing circles.

The sky had never looked so romantic, so inviting, so infinite and so utterly mysterious.

And then she understood the meaning of *Nevis Rue* – a clever name for the *universe*, an anagram of the very *word* itself.

What better place to build such a magnificent hotel than here, on *Mars!*

\* \* \*

Kelly Rideout wrote her stories and took her pictures, but she never returned to the employ of *The Daily Encounter*.

In less than three months she had become the director of *Martian Media* for the entire *Nevis Rue* hotel chain – other hotels would soon be under construction – and took responsibility for organising extraordinary tourist attractions and activities.

High on the list was Dust Surfing down officially authorised mountains, especially following major dust storms.

For those eager and fit enough to travel in the opposite direction, *Nevis Rue* offered its guests the opportunity to climb *Olympus Mons* – the tallest mountain in the solar system at 21km above zero-elevation.

* * *

*'Book a trip to the North or South Pole, seasonal ice cap permitting'* . . . said the promotional literature . . . *'with our subject matter expert on Martian weather, from gas and snow to dust clouds, storms and wind'.*

*'Hop aboard a Martian Rover and visit the famous landing sites of previous space missions to the red planet: Viking, Pathfinder, Spirit, Opportunity, Phoenix, Curiosity, InSight, Perseverance and a host of others'.*

*'Experience the ultimate romantic meal or life amongst the stars on the Martian plains, from the privacy and comfort of a Nevis Rue sightseeing pod – portable, pressurised and perfectly poised to offer the experience few of us will ever know'!*

In appreciation of her commitment and unwavering loyalty, Kelly Rideout had been given the penthouse suite unconditionally and without charge to live in.

Mars was now her home.

There she remained, happy and fulfilled, with a bird's eye view of the universe and its infinite wonder.

"If anyone stops to ask what we're doing, don't say anything and don't ask for any help. You never know who's on the road at this hour. Bog rolls are like gold dust. We wouldn't want to be hijacked, would we? This Coronavirus thing is shocking news. Criminal disorder . . . the collapse of society . . . you know what I'm saying?"

# The Allotment Business

It was 2:30am.

A procession of three empty school buses rounded the bend. The two-lane road was clear of traffic in both directions, save for a stationary lorry parked half-a-mile ahead.

The lorry listed noticeably to the left like a ship that had run aground in shallow water.

The buses slowed down and stopped on the hard shoulder directly behind the disabled lorry. Their doors opened simultaneously. The three bus drivers stepped down on the same beat.

"Good morning," said the lorry driver. He was tall and broad-shouldered, the kind of person you'd expect to see working in a London club to keep it safe, secure and orderly.

"Good morning," replied *busman one*. "What seems

to be the trouble?"

"Two blown tyres. Nearside front and rear."

"Where are you heading?"

"I have to get this load to the distribution centre by seven. I've only got about twenty-five miles to go. Hell of a place to break down."

"Can't you phone ahead and get someone to come out for you?" asked *busman one*.

"My phone battery is dead, mate, and I haven't got any charging cable."

"What are you hauling?"

"Toilet paper. This new virus that's going around – what's it called again?"

"Coronavirus."

"Yeah, that's it. People have started to panic like the end of the world has arrived. I think they enjoy the hassle of being inconvenienced."

"It happens everywhere. You don't have to be British to queue for a bog roll," said *busman one*.

"One roll is more valuable than one toner cartridge," said the lorry driver. "Just ask my wife. She'll tell you!"

The three busmen laughed as they huddled by the side of the lorry.

"I didn't expect to see a school bus at this hour, let alone three of them!"

"We had a bit of engine trouble with two of our buses just before we left. It took longer than we expected. It's no big deal, though."

"Where are you heading?" asked the lorry driver.

"Back to our yard. All the schools have closed. I heard it on the radio. The Government wants us to return home and isolate – *'slow the spread by reducing unnecessary social contact'* they said. We've also been told to work from home, if possible, until further notice. Driving a school bus at home – well, you can see the problem! Looks like you've still got a job, mate. It's a shame that *we're* not lorry drivers. You say you're hauling loo paper?"

"Yup."

"How much you got? We might be able to help you out."

"Hang on, I've got the consignment inventory in the cab."

When the lorry driver was out of earshot . . .

"What are you playing at?" asked *busman two*. Do you have any idea what time it is? I was looking forward to seeing my wife before the sun comes up AND I'm hungry!"

"Shhhhhh! Leave everything to me," said *busman one*. "I've got an idea. We could be in with a chance. I've got to think quickly. Let me do the talking. Don't forget, we're now unemployed. We still have to the pay the bills and look after our families."

"Right. Let's see . . . I've got thirty pallets . . . forty-five cases to the pallet . . . and thirty-six rolls to the case," said the lorry driver. "Fortunately, all the figures are written down on the inventory. Right then . . . that comes to 48,600 rolls. And they're all three-ply and white, as well."

"Much better than lime green – which I might add, you can still buy!" said *busman one*. "Still, thousands of people have to wipe their arse sooner or later!"

"Any chance of calling ahead for me?" asked the lorry driver. "A replacement truck is the best answer. I can give you all the contact details."

The lorry driver checked his watch. The busmen looked at each other for someone to take the lead. It was too dark for the lorry driver to see the blank reaction on their faces.

"Of course, we will," said *busman one*. "Or we would do if we had our phones. They went missing this afternoon, right inside the school grounds. It's rather embarrassing."

The other two busmen looked straight ahead and said nothing.

"What happened?" asked the lorry driver.

"We shouldn't have left them inside the buses. That's what you get when you don't lock up. People take things that don't belong to them."

"Everyone's gone crazy with this virus, I can tell you. You can't trust anyone," said the lorry driver. "Say, do you have any heavy goods vehicles for hire? That would be magic if you did. Happy to pay whatever you want."

"Sorry mate. We're a small family business. These are the only vehicles we have – just the three buses. I do have an idea, though. We can still give you a hand."

"That would be brilliant. I'm Jesse Street."

"I'm Good . . . Tom Good. This is Dick and Harry. We're brothers – the Good brothers. We run a local bus hire company. Better not shake hands, though."

The darkness concealed the befuddled reaction of Dick and Harry.

"Nice to meet you fellas. It's a lucky thing you stopped, Tom. Thanks."

"Can't leave a fellow driver stranded, definitely not with 48,600 rolls of toilet paper!"

"Cheers, mate. What have you got in mind? I've got a delivery to make by seven this morning. So, anything you can do to help . . ."

Tom winked at Dick and Harry.

"The way I see it, you've got a lorry with two flat tyres, a phone with no battery power and a shitload of loo paper to deliver, figuratively speaking. We have three empty school buses in perfect working order and happen to be going in the same direction. You're going to require something much bigger and more powerful than a school bus to tow you even without flat tyres. Look, it's nearly three o'clock. The four of us can transfer your entire shipment onto our buses. It can't take us that long. I'm sure we can manage. The distribution centre, you said, is only twenty-five miles from here. We should make it with enough time to spare. It won't cost you a penny either. We're already going in that direction. and as soon as we arrive, we'll make sure someone comes out straight away to recover your vehicle."

"That sounds reasonable to me," said the lorry driver.

"No trouble," said Tom Good. "It might be your only option, if I'm honest."

"Thanks for the help. I appreciate it. Do you have a map? Do you know where we are?"

"Of course. I know every inch of this road. They'll find you, don't worry. Leave it to us."

"What about your buses? You said you had engine trouble earlier on."

"It's been sorted. These buses are ready for another twenty-five thousand miles, let alone twenty-five!"

"Let's do it," said the lorry driver. "By the way, why isn't your name on the side of your buses?"

"That's exactly what I was thinking about this morning. Thanks for the good advice, though. No pun intended!"

Dick and Harry shook their heads.

"Where's your yard?" asked the lorry driver.

"Are you familiar with this area?" asked Tom.

"No, I can't say that I am."

"No worries. I'll leave our contact details at the distribution centre for you."

"Much appreciated."

"My pleasure."

"If anyone stops to ask what we're doing, don't say anything and don't ask for any help. You never know who's on the road at this hour. Bog rolls are like gold dust. We wouldn't want to be hijacked, would we? This Coronavirus thing is shocking news. Criminal disorder . . . the collapse of society . . . you know what I'm saying?"

Dick poked Tom in the ribs with his elbow. Harry shook his head, wondering where this was all going to end.

"I thought you said you had 30 pallets?" said Tom as he climbed into the back of the lorry.

"I do! There's a shortage of timber, so the pallets are secured with twine. They just look different. The next thing you know, there won't be any petrol to put in your car or paper to print books! The world's gone mad."

"Let's hope we never run out of this stuff!" said Tom as he took pleasure in squeezing a case of toiler paper rolls.

It took nearly three hours to complete the switch. Inside each of the three buses were 450 cases, or 16,200 rolls, of toilet paper. They occupied every square inch of space: floor, seats and aisle. Only the top halves of the windows were visible.

"Never underestimate the weight of bog rolls," said Tom. "It all adds up, I can tell you. At least the ride back will be quiet – no screaming kids! Don't worry, Jesse. Go back inside your cab and get a bit of rest and leave the rest to us. Best to sit tight and not leave your vehicle."

It was nearly 6am.

A restless Jesse Street paced back and forth along the side of the road, alone and unsure of his decision, as the three buses departed and faded into the soft, scattered light of a new day like battery-powered model toys.

No wrongdoing had been committed except for the decision of lorry driver, Jesse Street, who handed over his precious consignment to three school bus drivers – three strangers – who had given their names as Tom, Dick and Harry Good.

There was no proof or receipt given to the lorry driver for the transfer of his stock, just one man's promise – busman Tom Good – to deliver the shipment and arrange help for the stranded lorry driver.

If there was a second offence that played out on the

side of the road, it would be one of dishonesty, if not blatant deception. Two simple, yet revealing lies had been told.

Firstly, Tom, Dick and Harry Good – the names given as the three busmen *and* brothers – had been fabricated on a whim following the chance encounter with a lorry driver hauling 48,600 rolls of pristine white, three-ply toilet paper. Their real names are irrelevant.

Secondly, no busman's phone had been misplaced, lost or stolen. It was, simply, an impulsive ruse to manipulate the will of one man, lorry driver Jesse Street, who happened to be down on his luck.

That the three buses were legitimately owned and operated by these three gentlemen – though they were emphatically not brothers – was true enough, as was the engine trouble that had delayed their journey home to see their wives and kids, find something to eat and sleep at least until noon.

The three buses turned off the main road before reaching the exit for the distribution centre and drove in the opposite direction. Although Tom had not yet shared his plan with the others, Dick and Harry knew exactly what was going on.

The import of what they were about to do was overridden by the exhilaration of opportunity and the potential available to them.

In a word – *money!* The three busmen had taken what didn't belong to them and planned to keep the spoils for themselves. They had stolen a valuable consignment of merchandise with the sole purpose of selling their treasure to anxious, panic-stricken people whose obsessive demand for such household essentials was quickly spiralling out of control.

For this fact alone, the three busmen somehow felt vindicated by their own delinquent action.

Once the busmen explained what they had done – much to the unexpected and unanimous support of their wives and the unyielding promise of their children to keep their mouths shut – their sense of purpose focused on transferring the stolen toilet paper from the three buses to a suitable hiding place. They could think of nothing better, or more secure, than hiding an equal number of cases where they lived.

During the next seven days, and under the cover of darkness, they cleared the stolen rolls from the three buses. They loaded and re-loaded their cars until each house was bloated with three-ply, white toilet paper.

They had crossed an imaginary line. Their crime was gathering pace.

Feeling safe and confident that no one knew what they were up to, the three busmen and their wives drove to different neighbourhoods where homeowners didn't recognise them.

They knocked on everyone's door, wielding thirty-six-roll cases of toilet paper in front of strangers for the sum of £40 per case – at least double the pre-pandemic rate. The busmen and their wives were greeted with smiles and laughter.

No one asked any questions. No one berated them or shut the door in their faces. And no one argued about the price. When their cars were empty, they returned home to collect another batch of supplies and started knocking on doors somewhere else.

"At this rate," said Tom Good to his wife, "we could soon net a tidy profit £54,000 – that's £18,000 apiece! Let's call it unemployment benefits."

On the fourth day of the crime, the busmen's wives conceived a clever strategy to widen their distribution network.

In addition to their own plot of land on the local allotment where they enjoyed growing fruit and vegetables, they each had a shed at their disposal: ten feet long by eight feet wide.

The busmen and their wives waited until midnight before moving a considerable quantity of cases onto the allotment and stashing them in their sheds, keeping them stocked to capacity. They also had to be careful, cautious and cagey, and only sell to people they knew and trusted.

No emails, no texts and no phone calls they reminded their customers. And no queues at any time on the allotment. As for a friendly discount – that was a hearty 'no' as well.

\* \* \*

For her seventy-fifth birthday, Ada's daughter bought her an expensive pair of binoculars and tripod intended for year-round stargazing and, more specifically, to help pass the time during the Covid lockdown.

Astronomy was one of Ada's passions since she was a young teenager. Facing a lockdown of uncertain duration to stem the virus, Ada had the freedom to peer into any pocket of the night sky from the comfort and safety of her eighth-floor balcony and magnify whatever she saw to an impressive twenty-five times its normal size.

Ada had an enquiring mind. She enjoyed meeting people and learning new things about life. Resigned to staying put in her block of flats alone, there was no better way to see what was happening round her, she reasoned, than through the high-resolution 70mm lens of her birthday binoculars. There was no law against it and given the circumstances, she didn't care what people thought.

Despite the lockdown, people remained free to visit their allotment as and when they liked. Although gardening was of little interest to Ada, she still enjoyed watching others tend to their precious plot of land.

On the fifth day after the crime and just before midnight, Ada settled into her favourite chair. Through her binoculars she surveyed what she liked to call the observable universe and, in particular, *Shadow Glen* – the local neighbourhood allotment located directly across the street.

*'Now that looks interesting'*, she mumbled to herself. A dull yellowy light, partially obscure by net curtains, glowed from three sheds. An array of solar panels was clearly visible fixed to their roofs.

Two young boys, each grappling with an oversized suitcase, emerged from behind shed one. The front of the outbuilding faced away from Ada's viewpoint. She didn't recognise either one of the boys and wondered what they were doing there at this time of night and why they were trying to walk so quickly.

An elderly man appeared in Ada's line of sight from the side of shed two. He too stepped lively with a large suitcase to hand. A cloth cap angled to one side concealed much of is face. Again, the front of the shed was hidden from view.

The door of shed three opened wide. This time, Ada had a clear view of the front. A middle-aged woman marched along the same path and towed a suitcase behind her. One of its wheels was bent out of alignment. Ada smiled at the clarity of what she was able to see through her binoculars. She didn't recognise this person either.

But she did see what was inside shed three – a heap of toilet paper stacked tightly from floor to ceiling.

The light in shed one went out, then shed two and shed three in succession. All was quiet until Ada saw what looked like a tall, burly man walking away from shed three. He looked back over his shoulder and appeared to say something. His coat was pulled up to his chin, but there was not enough light to see what he looked like.

Ada scanned the allotment from left to right, then from right to left. It was an eery picture. There was nothing else of interest to see. Although it was well past midnight, Ada had no intention of calling it a day just yet. She had other ideas.

Ada fetched a blanket pin, a small screwdriver, and a pocket-sized torch, grabbed her coat and dashed across the street back to the allotment.

She was fearless. Or, as others might be inclined to suggest, reckless.

At the entrance to the allotment, a hand reached out and touched Ada's shoulder. She was caught off guard. She spun around in an instant and, with her pocket torch raised above her head, was about to smack her would-be assailant to the ground.

"Mum! It's me, Carol!"

Ada shone a light in the stranger's face.

"Carol? Is that you?"

"Yes mum, it's me. Who else do you think it is?"

"I thought it might be him?"

"Who?"

"I saw this big fella in the allotment – I thought he might be following me. I could have been mugged."

I'll mug you myself in a minute if you don't tell me what you're doing here! I've been calling you all evening – your line has been engaged. I thought you might have fallen over."

"When was the last time I fell over? I'm not that old yet. I'm fit as a fiddle. I took the phone of the hook if you must know."

"Why did you do a silly thing like that?"

"I was looking through my wonderful binoculars. I didn't want to be interrupted. It's better than watching television. So, I took the phone off the hook. Big deal. People always call you back when the line is engaged. It worked for you and here you are!"

"I was worried sick about you. You ought to be thankful that I saw you cross the road just now or I would have called the police."

"You don't want to do that Carol."

"What are you doing here, mum? Do you have any idea what time it is?"

"You should be in bed, Carol. You have to go to work tomorrow."

"It's Friday, remember? What about you? Why are you skulking around an allotment in the pitch black? It's not safe. Besides, we're probably breaking Covid rules."

"Rules, shmules! I've seen something?"

"What? Seen what?"

"Come with me and I'll show you."

"Mum? What are you doing?"

"You'll see. Now, be quiet and follow me. They've got solar panels on the roof."

"What does?"

"The *sheds!* You won't believe what's inside. I bet the other two are the same."

"What other two? What are you talking about?"

"The *SHEDS!* There are three of them, all with solar panels on the roof. I saw a light in all of them. I know where they are and what's inside."

"Have you seen a crime – a *murder!* – through your binoculars?"

"Something better!"

"Stay close to me and don't wander off and don't say anything until I tell you to. There's nothing like a little adrenalin rush. Now, my dear, let's have a little fun."

Ada found one of the sheds in no time. She removed the blanket pin and small screwdriver from her pocket and set to work on the padlock.

"What are you doing?"

"Shhhhhh. Keep your voice down. What does it look like I'm doing? I want to open the door."

"With a blanket pin and a screwdriver?"

"It's easy. Don't you know how to do it?"

"NO!"

"Don't forget, your father was an engineer in the Royal Navy. You'd be surprised what I can do! I bet he's smiling down on us right now."

"He wouldn't have approved of your behaviour," said Carol with more than a hint of sarcasm. "You do realise we're breaking the law, don't you? Whatever possessed you –?"

"Shhhhhh. Not so loud. I don't think we're the first to commit a crime here."

"What do you mean? "

Ada opened the padlock and pulled open the door.

"Oh – My – God!" Carol was stunned. Where did all this come from? There must be hundreds of rolls –"

"I would say thousands, which is why we're going to borrow a few."

"You mean steal! Mum, you can't do that. That's against the law."

"I've seen people coming and going with suitcases from three different sheds, and I'm positive the three sheds are exactly the same. This toilet paper has already been nicked by somebody else, no doubt, with the help of friends. Stealing from thieves is not a crime unless you get caught."

"And punished!"

"Don't worry, I'm far too old to smack around."

"We'll see about that, mum."

"It's not like we're doing anything wrong. We're just moving a bit of stock along the chain to those who need it most."

"Such as? You? How many rolls do you need? You don't even go to the toilet that much."

"Never mind that, Carol. Make yourself useful. One case for you and one case for me and another case for you another one for me. I expect you can manage one in each hand. I make it 144 rolls from one shed alone!" said Ada.

"I can't believe I'm doing this! I was watching a charming film at home, in bed."

"This is much more entertaining! Hang on for a minute, I forgot to close the padlock. There! No one will ever know we were here."

They arrived back at Ada's flat without incident.

"I'd say that was a rather good haul, don't you? You'd better phone Simon and tell him not to worry. You'll be home a little later than expected. As a matter of fact, tell him that you're staying the night. We're not finished yet."

Carol was speechless. She stared at her mother in disbelief, knowing precisely what she had in mind. Carol was dead wrong. She didn't know the half of it!

It was well past one o'clock in the morning. Ada and her daughter made two more trips to the allotment before sunrise. This time, they brought suitcases – one for each of them.

"Look, Carol. This shed is identical to the first one. Chock-a-block with toilet paper!"

Ada used the same method as before to open the padlocks for each of the three sheds.

"Look, Mum. If we get caught, we're going to be in BIG trouble."

"Don't worry, the police aren't bothered with this sort of thing –"

"I'm not talking about the police –"

"Keep you voice down, Carol."

"I'm not talking about the police," Carol whispered again. "I am referring to the people who nicked this stuff in the first place. I don't want my husband – and my kids – reading about our little late-night adventure in *The Times*:

Mother & Daughter Unearthed
Strangled in Allotment!

"Don't be silly, Carol. Nobody likes to put their hands around an old woman's neck. We'd most likely die of stab wounds. Besides, they wouldn't leave us here for the police to find. Too close to their sheds and the toilet paper. They'd drag our bodies to another county and dump us there. We'd be on television within the hour. That's usually how it's done."

"And you know from experience?"

"Stop wasting time Carol and make yourself useful. Put another two of these 36-roll packs of toilet paper in each suitcase. When we get back, we'll unload, wash our hands and come back for the third shed. Then I'll make breakfast – bacon and eggs. Nobody will know that anything is missing. And if we're lucky, we can do

71

it all over again for the next two nights. That'll give us 432 rolls for each night's haul. Do you want jam or marmalade on your toast?"

"WHAT? You are crazy – bonkers. You must stop this nonsense, or I will take you directly to the police station myself!"

"No, you won't. How are you going to explain the loo paper in my flat?"

"That's your problem."

"Our problem. I couldn't have done it without you. You're my partner in crime. Too upsetting for the children. Bad publicity for the family."

"What are you going to do with all this toilet paper? Where are you going to put it?"

"I have a plan," said Ada as the two of them left the allotment and walked back. "For just three nights' work, according to my calculations – we'll have . . . I'll have . . . 1,296 rolls of toilet paper."

"Then what?"

"You're forgetting that everyone who lives in my building is over the age of fifty-five."

"So?"

"Work it out for yourself. Nobody should be going outside . . . shopping on the High Street for toilet paper. We must stay at home and shield, wash our hands and wear a mask. Mustn't catch the virus, especially when you get to our age."

"Speak for yourself, mum."

"Given the dire circumstances we find ourselves in, £2 per roll is a fair price. Believe me, they can afford it. I'll send out a personal, hand-written note to each flat and tell them they can buy as many rolls of toilet paper from me as they want. No limit and first come, first served. We'll all wear masks and gloves and keep our distance. You'll soon learn that people of a certain age are, shall I say, discreet."

"That's criminal."

"No, it's not, Carol. It's good business. Your father would have been extremely proud."

"He would have called the police!"

"Don't be silly. How many rolls would you like, my dear? No charge of course! Help yourself."

"This is insane, mum. I can't believe I've been a part of this."

"It's all for a worthy cause, Carol. We have to look after our family, friends and neighbours in this crisis."

"This allotment business has gone straight to your head. What exactly are you going to do with all this money, then?"

"Oh, haven't I told you? I'm going to have a new cloakroom. I've been saving and planning to replace the old one for the past three years. Now I can do it! I've already selected the wall tiles, flooring and the sink – new lighting as well. Wait until you see the toilet, Carol! You'll love it!"

"... there is a priceless artefact in the Upper Hall just below the tower that no one has laid eyes on for nearly four thousand years! It's mentioned in the Bible ... something about a woman who was turned into a pillar of salt by God!"

# Mystery Weekend

Surprises can be pleasurable or hazardous. Either way, they will set your adrenalin alight and rattle your bones to the core.

With this expectation in mind, five individuals – call them *participants* or *victims* – paid handsomely to attend a luxury, mystery weekend at *Chillgrave Castle*, an imposing residence situated on a small island off the west coast of Scotland.

The exact location of this isolated residential setting and the name of the loch surrounding it, was of no consequence to the travellers, all in their twenties, and had specifically not been disclosed to them.

The cost of the weekend – £3,500 per person for three nights – included a chauffeur-driven limousine to and from *Chillgrave Castle*; bedchambers fit for the Lord of the castle; gourmet cuisine including grand *cru* wine and spirits; personalised, hand-tailored attire to keep and take home; and a souvenir group photograph presented in a sterling silver picture frame.

The last stage of the journey – fifteen minutes at best – was completed in a small private yacht and provided the first opportunity for the guests to meet one another. There were four men and one woman.

It was unseasonably warm, even for mid-August on this Friday, and especially for Scotland as the setting sun played across the castle's façade. Through the coppery shimmer of fading light, the household staff looked like blurry cardboard silhouettes as they peered through the windows for a sneak preview of the arrivals.

The mystery weekend guests were escorted into the Great Hall. Dulcet sounds of a string quartet filled the commanding space with surprising volume and clarity. The majesty of the room, with its large bay windows, was striking.

The intricate wooden-beamed ceiling measured sixty feet long, thirty feet wide and forty feet high, from which radiated three magnificent chandeliers. Portrait paintings – a gallery of *Chillgrave's* ancestry – were artfully arranged along both sides of the hall.

A tall, broad-shouldered man smiled as he presented a glass of pink champagne to each of the five guests. He was dressed in a black suit and waistcoat, a white shirt with a Windsor-cut collar, and a silk grey tie with matching Windsor knot. In his left lapel buttonhole, he wore a black and white boutonniere. On the opposite side was his name badge: *Butler*.

Although his well-knit smile gave nothing away, the sparkle in his narrowing eyes foretold a weekend of the unexpected.

The full complement of household staff formed a receiving line as they bowed to their weekend lodgers. They too sported name badges: *Housekeeper*; *House Steward*, *Chambermaid*; *Chef*; *Server One* (female); *Server Two* (male); and *Nurse*.

The intoxicating aroma of food swirled throughout the Great Hall much to the delight of the hungry guests. Leo Manners looked at his watch and wondered when dinner would be served. He was hungry. He drank his champagne too quickly and felt embarrassingly light-headed within minutes. He swayed from side to side like a tree branch in the wind. He hadn't eaten anything since breakfast.

"Are you all right?"

"I don't think champagne agrees with me, especially on an empty stomach," replied Leo.

"I know what you mean. Do you need a doctor?"

"I think the worst is over. Thanks for asking."

"It would be a shame if you missed dinner."

"There's no chance of that happening," Leo said with authority.

They smiled at each other.

"By the way, I'm Alice Storey."

"Hi. I'm Leo Manners. Glad to meet you."

"I didn't get a chance to say hello properly on board the yacht. It was all a bit frantic."

"And noisy!"

"Is this your first mystery weekend, Leo?"

"Yes. It's a birthday present from my fiancée."

"Well, happy birthday and congratulations. When is

the wedding?"

"Sometime in April next year. We haven't decided on the date yet."

"Why didn't both of you come here? It's no fun being on your own."

"I like mysteries and Claire likes musicals. Besides, she's busy doing other things. Have you been on one of these weekends before?"

"No. It's the first one for me, too. Sadly, it's not my birthday today and I'm not getting married either."

They both smiled.

"My birthday is on Monday!"

"Is it a special one?"

"Twenty-five!"

Alice applauded.

"Do you have any idea what the mystery is or what's going to happen?" Leo asked, eager to change the subject as he scanned the room, trying to make eye contact with his fellow guests.

"I don't have a clue. That's why they call it a mystery weekend! I expect we'll be asked to solve a murder. A good, old-fashioned whodunnit is not the same without a scandalous murder plot, especially in a place like this!"

"It better be. It's costing enough money!" said Leo. "I wonder if there's a prize for solving the crime, or whatever the mystery is? The winner might get his or her money back."

"It's a clever idea. More likely, you don't get killed!"

Alice chuckled at her own joke.

"Just kidding, Leo. You can't take part in a mystery

weekend without a twisted sense of humour!"

Leo grinned. He was grateful for Claire's thoughtful and extravagant gift. He also felt a stinging prick of guilt for travelling without her. No doubt he would never forget the experience. It would have been so much better, he thought, if Claire had been here to share the memories.

The Housekeeper was a stout woman in her late fifties, whose matronly expression was etched on her face like a cheap Halloween mask. She wielded a large brass bell and rang it briskly. The quavering shrillness, amplified tenfold by the stone floor and breadth of the room, caught Leo and the others by surprise, bringing a hush to the proceedings.

"Welcome to *Chillgrave Castle*," she said quietly and without fanfare, clearly Scottish by inflection.

Leo and his fellow weekenders braced themselves, took root and concentrated on every word.

"*Chillgrave* was constructed in 1489 by *Lord Bonnie the Tranquil* as he was known and is owned today by Sir William Riley McCallum. He is the internationally renowned archaeologist, adventurer and historian. Sir William and Lady Jane McCallum still reside here throughout the year. They're presently on an expedition in South America. Shortly, you will be escorted to your bedchambers where your luggage awaits you. Dinner will be served promptly at seven o'clock this evening, here in the Great Hall. Do not be late! There is no television, radio or internet connection at *Chillgrave*. If you need to make contact with the mainland, I will deal with your request directly."

* * *

A ten-foot long, peg-jointed oak trestle dining table with matching benches either side – clearly hand-cut and planed – took pride of place in the centre of the Great Hall.

Alice insisted that she sit next to Leo and was the first to introduce herself to the group. As she swept her long blonde hair back from the side of her face, the sweet scent of her perfume was all too noticeable: jasmine fused with orange blossom.

More alluring was her silver, deep-'V' wrap-over sequin dress that sparkled in the candlelight like distant stars in the night sky.

Leo smiled with parted lips. He shifted uneasily along the bench away from her, pretending not to show any reaction. It was a subtle move and went unnoticed. Although he tried not to think about the *word* itself that shaped his thoughts, it reverberated in his mind like the pluck of a bass guitar distorted by excessive volume.

Alice was a *flirt* . . . and *flirting* . . . her sensuality was radioactive. He thought about Claire and wondered what he was going to tell her about his weekend adventure that had only just begun.

Attired in midnight blue tuxedos with black shawl lapels, matching trousers and black silk bow ties, the rest of the weekend quintet sat opposite Alice and announced themselves in turn: Byron King, Curtis Riddle and Rafe Pallister.

Towering ornate wrought-iron candelabras – there

were at least a dozen in number and spaced evenly on the stone floor – dispensed an eerie luminosity during the sumptuous dinner.

"Well, this is positively most unusual," said Leo. "I can't say that I've ever eaten in a restaurant quite like this before!"

Bookended by the stark emptiness of the room, his words took wing, reaching every crevice of the Great Hall before bouncing back as muffled echoes.

"It's a bit spooky in here if you ask me," said Alice. "I like bright lights and modern décor! I also like to see what I'm eating."

"It's got to be atmospheric for the occasion," said Curtis. "This is fantastic! You have to get something different for your money these days. The main course is Beef Wellington in case you hadn't noticed!"

"When are you ever going to have a room like this all to yourself?" added Rafe. "I'm sure this mystery weekend is going to be brilliant!"

"Don't worry, Alice, the four of us will protect you from the evil demons of *Chillgrave Castle*," said Byron endeavouring to imitate Boris Karloff, the English actor in his role as *Baron Boris von Frankenstein* – the 'Mad Scientist'.

"Do you guys know each other?" Leo asked of no one in particular. "Are you all friends, or something?"

He looked from face to face for a response.

"No, not at all," replied Rafe.

"I'm a pharmacist from St Albans," said Leo, in a bid to kick-start the conversation. "I work for a big chain in Hertfordshire. I hope to build up my own business in the next year."

"He's also getting married next year!" said Alice.

"At least you've got your tuxedo for the big day!" said Curtis. "I work in the City – investment banking, primarily."

"What about you, Rafe?" Leo asked.

"I buy and sell second-hand luxury cars. I'm based in Manchester, originally from Brighton."

"And I've got my own building company in Cardiff," said Byron. I started out as a plumber and managed to grow the business from there."

"What about you, Alice? What kind of work do you do?" asked Curtis.

"I'm a travel writer. I have a remarkably successful and internationally read travel and adventure blog. I'll give you my details."

"Where are you based?" Leo asked.

"London."

"Are you planning to write a story about this mystery weekend, then?" queried Byron. "That's something I would definitely read!"

"Absolutely! I'll send you a link after it's published."

"Are you allowed to write about it?" asked Curtis.

"Why not?"

"Well . . . I mean . . . it's all supposed to be a mystery. If you write about your weekend experience, you'll let the cat out of the bag. Where's the fun in that?"

"Don't worry, I'll try not to give too much away."

"Well, I must say, this is a most interesting group!" replied Leo. "Does anybody know what we're doing tomorrow? Is there a programme of events or itinerary we should know about?"

"Not that I am aware," said Rafe. "It seems we're all in the dark. Pardon the pun."

"It could be that we're not supposed to do anything. Just eat, sleep and wait for the crime to find us!" said Byron. "Then, all we have do is guess who the murderer is!"

"Who said anything about murder?" asked Rafe.

"A mystery weekend would be ridiculously dull if there was no murder to solve!" said Byron. "It has to be the *Butler*. It always is, you know."

"Maybe nothing happens at all!" added Leo. "Now that would be an interesting mystery!"

"And a waste of money!" moaned Curtis.

"At least the food is five-star."

"Actually, I did have a word with the Housekeeper before dinner," said Alice. "She's a nice lady."

The others stopped eating and stared at Alice, who hadn't yet noticed.

"What do you know that we don't?" asked Curtis.

Alice put her knife and fork down and propped her chin in the palm of her left hand.

"She couldn't – or wouldn't – tell me anything about tomorrow. However, the House Steward will be giving us a tour of the castle later tonight."

"Imagine spending three-and-a-half grand for a tour of an old building!" grumbled Rafe.

"Except for one thing," said Alice.

They stared at her.

"Apparently, there is a priceless artefact in the Upper Hall just below the tower that no one has laid eyes on for nearly four thousand years! It's mentioned in the Bible and is quite famous! And we – I'm told – are going to be the first to see it! Apart from the man who found it!"

"Did she tell you what it was?" Leo asked.

"Something about a woman who was turned into a pillar of salt by God! The woman's head is on display in the Upper Hall! It's been insured for twenty-five million pounds!"

"Well, that sounds promising," said Rafe. "I think our mystery weekend has just begun!"

"I wish my head was worth even half as much," said Curtis. "I'd sell it in a heartbeat!"

"I'll see what I can do," said Rafe, "as long as you give me a commission!"

* * *

The Upper Hall was surprisingly small and sparse with only a single window to capture the north-facing light of day. In the evening, two low-wattage table lamps cast a buttery-yellow pallor over the ancient interior. It smelled musty and unused.

In the centre of the room was an old wooden table and on it was a large, hand-blown, solid glass bell *cloche*. The object it covered was the only item in the room that commanded everyone's attention.

The five *Chillgrave* companions gathered around the table. It was just after 10pm on the first night.

"Good evening, *lady* and gentlemen. You are the privileged few to be given access to this special room," said the House Steward as he grinned at Alice. "What you are about to see under the glass dome is one of the most significant archaeological finds in centuries!"

He enunciated every word with the precision and theatrical vitality of an experienced *compère*.

"About four thousand years ago, there were two legendary cities of ancient Palestine known as *Soddom* and *Gomorrah* along the south-eastern coast of the Dead Sea.

"According to the *Book of Genesis*, the men of Soddom were corrupt, immoral and degenerate human beings, who provoked God's anger for their sinful behaviour."

Everyone was wide-eyed and speechless.

"However, there was still one good man – one righteous individual – living in Soddom. His name was Lot. Two angels were sent by God. They told Lot to leave Soddom at once with his wife and their two unmarried daughters before the wrath of the Almighty – fire and brimstone – laid waste to everything before them. '*Escape for thy life!*' 'they were instructed in no uncertain terms. '*Look not behind thee . . . lest thou be consumed!*' Things did not go to plan. Lot's wife did not do as she was told. She hesitated . . . flinched, then turned and looked back at Soddom as she fled. And, for her disobedience – for this single reckless act alone – she was turned into a pillar of salt on the exact patch of ground she stood!"

Everyone took a step forward for a closer look as the House Steward raised the glass dome.

"What you are looking at is the head of Lot's wife!

Some say her name was *Ado* or *Edith*. It is quite valuable. Please do not touch it!"

For an archaeological find of this age, it was in remarkable condition. Although the top and back of the head was understandably pitted and irregular, the overall contour of the skull was symmetrical and easily identifiable as a woman's face.

Her neck had endured in its original profile. Yet, it was angular, almost twisted in attitude as if stretching, turning straining . . . her attention plainly arrested by a frightful disorder crashing down from all directions.

Her mouth was deformed and parted in a macabre expression, her eye sockets distended is if looking into the unfathomable abyss of hell itself!

"Oh my God!" shrieked Alice. "This is insane."

"I don't believe a word of it," said Byron.

"Forensic tests have shown without any doubt, human DNA material – cells and molecules, for example – embedded within the calcified remains that you see in front of you. All of which dates to the time period I have described. What's more, it has been authenticated by two unnamed biblical scholars in the Middle East. I can also tell you that Sir William has already received an offer of £30 million pounds for the head from a French investor."

"I didn't think anyone was allowed to physically *remove* artefacts of this nature from certain places . . . countries," said Curtis. "Isn't that against the –?"

"I can't answer that question. I can tell you, however, that detailed negotiations are, in fact, taking place about the legality of Sir William's discovery as I speak. The situation is volatile as you can imagine – religious passion and all of that – and in view of the extremely sensitive nature of this artefact and murmurings of a plot to steal it back. I can only say that the head will be moved to a more secure location when Sir William returns next week. For the moment, it's as safe as can be right here in Scotland and on this island. And please, NO pictures!"

* * *

*Friday night.*

There was a knock on Leo's door.

"Who is it?" he asked, rubbing his eyes and yawning.

"It's Alice."

"What time is it?" he asked through the locked door.

"Half-past two! I'm sorry to bother you . . . I heard a noise outside. I didn't know what to do."

"Outside where?"

"My window. I saw someone in a boat."

"A boat! What do you mean?"

"Open the door and I'll show you. Please!"

"OK. Give me a minute."

Leo and Alice wore matching dressing gowns: royal blue with *Chillgrave Castle* embroidered in gold on the garment's lapel. This too was a take-home gift.

Alice locked arms with Leo and wheedled him to her room.

"Quick! Look out of the window. Can you see it?"

Leo leaned out as far as he dared and instinctively gazed up at the full moon. It was like a lighthouse beacon that illuminated everything around him. He peered long and hard towards the unobstructed view of the north-eastern coastline, only a stone's throw from the castle itself. Then he cupped a hand behind his ear and listened for any unnatural sounds.

"I can't see or hear anything. Certainly not a boat."

"I definitely saw something, Leo! It was small, like a motorboat. It wasn't the yacht we arrived in. I'll tell the House Steward in the morning."

"Did you see who was in it?"

"I saw a hand and a foot. I don't know if it was from the same person. It could have been. There might be several people in the boat!"

"There's nothing else we can do about it tonight, unless you want to wake everyone up! We better get some sleep and sort it out in the morning. I'm sure there's nothing to worry about."

"Thanks, Leo. I'm terribly sorry for knocking on your door so late and for making such a commotion."

"That's OK, Alice. No problem. It's better to be safe than sorry. Good night."

"Good night, Leo."

Leo had already closed the door and bolted it before Alice could utter another word.

\* \* \*

*Saturday morning.*

After a full Scottish breakfast, Byron, Rafe, Curtis, Alice and Leo were encouraged to explore the castle grounds given that it was a fine Saturday morning.

Verdant woodland mingled with well-worn, narrow trails and occupied the majority of the square-mile island, providing a cool refuge from the noon-day sun.

Byron took the lead and was virtually out of sight of the others.

"I didn't want to say anything during breakfast," said Curtis as the group rambled along the first path they encountered. "What did you guys think of last night's show and tell?"

"I'm not sure what to believe," said Rafe, "though it could be part of this mystery weekend. You never know."

"I think the whole thing is a load of tosh, if you ask me," said Curtis. "I mean, a four-thousand-year-old head made of salt! We're no fools, you know. I agree with Rafe. It could be part of the mystery we're here to solve."

"I wouldn't jump to any conclusions," said Alice. "I made some phone calls last night and –"

"How did you do that?" asked Curtis. "There's no signal on the island! I've already tried."

"There is if you have a satellite phone! And for goodness' sake, don't tell anyone! I need it for my job. You know, travel-related research. It might come in handy if we're forced to leave in a hurry!"

"What's going on?" asked Curtis. "Do you know something we don't? What did you find out?"

"First of all, I can tell you that the Bible story is true in every detail. So is the head's discovery by Sir William what's-his-name. My sources also told me that certain unnamed individuals said the head was taken

89

without permission – pilfered, they said – and that they were eager to get it back, although they didn't exactly phrase it quite that way."

"Who are *they* and what exactly did they say?" Leo asked.

"My sources didn't want to go into too detail, only that they believe hallowed ground had been plundered and defiled by greedy western zealots obsessed with commercial gain and greed . . . and that they would stop at nothing to bring the head back to its original resting place before it was destroyed by those demented with grievous arrogance! Something like that. And don't believe that the motorboat, or whatever it was, that Leo and I saw last night wasn't real."

"Hang on a minute, Alice," said Leo. "I never said any such thing. There might have been a motorboat, but I didn't see it. Your window is near the castle dock, remember? It could have been the yacht."

"Well, at least you can't say it wasn't a motorboat that –"

Before Alice had a chance to finish, Byron let out a piercing shriek. The others ran ahead to find him. He was lying on the ground, clutching his ankle and writhing in agony.

"Oh my God," said Alice. "Are you OK?"

Byron was slow to answer.

"What happened?" asked Rafe?

"I was pushed. I'm sure of it. I lost my balance and tripped over that gnarled tree root sticking out over there by the side of the path!"

"Who could have pushed you?" asked Leo. "There's

no one else around here except us! And none of the staff would do anything like that!"

"I was pushed. I felt a hand, or something, pressing against the small of my back."

"You probably got tangled up in a bush," said Alice.

Byron was in too much pain to argue.

"Is it broken?" Curtis asked.

Byron was breathless.

"I don't know. I don't think so. I hope not. It feels like a sprain – and a bad one at that! There goes my weekend!"

Curtis turned to Leo.

"You and Alice had better alert the Nurse straight away. Rafe and I will help Byron back to the castle."

As soon as the Nurse declared that Byron's ankle had sustained serious ligament damage, Curtis and Rafe took the time to pack Byron's belongings. The private yacht was brought round, and Byron was whisked back to the mainland for treatment.

Alice's alleged sighting of a motorboat from her window and Byron's version of events leading up to his fall were reported to the Butler, who said he would treat both accounts with the utmost care and attention.

"Don't worry about a thing," he said.

* * *

*Saturday night.*

There was a knock on Leo's door.

"Is that you, Alice?" he asked, reluctant to open the door.

"Yes. Please let me in."

"Have you seen something else this time?"

"No, not this time. I did hear voices, though! Please, let me in. I'm scared!"

Leo slipped on his dressing gown and unlocked the door. He turned the handle slowly and pulled the door towards himself until he saw the side of Alice's face framed neatly by the slender opening he was eager to defend.

"What time is it?" he asked.

"It's just after one o'clock."

Leo side-stepped his way into the hallway and closed the door behind him.

"What about the others – Rafe and Curtis? Have you checked with them?"

"No. You're much closer. Besides, they think I'm crazy. They don't believe anything I say. You do, don't you, Leo?"

"Well, I don't know . . . I mean –"

"What about the plot to recover the head and Byron's accident? I didn't make any of that up, did I?"

Alice was close to tears.

"You said you heard voices. When? Where?" Leo asked.

"About ten minutes ago. I heard at least two voices. I'm not sure if they were male or female. So, I opened my door. I think they came from the Upper Hall."

"Why didn't you tell the Butler or the House Steward instead of me? Surely, they need to know! It's not up to us."

"Oh, for sure! First, we ought to find out if anyone is

up there, so we know what we're talking about."

Leo was struggling to remain focused, objective.

"Perhaps the owner has already returned early from South America and is talking to the Butler or the House Steward about the security of the castle or the threat being made against him personally," said Leo. "This is supposed to be a fun weekend. It's possible that we might be in the wrong place at the wrong time. We should ask for a refund and get the hell of out of here. At least you've got a phone that works. Can you send a text to Claire?"

"First things first, Leo. We must do something. We can't simply ignore what's going on."

A heartbeat later, she wrapped her fingers around Leo's wrist like a pair of hose clamp pliers and pulled him away from his room towards the Upper Hall.

"We have to investigate," said Alice.

"Why? It's none of our business!"

"Yes, it is. Look, this could be an incredible story and I'm going to write about it! This is what I've been dreaming about: a remarkable relic from the ancient world that no one else has seen for nearly four thousand years and a plot by religious fanatics from the Middle East who intend to steal it back."

Leo couldn't help himself as he accompanied Alice to the Upper Hall. He was ensnared by the situation, attracted by the intrigue and potential danger of the unknown. It was the supreme adventure of his life.

"Don't worry, Leo, it'll be all right. You can be in my story too. I'll give you a credit."

The lights were on in the Upper Hall.

"See! I told you so," said Alice. "Someone has been up here tonight. The Butler – or whoever – would have turned off the lights."

Alice went to the window.

"Leo! Come here. The window is off the latch. I'm sure someone has been here or at least tried to get in."

"Can I suggest we leave here immediately and tell someone what's going on? I don't want to be thrown out of a window in the middle of the night."

"Don't be so melodramatic, Leo. Nothing is going to happen to us."

"What are you doing?"

Alice lifted the glass dome and picked up the head.

"What are you doing?" Leo repeated a second time. His tone was a pitch higher. "Are you crazy?"

"I just want to see what it feels like. It's much heavier than I thought – like a bowling ball. Funny smell too, like charred matches. Fancy a whiff?"

"No thanks. If either of us damage or drop it –"

Before Leo finished talking, Alice thrust the head into his stomach. Leo grabbed it with both hands like a footballer as if his life depended on it. His fingers splayed to their limit like a goalkeeper, who had just saved a penalty in the last minute of the game!

Alice moved swiftly, took her place beside Leo and took a selfie of the two of them. Then she grabbed the head back and told Leo to take a picture her holding the prized treasure.

\* \* \*

*Sunday morning.*

Leo, Rafe, Curtis and Alice were woken up an hour before breakfast. The Butler pounded on their doors abruptly and asked the four of them to gather in the Great Hall immediately.

"No need to dress formally and please be quick about it!" the Butler advised.

The seriousness of the occasion was marked by a meeting with the entire staff supervised by Sir William Riley McCallum himself!

He turned to face Alice and Leo. His jet-lagged eyes drilled into them. He spoke slowly and quietly, his voice humming with overtones of indignation.

"WHERE is the head of Lot's wife – MY head! It is m-i-s-s-i-n-g! I've had a long flight home and am in no mood for any bullshit!"

Before they could respond, Sir William raised his hand and put a finger to his lips. The Housekeeper walked up to Sir William, extended her arm and handed over Alice's mobile phone. Alice was furious.

"The Butler has also given me a detailed written account – Alice – of your late-night encounters with Mr Manners. My staff is well trained to keep an eye on everything that goes on under my roof. If you want to pair off, that's none of my business. It is my business when you disrespect valuable property that doesn't belong to you."

Alice defended Leo and herself without wavering, proclaiming that Sir William's conclusion was utterly hollow, wanting of any real facts. Alice also knew that pictures don't lie and that explaining the images on her phone would not be easy.

Sir William ordered a thorough search of all the rooms including those of the staff.

"If the head is not found before midnight tonight – Alice and Leo – the Specialist Crime Division of Police Scotland will be notified first thing tomorrow morning and I imagine you will be held for further questioning. And don't forget, the Butler's written statement and the pictures of both you and Leo in the Upper Hall holding the head will be used as evidence.

"If you have anything more to say to me or the police about your actions, I suggest you hold your tongue until tomorrow. There will be enough of time for chit-chat."

*A great birthday this is going to be*, thought Leo, with a dash of sarcasm.

"I'm sure you won't mind, Alice, if I give your phone to the Butler for safe keeping, or until the police have had a chance to examine it. If the head *is* returned to me, rest assured that I will not take this matter any further. The four of you will be free to go and all will be forgotten. I may even refund your money."

"Can I at least call Claire? Please!" begged Leo.

"His fiancée," added Alice.

"I'll think about it."

* * *

*Monday morning, 5am.*

The Chambermaid screamed. Then a second outburst in quick succession. High-pitched, raw shock waves consumed the sweet tranquillity of a new day.

When the rest of the household staff arrived on the scene, they found the Chambermaid standing over the Butler. She covered her mouth with both hands. Alice and Leo were the last to appear.

"Oh my God, what happened? shrieked Alice.

The Nurse was scrabbling for position over the body. The Butler lay sprawled on the castle dock next to the yacht. One side of his face was daubed in blood.

"Is he dead?" asked Sir William.

Leo began to tremble. His body shuddered like a car engine whose spark plugs had worn out.

A minute passed before anyone spoke.

"I'm afraid he has no pulse," said the Nurse. "He's been struck on the head. Yes, he's dead!"

Alice covered her eyes. She started to cry, then lost her balance as if on the verge of fainting. Leo grabbed her with both hands and hugged her tightly. With due diligence, Sir William and the Nurse lifted the stricken man off the ground and carried him onto the yacht.

"Everyone else, please go inside," said Sir William. "No one will be permitted to leave *Chillgrave Castle* until the head of Lot's wife is returned to me safe and undamaged. The Nurse and I will see to the Butler and contact his family immediately. I will return with the police as soon as possible! I suggest our four guests start packing and that you all remain in your rooms until the police arrive. The House Steward will ensure you do as you're told."

\* \* \*

*Monday morning, 8am.*

"LEO MANNERS!" bellowed the Housekeeper through a closed door. "You are wanted at once in the Great Hall. The police would like to interview you."

Leo opened the door slowly. He was in no rush. With stooped shoulders and luggage to hand, he stared at his feet as they dragged along the floor towards the very moment he was dreading.

"Have you seen Alice? I mean, is she all right?" His voice was surprisingly weak.

"They are all waiting for you, Mr Manners," said the Housekeeper. "Come along now."

Leo looked up at her. There was something about her expression, or was it the way she spoke to him that sparked a cautionary note of optimism in his heart? He felt a trickle of adrenalin seep into his spirt. All manner of possibilities crowded his brain like bumper cars colliding with each other at an amusement park.

*Maybe, just maybe*, he thought: *They found the head of Lot's wife AND the person who killed the Butler. Maybe someone has confessed. Was it Alice? It must be her! Or the Butler himself? Yet how – he's dead! Rafe and Curtis are innocent enough. And Byron, well he couldn't possibly – I haven't done anything dishonest or illegal, other than hold a four-thousand-year-old head in my hands, and that was my own stupidity.*

When Leo reached the Great Hall, the Housekeeper stepped in front of him and opened the door. Everyone was there: Curtis, Rafe and Alice . . . Sir William, the House Steward, the Chambermaid, the Chef and his two Servers, the Nurse and a Police Detective.

"Come in, Leo," said Sir William. His voice was cold and sombre.

"You have a lot of explaining to do Mr Manners," said the Police Detective. He pointed to a chair. "Now sit down."

The silence was bedevilling. Leo was confronted by a steely-eyed audience who bored down on him with unrelenting scathing.

Then Sir William turned to Alice and nodded.

Surprises can be pleasurable or hazardous. Either way, they will set your adrenalin alight and rattle your bones to the core.

The stupefied, punch-drunk look of surprise on Leo's face was simply unforgettable.

Sir William stepped forward, clutched his face and at once began wrenching at his skin, rending, yanking and pulling it in all directions: first his forehead, then his cheeks and chin.

It was a gruesome exhibition, until Leo understood. It was a convincing, wily disguise. Sir William smiled – only it wasn't *him*. It was *Byron* and in perfect health! He bowed and stepped back.

Next to step forward was the Police Detective. He, too, had befuddled the innocent Leo Manners – for it wasn't a Police Detective at all. It was the *Butler*, also in disguise and in fine fettle!

Everyone, save for Leo Manners, applauded, for Leo thought he had just seen a ghost, or at least a dead man walking! The *Butler* patted Leo on the back and smiled.

"What's going on?" Leo pleaded. His hands clasped firmly against the back of his neck, then rifled through his hair vigorously as if trying to massage a bit of sense into his brain.

Byron – *aka Sir William* – came forward and put his arm around Leo's shoulder.

"We all owe you an explanation, Leo."

He spoke with an American accident.

"May I present *The Mystery Weekend Players*!" They smiled and bowed.

"We are all actors and actresses and have put on a little act for you this weekend. Your fiancée did pay for the show. I do hope you enjoyed our little performance. My real name is Jason Conway, from Scranton, Ohio. I own this castle and the yacht. I am also a professional stunt man and have appeared in a dozen films, both here and in America. Alice is an exceptionally talented actress, who also specialises in special effects and prosthetic makeup."

"Oh my God. This is crazy! What about the head of Lot's wife?" Leo was flummoxed.

"Oh, the story is true enough. You can read the *Book of Genesis* for yourself, except for the head you saw in the Upper Hall. My son made that for me. He's a professional sculptor."

"We have one more surprise for you Leo," said Alice.

The entire ensemble broke into voice with a hearty rendition of *Happy Birthday*. A three-tiered birthday cake, boasting twenty-five candles in full flame, was carried into the Great Hall.

Leo stood up and turned around. He could have leapt into the air with jubilation. And he did!

"Happy birthday, Leo," chimed Claire as she joined in and began to sing.

"The clock does not give its owner immortality, Mr Weekes. This is most certainly impossible. The clock simply prevents you from growing older, provided you follow the instructions and wind the clock back twenty-four hours before each new day begins or time will catch up with you in a single breath and take back what it has lost to the clock."

# It's
# About
# Time

It was a cold and windy November evening. Abel
Weekes had just finished having dinner with his wife.
The knock on the door was unexpected.

"Hello, can I help you?"

"I am terribly sorry to disturb you. I am looking for
Mr Weekes – Abel Weekes."

"Yes, I'm Abel Weekes."

"My name is Rufus O'Shea."

He was a young man, not more than thirty, about the
same age as Abel.

"I have something for you. It belonged to your great-
grandfather, Bertram Weekes. I thought you might like
to have it."

"Bertram Weekes!"

Abel stared at Rufus before uttering a word. His eyes
glowed at the sound of his great-grandfather's name.

"I hope you do not mind me barging in on you like this," said Rufus. "I came across the article you wrote on the *Boer War*. I read it about six weeks ago in one of the Sunday magazines. It took me a while to find out where you lived, and here I am. It is important that I talk to you."

"Who is it, darling?" asked his wife.

"Rufus . . ." Abel couldn't remember his last name.

"O'Shea. Rufus O'Shea," said the stranger so all could hear.

"You'd better come in then, Mr O'Shea," said Abel. "There's no sense standing outside."

"That is kind of you. Please, call me, Rufus."

"Have you travelled far?" asked Abel.

Rufus spoke slowly.

"I have come from *Little Dewsford*. It is about ten miles from here if I am not mistaken. I am renting the old schoolhouse in the village. It is a quiet part of the country. Peaceful and serene."

"Yes, I know it well."

Rufus O'Shea was about six feet tall, smartly dressed in highly polished shoes and cuffed trousers with pin-sharp creases. A royal blue scarf matched his long coat. He carried a small wooden box by a handle made of braided hemp.

"Sorry, Abel – I'm afraid I'm late again," said Jennifer Weekes. "I have to leave."

"I'll see you later, Jen. Say hello to the lads in the band."

"I will," she replied as the door closed behind her.

"Is your wife an entertainer?"

"She sings in the local pub, *The Barking Goats*, two nights a week.

You might want to stop in and see her perform. She has a wonderful voice!"

"I must just do that if I have time. Are you also a musician?"

"No. I teach history and math at the local sixth form college," said Abel. "What about you? How is it that you have an interest in the *Boer War* and my great-grandfather specifically?"

"I have come to see you about *this*, Mr Weekes."

Rufus raised the wooden box head high. The box was about the size of an A4 sheet of paper along its length and width and about six inches in depth.

He put the box on the table.

Rufus opened the box as quickly as he dared without damaging its contents. Inside was a hand-crafted, self-winding carriage clock with a skeleton movement set into a black iron case. The hours were marked by classic Roman numerals, and atop the clock was a mushroom-shaped brass bell.

"It is fairly discoloured, I am afraid, and well-worn around the edges as you can see. Considering its age, it is still in working condition," said Rufus.

Abel sat down in front of the clock and examined it in more detail.

"Are you telling me that this clock belonged to my great-grandfather, Bertram Weekes?"

"Please, take it. I want you to have it."

Rufus stared at Abel.

"I believe it was mentioned in Bertram's letters in

detail and quoted in your article," said Rufus. "He carried the clock in this wooden case everywhere he went. He said it was a blessing."

"Yes, there was a clock of this exact size and design mentioned in the letters. How can you be so certain this is the very *one*? Do you have any proof? Do you have documentation?"

"Only my word."

"I'm sorry, I don't understand."

"Please hear me out. As a teacher, I hope you can keep an open mind. It is a matter of life and death."

Abel's face was ashen.

"It happened during the *Battle of Paardeberg* on the banks of the Modder River near Kimberley. There was a great number of casualties on both sides. Bertram wrote letters about his experiences and, more to the point, how his life had been saved by a fellow soldier on the very first day of the conflict, the eighteenth of February 1900. No one knew who this person was."

"Yes, I know the date well."

"Weeks later, Bertram discovered the identity of the soldier who had saved his life and gave him this clock as a token of his profound gratitude. A picture was taken of the two men at the time by a newspaper photographer. It was never published."

"Why not?"

"The camera fell from the photographer's grasp and smashed into a thousand pieces."

"I see. Why should I believe your story? Where is your proof? And how could such a clock have survived all this time?"

"The soldier who saved your great-grandfather's life is my source! Surely, there can be no better evidence than that?"

"Your source? No one knows who this person was! His identity was never revealed. I know nothing about the existence of such information, unless of course this mystery soldier had also written letters of his own and written about the incident."

"There are no letters. Just the word of one man, who had saved the life of your great-grandfather. I know him well."

"You're talking in riddles. Do you know the name of this soldier or not? Can you prove it? I will make you an offer to buy his letters, or whatever evidence you may have unearthed."

"I have not come here for money. It is the clock that concerns me. The soldier's name was *Rufus O'Shea*, British 6th Division, under the command of Lieutenant General Herbert Kitchener. It was I, who saved your great-grandfather's life! *He* gave the clock to *me*!"

Abel stood up. He took a step forward. His eyes bore down on his guest, who remained in his chair.

"If you think I'm a fool, Mr Rufus O'Shea, then you are sadly mistaken! I don't know what you're playing at. If you're not after money, then what exactly do you want?"

"I have come to see you about *time*, Abel, not about money."

Rufus reached into his pocket and held a piece of paper in the palm of his hand. The document was yellowed around the edges, and all save one corner was still intact. He unfolded it slowly with great care and handed it to Abel.

"You can keep it if you like, it is of no further use to me. It's my birth certificate from the General Register Office for England and Wales."

Abel's attention drifted between the words on the document and the face of Rufus O'Shea.

"Is this another brainteaser?" asked Abel.

"Mr Weekes, I can assure you that the piece of paper you hold in your hand is original and legitimate. I have kept in an envelope all this time. As you can clearly see, I was born on the 2nd of May 1882!"

"Who are you, Rufus O'Shea?"

"A man, just like you."

"No sir, you are unquestionably not like me!"

Rufus paced around the room, all the time looking at the watch on is wrist.

"I have not let your great-grandfather's clock out of my sight for more than a day and have kept it in this same box you see. When the war ended on the last day of May 1902, I returned home to England, and had the clock restored to working order in the Kings Road, Chelsea. I sat in the shop and waited for it to be mended. When I paid for it, I was handed a piece of paper that had been found wedged under the bell. The writing was badly stained and barely legible. I managed to re-write the message as best I could. You'll find it under the bell."

Abel tilted the clock and removed the message. He took his time unfolding the piece of paper, then sat down in a chair before he read it aloud:

Don't forget to extend your stay.
Round it goes for an extra day.
Count the days and you will find
That one in seven, you must wind.

Move the hands before the morn.
Fifteen minutes is just the norm.
Left is right as time will tell!
Wait your turn to hear the bell.

If you stop to end your stay,
Time will call and have its way.
Your flesh and bones will be no more.
Death will come to settle the score.

"More cryptic nonsense!" muttered Abel. He placed the clock on the table and raised his hands in dismay.

"Fifteen minutes before the midnight bell," said Rufus, "you must turn the clock's hands anti-clockwise a full twenty-four hours. If you do as the note says, every day without fail, then you will not grow a minute older in body or mind. The world will go on and age as it always has, except for you. However, you must also remember to wind the clock every seventh day to keep it ticking. However, if you should fail or forget to do any of these things, or merely shorten your extended stay in this world, then time will take back what it is owed."

"Nonsense!"

"You do not look convinced."

"Did Bertram say where he got the clock?"

"No."

"Or who made it?"

"No."

"You have no idea?"

"How could I know?"

"What about the shop on the Kings Road? What did they tell you?"

"It is a common timepiece. It looks like any other mechanical carriage clock of its age."

"Why did Bertram give it away?"

"I have already told you. For saving his life! Your great-grandfather had no idea what he had in his possession. But I did as I discovered over time. No one else knows except me. At first, I thought it was a prankster's game for fools, so I played along for the fun of it. Every night, fifteen minutes before midnight, and as instructed, I turned the hour and minute hands anti-clockwise twenty-four hours. As the weeks, months and years went by, my body never aged. I could have stopped then and there and paid a small price for my youth. I didn't. The dream of never growing older was far too strong to resist. My wife and two children thought I had become an evil spirit. My children did not speak to me and would hide in their rooms. When I finally told my family the truth, they laughed at me and told me to leave. They had become frightened of me and said they couldn't live with me any longer. In my heart, I had no choice, so I packed my bags and have

110

been travelling ever since, from city to city, country to country, working to make ends meet, and never staying long enough to make friends. I never saw my children grow up, nor did I grow older with my wife. We had become two strangers, lost, and separated by time. They have long since died."

"Didn't you re-marry?"

"How could I? By then, I was trapped by the clock. Damned if I kept it and damned if I didn't. I changed my name to Waldo Hill. It was as good as any I could think of, though I have always preferred my given name. I also changed my identification documents – passport, driving licence and everything else, including a new birth certificate. I met good people along the way who helped me take on a new identity. I paid them well, of course, for their time, and never told them why I needed to be someone else."

"This is madness. Eternal youth . . . immortality?"

"The clock does not give its owner immortality, Mr Weekes. This is most certainly impossible. The clock simply prevents you from growing older, provided you follow the instructions and wind the clock back twenty-four hours before each new day begins or time will catch up with you in a single breath and take back what it has lost to the clock. You must also understand that time without ageing will not stop you from getting sick with the common cold or succumb to unspeakable, life-threatening diseases. And will it not save you if you are hit by a car or bus. Surviving such calamities is not up to the clock."

"What happens then?" asked Abel.

Rufus shrugged.

"I am sure I will be the last to know. Whether or not you believe me or keep the clock is up to you."

Abel thought for a moment, then asked.

"Why don't you sell it? You could name your price."

"Time has no more value to me. It is worthless."

"Why give it to me?"

"You have a connection to it. I thought it only right and proper that you have first refusal."

"Will it work for others? What about Jennifer? Will it work for her as well? And for our future children?"

"You may be more fortunate than I was. I have no way of knowing. I am just one man, the same as you. I have no way of knowing the future."

Rufus looked at his watch.

"I have to go now. After midnight, it will not matter anymore. I have something else to give you. This is a duplicate key to the old schoolhouse in *Little Dewsford* where I am living. Please take it. I would be extremely grateful if you could stop by tomorrow morning. Let yourself in. Not too early. Ten o'clock would be fine. Arrangements that need to be made."

"I don't understand. What arrangements?"

"I have left instructions for you. Will you help me?"

Abel felt cornered. He had no choice.

"Yes, of course. I will come. I will do that for you."

Abel looked at him with compassion.

"Where are you going?"

"Home."

"What will happen to you?"

Rufus shrugged. Tears formed in his eyes.

"At midnight, I will be dead.

"Why don't you keep the clock, stay a while longer? I'm sure Jennifer would love to meet you. She could introduce you to our friends. We could have a pint or two at the pub. Better yet, I'm sure the college would take you on as a teacher. I'll write a reference for you. I promise not to mention the clock to anyone. It will be our secret."

Rufus grinned. His expression was hollow.

"You are a kind man. It is a shame that we did not meet under different circumstances and in another time. I have grown tired of saving time. The world keeps changing. It is complicated and cruel, and it has been difficult keeping up with it. I think about my wife and children every day and wish I had never saved your great-grandfather's life! There would be no clock and I would now be lying beside by wife. Time would leave us alone and continue with its normal business. I can still dream like anybody else, can I not?"

"You have experienced more than any one person could have imagined. Is that not of any consolation?"

"I have lost more than I have gained. Please give my regards to your wife. Unfortunately, I will be unable to hear her sing this evening. Thank you for taking the clock. So long, Mr Weekes."

Rufus closed the door before Abel could speak.

* * *

"I'll be back later," said Abel.

"Where are you going?" asked Jennifer. "It's nearly

113

four o'clock."

"The college."

"It's Saturday, Abel. No school today, remember?"

"I left a batch of test papers there. I thought I'd mark a stack of test papers this weekend."

"You won't be long, will you?"

"I'll be home as quickly as I can."

"By the way, I meant to ask you about that clock."

"What clock?"

"The one on your office desk. I hadn't noticed it before. Is it new?"

"Rufus O'Shea gave it to me yesterday after you left for the pub. I forgot to tell you. He's a history teacher, just like me. He found the clock at an estate sale in Australia. After he bought it, he discovered that it had belonged to my great-grandfather, Bertram – you know, the one I wrote about, who fought in the *Boer War?*"

"Surely your friend didn't fly here from Australia just to give you a clock?"

"No, of course not. And he's not my friend. I met him for the first time yesterday. Remember? He's in the process of moving back to England and thought I'd like to have the clock for my collection. He read one of my articles in a magazine."

"How much was it?"

"What?"

"The clock!"

"He said he didn't want any money for it. He was stubborn about that. He wanted to find the right home for it and wanted me to have it."

"That was thoughtful of him."

"Yes, it was."

"How did he know where we live?"

"I have no idea. I never thought of asking him. Besides, it's not too hard finding someone with a name like Weekes and the connection to the *Boer War*."

"Are you going to see him again?"

"There's no need. Besides, I forgot to ask him where he lives. Anyway, I'd better be off, Jen. I'd like to get back before dark."

There would be more lies.

Abel drove directly to the old schoolhouse and let himself in with the key that Rufus had given to him.

"Rufus? It's Abel. Jennifer has invited you to lunch. We both have. She'd like to see you again."

No reply. He repeated the call.

Abel was nervous. He walked slowly throughout the house, saving the bedroom for the last.

Rufus – or so Abel assumed – was lying on his back and was covered to his neck with a blanket. His head was resting squarely on two pillows, face up. Hollow, black eye sockets were trained on the ceiling. His skin looked like a threadbare rag and was without shape or form. His nose and mouth had become visible bone.

Abel approached the corpse slowly and reluctantly. He extended his arm at full stretch and peeled back the blanket. Abel choked as he sucked in a mouthful of air. He dropped to the floor on one knee, coughing without release, trying to catch his breath.

The body was squat and devoid of air and blood and was flat like a two-dimension cardboard caricature of its original self. It had no connecting arms for they had been severed cleanly from the scapula like desiccated tree branches, snapped off under their own weight. Abel covered the gruesome remains with a blanket.

His attention turned to the bedside table, where an envelope had been placed next to a framed photograph of the victim's wife and children. It was addressed to Abel Weekes.

Dear Abel:

Thank you for keeping your word. Please accept my apologies for involving you in my life and now my death. I had no one else to turn to at such a late hour.

In the envelope, you will find the keys to my car and the relevant documents, which I have signed over to you by name. You may keep the car or sell it to pay for my funeral, as you wish. I have reserved a place at the local church. You will find the necessary details below.

Please tell Mr Wainright that I am terribly sorry for leaving and that I will not be able to carry on with the monthly rental payments due to unforeseen circumstances.

I hope the clock brings you and your family the best of luck and good times in the years ahead.

Remember, your fantastic tales through time can never be told.

I have one last request. My sudden death requires a believable explanation. A heart attack or stroke should be satisfactory. Whatever you decide to do, you must NEVER mention the clock!

You are a generous man, Abel Weekes. I enjoyed meeting you and your wife.

Best wishes for a long life
Waldo Hill (Rufus O'Shea)

Time had consumed the life of Rufus O'Shea, stripping him of everything he had ever been.

Abel folded the letter, put it back in the envelope and stuffed it in his back pocket. He stood beside the bed, thinking. Rufus must not be discovered by anyone, not like this. There could be no explanation of his death, no mention of the clock and no connection between the two of them.

The remains of Rufus O'Shea had to be moved, hidden and buried. Whether Abel liked it or not, he had become embroiled in a crime scene – a human being was dead – and at the moment he was a key witness, if not a suspect!

Abel sat in the kitchen, staring down the corridor at

the open bedroom door and having a tacit conversation with himself.

'Exactly what crime has been committed? What have I done? NOTHING! Yesterday, Rufus was alive and well and now he's dead. I didn't kill him. He killed himself. If there's been a crime, then it's THAT. Suicide! Better yet, assisted suicide. Killed by *TIME!* I could be questioned, searched and arrested, then charged with something serious. How do I explain his birth certificate and the letter he wrote to me, not to mention his keys! Hell! I have a spare key to the old schoolhouse and the keys to his car. Burglary, trespassing, theft . . . murder! What am I supposed to tell the police? Who's going to believe my story?'

*'Mr Weekes: how long have you known Waldo Hill, the dead man?'*

'I only met him yesterday for the first time, less than twenty-four hours ago. His real name is Rufus O'Shea.'

*'How do you know that?'*

'He told me. He gave me his birth certificate. Have a look for yourself.'

*'Why did he do that?'*

'It's about time – the clock. I didn't believe him at first. Now I do.'

*'What clock? What are you talking about, Mr Weekes?'*

'Rufus O'Shea was born on the 2$^{nd}$ of May 1882. That's what he told me. Look at his birth certificate. He fought in the *Boer War* alongside Bertram Weekes, my great-grandfather. He gave Rufus this clock in gratitude for saving his life. There was a note stuffed under the bell of the clock. Bertram knew nothing about the note in the clock. Never mind, it's too complicated to explain. It's just that, well, Rufus discovered that if he turned the clock's hand to the left – you know, the opposite way – he would never grow older. It sounds crazy, I know.'

*'Mr O'Shea doesn't look very young to me, does he, Mr Weekes? In all my years on the force, I have never seen anything like it. How did you do it? Have you done this before?'*

'Do what? I didn't kill him or anybody else! Why would I do that? I hardly knew the man!'

*'That's why we're here. To find out.'*

'It was suicide.'

*'How do you know that? I suppose he did this to himself?'*

'Yes, precisely! He told me. It's a long story. He was desperately unhappy. He didn't want to live like this – never getting any older – so he stopped using the clock. He knew time would kill him in the end. It was his choice. He asked for my help. It's in the letter he wrote. Here, read it. He wanted me to make the arrangements for his funeral. I said yes. I promised I would help him. That's why I'm here. To help.'

*'I think you'd better come with us, Mr Weekes. Call your wife and tell her you may be home later*

119

*than expected. We need to see this clock of yours!'*

Abel waited until the afternoon light had dulled before driving home and wondered if anyone had seen him enter or leave the home of Rufus O'Shea.

"I wish I'd never come here," said Abel aloud.

\* \* \*

Jennifer had been asked to sing at *The Barking Goats* that same evening as the pub's regular weekend singer was ill. Jennifer was in two minds about accepting, but Abel persuaded her to take the gig.

"You should do it, Jen."

"What about our dinner reservation? I was really looking forward to a steak dinner tonight."

"I'll re-book the restaurant for tomorrow. Besides, I can use the time tonight to mark the test papers."

More lies.

Abel waited thirty minutes, then drove back to the old schoolhouse in *Little Dewsford*. Once inside and using a pocket-sized torch, he drew the curtains in every room, then headed to the bedroom.

He carried the body to his car and placed it on the back seat and locked the car door. Rufus was no heavier than a daily newspaper. Then Abel searched the dead man's car for anything that might connect the two men – Abel's address or directions to his own house.

When Abel was satisfied there was no such evidence, he went back to the old schoolhouse. He examined everything that came to mind: the bedside dressing

120

table; the sideboard and the chest of drawers; every bookshelf front and back and even the wastepaper bin. He was careful and methodical, all the while looking at his watch and the swift passage of time. He had to be certain there was nothing in the old schoolhouse that connected Rufus O'Shea, aka Waldo Hill, to Abel Weekes or his great-grandfather for that matter.

He rifled through a stack of *National Geographic* magazines from 1940 to 1959 and was tempted to take one as a souvenir. He didn't.

Hanging on the wall was a framed picture of the *Evening Standard*, August 1966. The cover headline in capital letters, read: 'CHAMPIONS of the WORLD' Wedged under the glass on the bottom-left corner was an autographed Polaroid picture of Bobby Moore, the captain of England's winning World Cup team.

Abel found a treasure trove of other timeless memories from the life of Rufus O'Shea: a furled poster of *The Jazz Singer* starring Al Jolson – the first feature-length movie with synchronized dialogue made in 1927; a sales brochure for the 1933 *Lincoln K Convertible Roadster*; numerous boxes of Super 8mm film – one was labelled 'The Launch of Apollo 11'; *The Guardian* newspaper, wrapped in a thick plastic bag. Published on 14 December 1911, it featured Roald Amundsen's record-breaking trek to the South Pole; one ticket from the 1936 *Olympic Games* in Berlin – valid for the Olympic Stadium only; a copy of the 1964 Beatles record album: *A Hard Day's Night* signed by the four band members; coins, hats, postcards and souvenirs collected over the decades from more than a dozen countries, and bags of family pictures.

Abel knew he had to leave quickly. He found a towel and wiped his fingerprints clean from everything he had touched, or remembered touching, including the two keys: one for the old schoolhouse, the other for Rufus's car. Using a tissue, he put one key on the bedside table and the other key in the kitchen.

He checked his pockets for Rufus's birth certificate, his car ownership documents and the letter he had written to Abel. He had them all.

Abel was making it up as he went along, minute by minute. He had no specific plan in mind other than getting home as soon as possible without being seen or arrested. First, he had to tie ups the loose ends.

\* \* \*

He drove to *Dewsford Marsh*, a small, wooded area about a mile from *Little Dewsford* and parked by the side of the road.

There was no one in sight.

He was safe.

He carried the remains of Rufus O'Shea to the far side of the woodlands and hid the body under a pile of fallen leaves. A half-moon in the clear night sky provided ample light. Even if Rufus were found, identification would be impossible.

He walked another twenty paces, or so, from the burial site, hid behind a tree and fell to his knees. He bundled together all the incriminating documents – Rufus's birth certificate, car ownership and letter – and burned the lot. Luckily for Abel, he carried a lighter found in the pub the previous week.

He watched the last page turn black and disintegrate into dust amongst the leaves. He stirred the leaf-litter with a stick like a chef mixing a grand Caesar salad.

Abel Weekes was free and clear.

There could be no connection between the two men.

He would be home before Jennifer returned from her Saturday night gig and vowed never to speak of Rufus O'Shea, *or* Waldo Hill, again.

\* \* \*

It was a short drive home from *Dewsford Marsh*. Abel was bursting with questions that needed answers and a big decision to make before midnight.

*What should I do about the clock? Should I tell Jennifer? What do I do if she's against it? Will the clock work for both of us? What about our future children? Should I hide the clock from everyone?*

Abel knew everything and nothing about the clock. With Rufus dead, Abel was now in charge. Yet, there was no way of knowing the answers to any of these questions. There was no one to ask for advice, not even Jennifer.

So, before he walked through the door, he decided to say nothing! He kept the clock on his office desk and followed the instructions to the letter. He often worked late into the evening, so being at his office desk until midnight was not unusual.

Once he started to use the clock, he could not stop.

Nor could he leave the house or go on holiday unless he took the clock with him. Although Jennifer would laugh at Abel's peculiar behaviour, she never took his obsession about the clock seriously . . . until the day she broke it fifteen years later! It was an accident. The vacuum cord swept across the top of Abel's desk and, in the process, hurled the clock and its components across the room.

Abel was demented. He walked the full length of the Kings Road searching desperately for the repair shop that had once mended the very same clock for Rufus O'Shea. It started to rain. The brown paper bag in which he carried the clock unravelled in seconds. The contents fell from his grasp and lay scattered on the pavement.

Abel returned home in a taxi. He sat calmly in the backseat, knowing that something bad was going to happen to him after midnight, and prayed that time would take pity on him.

The following morning, something bad did happen. Abel's muscles and bones twisted and distended. His back stooped at an acute angle. His shoulders slumped into a deformed-looking arc. His skin had crimped, its fleshy pleats now embedded into his face.

His voice grew weak, hoarse and without the words to apologise for his selfish deeds. His eyes were tired and sad for they had seen what he done to himself and those he loved.

He told Jennifer the entire story. No gruesome detail had been spared from his account, including the day he buried Rufus O'Shea in *Dewsford Marsh*. As he

124

begged for pity and understanding, his two children ran from the house.

Jennifer left Abel, not because he stayed young and unchanged for fifteen years, and not because he had morphed into a deformed and grotesque human being, but because he had lied and deceived the woman he married and the children he fathered.

Abel Weekes never saw his wife or children again and lamented a simple truth: time cannot be borrowed, bought or stolen, and it cannot be given away for free by a clock!

"The world would be a much happier place if we didn't complain so much. When we are dissatisfied or find fault with something, we express resentment. In other words, we complain! We protest, moan, criticize and kick up a fuss . . . We are squawk boxes, each and everyone of us! There are more than one hundred words for complaining!"

# What's Your Complaint?

The TV studio is packed to capacity.
Lights dim to total blackness.
Applause signs illuminate.
Handclapping – loud and sustained.
Spotlights dazzle the eyes.
Out from the shadows – stage left.
The host of the show appears.

"Thank you, ladies and gentlemen . . ."

He holds up his hands for quiet.

"Welcome to the *Jimmy Dreem Show*. I'm Jimmy Dreem from *Times Square* in New York."

More applause and whistles.

"Glad you could join us. We have a fabulous show for you tonight. I'm sure you all know who my first guest is –"

Sustained applause.

"Please . . ."

He holds up his hands again for quiet.

"My first guest has been hailed as one of Britain's top supermodels. Even from the age of ten, she glowed with the elegance and sophistication of someone well beyond her years and had already appeared on the front covers of Britain's leading fashion magazines."

Applause.

"After nearly twenty years at the top of her game, she found international success as a fashion designer. The award-winning *Nia-Rose* label was lauded for its exclusive and unique range of clothing for business women."

Applause.

"My special guest has a degree in Psychology and Language Sciences from *University College London*, has appeared in a Hollywood movie, and also speaks fluent French and Italian."

More applause.

"If you've seen the news this week, you'll know what I'm talking about. Just phenomenal! Would you please welcome the founder and CEO of *What's Your Complaint?* A colossal superstar and legend . . . the exceptionally beautiful and talented Nia-Rose Sale!"

A standing ovation.

Nia-Rose waves to the audience with both hands. Her gold and silver bracelets glitter under the bright studio lights.

"Thank you so much, Jimmy. It's a great pleasure to be on your show!"

She sits down on the cream-coloured sofa.

"I believe we've tried to arrange this before. I've either been out of the country or on location somewhere . . . modelling or filming."

"You're looking beautiful this evening."

"At my age, that's extremely kind of you."

Laughter.

Jimmy looks at the audience and smiles.

Applause and more laughter.

"Correct me if I'm wrong, but I don't think your age is the world's best kept secret."

Nia-Rose smiles.

"In fact, your latest venture was launched last week on your thirty-ninth birthday, was it not?"

Applause.

"Yes, it was. I've never kept my age a secret. I think women can achieve anything they want at any age, no matter who they are, where they live or what they look like, and can be proud of their success. We see their accomplishments every day!"

The audience cheers.

"I think confidence, ambition and determination are far more important."

"Talent and beauty can't hurt either," adds Jimmy.

Laughter and a trickle of hand clapping.

"Before we talk about your new website, which has taken the world by storm in just a week, and how a complaint-free society can improve our lives beyond recognition, I'd like our audience to know a little more about you."

Applause.

Nia-Rose smiles.

129

"I understand you have homes in a number of cities – Los Angeles, Paris and Geneva and are living right here in New York."

"Well, actually, I've recently sold my beach house in California as well as my Carnegie Hill townhouse in Manhattan. My permanent home, of course, is in London where I've been collaborating with my team on the new website."

"Which is where you grew up, right?"

"Yes, that's right."

"Do you prefer living and working in London, rather than here in New York?"

"I love New York!"

Applause.

"I'll always be a London girl. It was time to settle down in one place, re-establish my roots and reduce the amount of travelling I used to do. Besides, my twelve-year-old son, Étienne, lives with his father in Paris, so I can visit him more often – my son that is."

A squeak of laughter.

"Speaking of names, can you tell our viewers about your own name – *Nia*? We were talking about this before the show."

"*Nia* is a girl's name, of course."

Stifled laughter.

"It means *purpose, resolve, bright, lustrous* and originates from the Swahili language."

"A lustrous name for an equally lustrous woman!"

Applause.

Nia-Rose laughs.

"Thank you so much," she says.

"I understand that your new website – *What's Your Complaint?* – had more than one million visits on the first day, three million visits after the third day and, according to the news just announced this morning, more than ten million visits in the first week alone! That's incredible!"

"It's been overwhelming to say the least, Jimmy. We've also had tremendous financial support from advertisers!"

"You must be making a lot of money!"

"Yes, we are. But I don't receive any money from it personally. Our net profit – every dollar we make after running costs – is invested back into my charity: *Women Evolving* or WE. More than fifty projects around the world are being funded through the charity, from the arts to agriculture, in which women play an essential role to improve their local communities while enriching the lives of everyone around them."

Sustained applause.

"You have reached out and touched a nerve with people around the world without question. You are an incredibly successful entrepreneur yourself and are fast becoming one of the most famous agony aunts in history."

"It's much more than that. We're all agony aunts, to be honest."

"What do you mean?"

"Everyone here in the studio and watching at home has one thing in common. We all complain about one thing or another, every day, even you, Jimmy!"

Laughter.

"It's one of life's habits, part of human behaviour. It's wired into our brains. I don't think a day goes by when we don't complain about this, that, or the other. It's a question of expectation and reality. We generally complain in an effort to change something that we feel is unjust or just plain wrong. It affects us personally. We have a fixation for trying to make things right. We constantly wish for things we don't already have or don't necessarily need! This can be an expression of complaining as well. This is how people behave. It is at the heart of who we are as human beings. We are always looking for the perfect or idyllic state of mind every waking moment. People want all there is to receive. And if we are unable to achieve this state of exactness or completion – let's call it gratification – then we start complaining about it. At the same time, it is especially comforting to vent our frustrations and disappointments about our lives to anyone who has the time to listen."

"Do you agree with that ladies and gentlemen? Put up your hands if you have complained about something today?"

Jimmy scans the studio audience.

"Don't be shy. I want to see all the complainers. Nia-Rose and I won't tell anyone."

Jimmy puts up his hand first.

"I'll make it easy and go first. I did complain and more than once I might add, about the traffic on my way to the studio this evening."

He looks directly into the camera.

"Just be clear, New York taxi drivers are second-to-

132

none, so please, please don't think I'm complaining about your driving skills. No letters of complaint, please! I was simply expressing my angst about the city's traffic in general – the congestion and pollution we face on our city streets every day of the week and not only here in New York!"

Sustained applause. Jimmy smiles and turns to his guest."

"Your turn, Nia-Rose. You're among friends. What about you?"

"I was bullied every day, for one reason or another, as a young teenager. That's why I complained when I found success as a professional model. You could say it was my way of fighting back. It wasn't as glamorous as it may have looked. Being a model was a very stressful job as you can imagine. Everything had to be perfect – hair, make-up, clothes, the way I spoke –when I did television commercials or appeared in front of the camera for any reason. I needed to create my own perfect little world and if it wasn't as I wanted it, I complained until I got my way."

Sustained applause.

"Tell us about your new venture."

"Well, Jimmy, *What's Your Complaint?* is a forum that invites everyone – no matter where you live or what language you speak – to voice your complaint about things that trouble you. It's an online meeting place where people all over the world can share their day-to-day grumbles and grievances about their lives and comment to each other about anything that annoys them. We find comfort in the worries and anxieties of others and crave the sympathy that usually comes with sharing our displeasures. Complaining has become an obsession. We can't seem to get through the day without it. According to the studies I've read, the average person complains fifteen to thirty times a day."

Jimmy looks directly into the camera.

"For the record, I would never complain about our wonderful, hard working New York cab drivers."

Laughter.

"I just want to make that point perfectly clear."

He smiles.

"The world would be a much happier place if we didn't complain so much. When we are dissatisfied or find fault with something, we express resentment. In other words, we complain! We protest, moan, criticize and kick up a fuss. We disagree, condemn, bitch and make all kinds of accusations. We complain when we are discontented or unhappy. We fret and whine given the first chance to do so. We denounce and attack. We are squawk boxes, each and everyone of us! There are more than one hundred words for complaining! That's why I've launched the website. Everybody can complain and express their grievances with the world."

Laughter and applause.

"I've never thought about it before," Jimmy says.

"You should join the forum, Jimmy. I'm sure your fans would like to know what you complain about, apart from traffic. Speak your mind. Let everyone known what you think. Share your thoughts with your fans. It's quite simple. Each complaint we publish is checked carefully by our editorial board of experts for security issues, libel, use of language, and, of course, for length – there is a maximum word count as well – before it can be posted. We do the same thing for readers' comments."

"I thought complaining was healthy. Doesn't it make you work harder to solve problems, get things done, make your life easier somehow? Though clearly, it hasn't helped the traffic situation in New York City. Only joking, folks!"

Laughter.

"Apart from annoying and alienating your friends and family, constant complaining can also damage the brain," says Nia-Rose.

Jimmy looks at the audience and pauses before he speaks.

"If that's true, we may be in big trouble, ladies and gentlemen."

"Recognising the danger is far more important," says Nia-Rose. "We should be aware of, and prepare for, the challenges we face every day. We have to decide what matters to us, what's truly important in our lives, and let go of all the messy stuff that interferes with our happiness and causes us to complain."

"Is there a pill we can take?"

"No, I'm afraid not. Try the website. It's the perfect place to share your gripes and hear from other people who can help us to live better lives."

"Does complaining actually damage the brain? I find that hard to believe."

"It's true. Absolutely true, Jimmy, especially when it comes to problem solving and intelligent thought."

"Well, that would explain a lot of things going on in Washington!"

Laughter and sustained applause.

"Medical studies have found that complaining can affect our ability to learn and remember new things by shrinking the hippocampus. This part of the brain is embedded in our temporal lobe and when we complain, neurons are peeled away. We have a temporal lobe in each side of the brain – the right and left hemispheres."

"Start posting your complaints, folks," says Jimmy. "Make your voice heard. Become a better, more stable person and bring happiness to the world."

The audience cheers.

Laughter and applause.

"Who said Saturday night television was boring?" says Jimmy.

Applause.

"You must have had thousands – no, hundreds of thousands of complainers so far during your first week alone. Tell us, Nia-Rose, do men complain more than women? Can you tell us your top ten complaints?"

"We don't know all the details yet, Jimmy. We're still sifting through the data. Ask me back in six months and I'll have all the answers for you."

"I look forward to it!"

Applause.

"In the meantime, ladies and gentlemen, before we pause for a commercial break, I'd like to hear from *you* in the studio audience. What drives you nuts? What do you like to complain about? If you have a complaint to make, raise your hand. I'll try to get to as many people as I can in the next three minutes. Our lawyers are also in the studio audience, ladies and gentlemen, so please keep it short and don't mention anybody by name or we may not be on air next week!"

"You sir . . . in the blue shirt."

"Rats on our city streets."

Applause.

"And you sir, in the first row."

"The *New York Yankees*."

Boos.

"A diehard baseball fan. You must be a *Boston Red Sox* fan!" says Jimmy.

"*Toronto Blue Jays*!"

More boos and shouting.

Jimmy holds gestures for quiet.

"The lady in white at the back."

"Helicopters flying over Central Park on Sunday."

Applause.

"The lady with the blue jacket at the end of the row."

"The smell of pollution."

Applause.

"I'm with you on that," says Jimmy.

The studio audience is in full flow. Even Nia-Rose is surprised at the response. Every comment is punctuated by applause, cheering, laughter and booing.

"The weather."

"Cold winters."

"I hate the cold."

"And the rain!"

"What about the snow?"

"Getting lost."

"Sat nav that doesn't work."
"The cost of living."
"Money and Poverty."
"Landlords who increase the rent."
"The cost of car repairs."
"Car breakdowns."
"Electric cars."
"Appliances that break."
"Marriages that don't last."
"Lack of respect for one another."
"Dreams that don't come true."
"Children who scream and cry."
"Sisters and brothers."
"Mothers and fathers."
"The in-laws."
"Christmas presents."
"Birthdays."
"Being too young."
"OLD and ugly."
"Getting old."
"Men with beards."
"Being short or too tall."
"Overweight."
"Underweight."
"Clothes that don't fit anymore."
"Falling over!"
"Unable to sleep."
"The loss of people we love."
"And animals too!"
"Failing to achieve your goals."
"Lack of opportunity."

"People who criticise you."

"Missed phone calls on your cell phone."

"Athletes who lose."

"Teams that lose."

"Writing school exams."

"Covid lockdown restrictions."

"Wearing masks."

"Not wearing masks."

"Arrogance, ignorance and stupidity."

"Voting rights."

"Protesters."

"Dictators."

"Selfishness."

"People who lie."

"Biased newspaper journalism."

"Forgetting things."

"Loud music."

"People with loud voices."

"People who cough in the cinema."

"Scams."

"When computers crash."

"Identity theft."

"Slow service in restaurants."

"The taste of food."

"Bad television."

"Camping."

"Sleeping in tents."

"Sand in your shoes."

"Waiting to get on and off airplanes."

"Flying."

"Lost luggage."

"Your health."

"Medication."

"The cost of health insurance."

"Travel insurance."

"The cost of filling up your car."

"The cost of living."

"Standing in line at the bank."

"And post offices."

"And grocery stores."

"Waiting in line for anything!"

"Online banking."

"City traffic."

Jimmy smiles and claps.

"Bad driving."

"Terrorism."

"Incompetence."

"Crooked politicians."

"Government policy."

"All politicians!"

The audience cheers. Jimmy holds beckons for quiet.

"OK, ladies and gentlemen. We have time for one more complaint. You madam, over there, in the middle row."

"PEOPLE WHO COMPLAIN!" he yells.

Laughter.

Jimmy and Nia-Rose stand up to applaud.

"And *that*, ladies and gentlemen, just about sums up the human race in three minutes! Imagine how happy we'd all be if we didn't complain! Share your *angst* – that's my special word for the day – with Nia-Rose on her website, *What's Your Complaint?* Talk to fellow-complainers. Make new friends and be a happier person!"

Rousing applause.

"We need to take a commercial break – please don't complain about that – but when we come back, I will be joined by my next two guests who have devoted their entire careers to complaining. What do they do for a living? They are politicians of course.

Laughter.

"One Republican and one Democrat, who sit on opposite sides in the Senate. Stay tuned. I'm sure you'll enjoy this too, Nia-Rose, so don't you go anywhere either!

I leaned back in my chair and asked for a cup of strong black coffee. A quick dose of caffeine, I thought, would help to jump-start my sluggish brain and I could begin to make sense of what was going on. I couldn't very well tell the fat man that I had somehow stumbled into an oil painting! Who would have believed that? And yet . . . it was true!

# The
# Hotel
# Midnight

The room had no windows.

The miasma of malt whisky, cigar smoke and cheap cologne, stuck to the walls like paste. It was odorous, stale and sickly. I imagine you got used to it over time.

The door was closed, which didn't help.

A short, fat man with greasy black hair was sitting behind a desk. He was smoking a *Nat Sherman* cigar. He had just opened a new box and offered it to me. That's how I knew the brand.

I declined.

His fingers were pudgy and discoloured, and his nails were badly in need of a manicure. His aftershave smelled of sewage. The cigar smoke, with its creamy aroma of cinnamon helped to contain the reek, but it was losing the battle.

"Identification please."

"I left everything at home – money, wallet, ID."

"Was that on purpose or are you the forgetful kind?"

"It was late, and I was tired. I hadn't planned on going anywhere."

That was the truth. I had no reason to lie.

He puffed on his *Nat Sherman* in quick succession, then blew perfectly shaped smoke rings that skimmed the top of my head.

"And yet, here you are."

"I'm as surprised as you are!"

I wasn't ready to ask him where *here* was, although I had a surprisingly good idea, as absurd as it turned out to be.

"I assume you have a name?"

"Myles Jakeman."

"Tell me, Mr Jakeman, did you forget to bring your wife, as well?"

I saw him look at my fingers for a ring. There was none. The fat man was the nosey type.

"I work pretty much every night in different places until the early hours of the morning – nobody wants to be married to that, unless you know of somebody?"

He dismissed my pathetic remark without comment. I was barely in my mid-thirties and in no rush to get married.

"And what do you do for a living, Mr Jakeman?"

I saw no harm in answering, so I told him.

"I'm a musician."

"Well, well, what do you know about that!"

He steepled his fingers under his chin and closed his eyes, deep in thought. The crystal on his wristwatch was cracked from the *twelve* to the *six*.

"Was that the right answer?"

I couldn't help the sarcasm.

He opened his eyes and glared at me.

"What kind of a musician are you, Mr Jakeman? Do you sing or play an instrument?"

"As a matter of fact, I'm a trumpet player."

He stood up and began to pace around my chair, hands stuffed into his trouser pockets as far as they would reach. His lips were curled tightly around the *Nat Sherman* like a jumbo drinking straw. One shoe had a different coloured lace. It had obviously been torn and re-knotted.

"I'm a pit musician – musicals, operas, ballets . . . that sort of thing," I said to break the tension. "I prefer jazz, although gigs are hard to come by these days. I also do a lot of studio work to make ends meet."

I was seldom without work for more than a week or two and was proud of my record.

He stopped pacing and glared at me. At one point, I thought he was going to offer me a job right here in the hotel, playing trumpet.

"What brings you to *The Hotel Midnight?*"

I had never heard of the place by name and decided to keep this revelation to myself.

"I must have taken the wrong train."

He ignored my excuse.

"As a rule, we don't allow outsiders in, unless of course you are looking for a job. I may have spot for someone who can play the saxophone, but we already have a fine trumpet player at the hotel. I understand you

145

have no ticket for this evening's performance.

"*Yes* . . . I do not have a ticket. And *no*, I am not looking for a job."

I coughed. It was genuine and not surprising given the dead air in the room.

"Are you the manager?"

His reply was casual, almost a whisper.

"I own the hotel!"

"Let me know how much I owe you and I'll post a cheque to you in the morning," I replied in the same whispery tone.

"Do you have a club membership?"

"Not that I'm aware. What types of memberships do you offer? Do you have a club brochure that I could look through? I'll need your mailing address."

"I don't think I like your attitude, Mr Jakeman."

"And I don't think I like your questions, Mr –?"

He didn't say.

"As much as I'd like to stay and listen to the music, I am tired and would prefer to go home to bed if you don't mind. I can come back another time when I have a ticket."

"I don't know anything about you. I will have to check your background."

*Enjoy yourself with that*, I thought.

"I have a better idea. I'll play my trumpet for you – now! I'll do a twenty-minute set. I don't think the other musicians will mind. I can hear them playing now. That should make up for not having a ticket."

"I don't think so, Mr Jakeman. Not to tonight."

My trumpet was nowhere to be seen. *'I'm sure I had*

*it with me'*, I mumbled.

I was tired. I couldn't think straight.

"Look, I'm happy to pay a fine, but as I've already said, I have no money. I left home abruptly! It's a bit complicated if you must know. I'll use the back door if you don't mind. I don't want to cause a commotion."

\* \* \*

When I'd first arrived at *The Hotel Midnight* an hour earlier, I was seated within arm's reach of the piano player.

His black and white lace-up Oxford brogues looked spotless as if they had been removed from the box for the first time. His gold watch bracelet sparkled under the bright lights as his fingers danced gracefully up and down the keyboard.

Sheet music was scattered everywhere, from the music rack to the floor. Manuscript paper could also be seen protruding from the storage compartment of the hinged piano seat.

I could have stepped up onto the bandstand, reached over, and improvised a tune before he knew I was interloping.

All my attention, however, was drawn to the woman in gold. She was wearing a bias-cut, silk and gold lamé gown with a sweetheart neckline and a long strand of cream-coloured pearls. Her gown flared gently at mid-calf and splayed onto the floor.

She was young – beyond her late twenties, I'd say – though I couldn't know for certainty.

Long, tight-fitting satin white gloves complemented her tall and slender figure. One hand rested on the piano. The other caressed a copper and brass floor-standing stage microphone. To her left was the third member of the jazz quartet. His round, tortoise-shell glasses blended seamlessly with the rich veneer of his double bass that matched his height to the inch.

Hidden by the piano's extended lid and sitting next to the bass player was the drummer. He twitched and swayed to the accented rhythm and often hummed along with the melody.

It was a formal affair, to be sure. Engagement party? Wedding? Concert? I was lost in the revelry of the moment, and not particularly worried about how I was going to get home.

*The Hotel Midnight* was glamorous and imposing in every detail. The ballroom – for that's what I assumed it to be – was filled to capacity, mostly with young couples dressed and groomed with impeccable style and grace, and with manners to match.

They talked quietly amongst themselves and were eager to avoid the distracting clinkety-clank of their champagne glasses.

It was all about the performers and their music, and the respect they commanded.

Small, round tables encircled the bandstand. Each table had two chairs, white linen tablecloths, several bottles of champagne and a set of gold-trimmed, fluted stemware of bright pink tinted glass.

I sat alone.

In the distance, I saw a dozen couples dancing under

148

the luminous dazzle of a waterfall chandelier. Their faces were obscured by the protracted waves of cigarette smoke forever dangling like dust particles caught in zero gravity.

Waiters, in their neat and tidy tuxedos with black bowties, strutted with purpose from table to table with perfectly balanced trays of champagne bottles and glasses.

I turned round and caught the attention of a waiter by grabbing his forearm, nearly upending a full tray of champagne bottles in the process.

"Excuse me, sir. Where am I?"

"Shhhhhh!" replied a woman sitting behind me.

The waiter pulled away from my grasp sharply and carried on with his duties without pause or words.

It was, to be fair, a stupid question.

The lady in gold was halfway through her rendition of *It Don't Mean a Thing (If It Ain't Got That Swing)* when someone tapped me on the shoulder and forcibly escorted me to the room with no windows.

I would have worn a white shirt and tie, had I known.

No one looked in my direction, or seemed to care, except for the lady in gold. She gazed into my eyes and smiled as if she knew who I was and where I was going.

* * *

The events leading up to my unforeseen arrival at *The Hotel Midnight* and my interview with the fat man had been set in motion a month previously when I had been hired to play a gig for a private house party.

It was nothing lavish, a hundred guests at most. The host was an art dealer who was celebrating his fiftieth birthday. He liked our jazz quartet and the music we played and paid us in cash at the end of the evening. He also gave us an original, framed oil painting as a bonus – cash would have been better.

He said he found the painting amongst his private art collection and had no sentimental attachment to it. Nor did he know or care how much it might be worth.

He'd remembered buying the painting at an estate sale. He said the picture belonged a musician – a saxophone player. According to his friends, he had died of a broken heart. His name was Aldo Reed.

Nothing more was known about the picture, or its owner, except for the artist who signed his or her initials in the bottom left corner: 'M M'.

I'm not exactly sure what he expected us to do with the painting. Even with all my experience, this was a first for me.

I offered it to the other band members. No one was interested, so I kept it for myself, and gave each of the lads fifty pounds in cash, instead. At least that way, we all shared the bonus, such that it was.

The painting took pride of place in my music room. The frame was mostly bronze with fine black lines etched in the wood along the direction of the grain.

It was a large picture, measuring about three-foot square including the frame. It was rich in colour and texture. Even standing at a distance you could see the thick, raised swirls of paint, the bold brush strokes and the evocative scene brought to life by the artist.

The painting was chic and emotive in every detail – musicians performed on a bandstand; people embraced on the dance floor. Their faces were undefined and vague.

You could almost feel the energy of the space itself, as waiters in their neat black bowties patrolled the vast room servicing the customers with champagne and attending to their every need.

After I hung the picture on the wall, I sat on a bar stool and started to play. My confidence grew as I stared at the painting, and the music swelled. I was in full flow and soon the room was saturated with the most glorious sound.

I closed my eyes. Minutes later, I heard someone singing. It was the captivating voice of a woman and the unmistakable rhythm of swing. It was lively, spirited and addictive.

Had I left the television or radio on?

Was my window open?

Frankly, I didn't care.

I kept my eyes shut and began playing a duet with the mysterious female vocalist who felt close at hand. I didn't want the recital to end.

My forehead began to perspire. I needed to take a break and sit down, and yet I continued to play. My eyes remained shut and I thought of nothing else except the notes, the melody and the woman's voice.

A puff of cigarette smoke drifted by my face. Its aroma made me feel woozy. I hit a series of wrong notes in succession and lost my concentration. At first, I was unable to open my eyes. They were tired and

151

heavy. I wanted to lie down and sleep.

Everything went quiet. Then I heard the muffled hum of people talking. More music. A piano, a double bass, drums and a voice – a woman's voice, singing. I opened my eyes. In an instant, they were wide and eager to identify the source of such captivating music.

I was dumbfounded, unable to understand what had happened. I was no longer at home, but in a magnificent ballroom. I saw her standing next to a piano. She was the same woman in the oil painting – the lady in gold, with a long strand of cream-coloured pearls around her neck.

The scene was uncanny! *How did I get here?*

The framed painting on my wall *was* the ballroom at *The Hotel Midnight* in every detail, from the gold-trimmed, fluted stemware of bright, pink-tinted glass and the waiters in their neat and tidy tuxedos with black bowties, to those dancing beneath the luminous dazzle of a waterfall chandelier.

How was this possible? I had somehow fallen into the oil painting and was now part of its own story. And that's how I came to be sitting in the room with no windows, where a short, fat man with greasy black hair was sitting behind a desk smoking a *Nat Sherman* cigar.

*What had I done with my trumpet?* I wondered.

The fat man's interrogation continued.

"As I've said, Mr Jakeman, I'm afraid I can't allow you leave *The Hotel Midnight*."

"Why not?"

"For one thing, we have no idea why you've come. You haven't been invited as far as I know, have you?

152

We don't allow strangers to interfere with our business. Has someone given you permission to be here? I've already told you that there are no jobs at the hotel for another trumpet player, and you don't play saxophone by your own admission, so I can't imagine what you want! You could be a troublemaker for all I know."

I leaned back in my chair and asked for a cup of strong black coffee. A quick dose of caffeine, I thought, would help to jump-start my sluggish brain and I could begin to make sense of what was going on.

I couldn't very well tell the fat man that I had somehow stumbled into an oil painting! Who would have believed that? And yet . . . it was true!

This was no elaborate game, and I was definitely not dreaming, so I let the events unfold and the adventure begin.

"I must have taken the wrong train."

"So you've said."

"Look, I have no idea where I am or how I managed to find this place. It was a complete accident. That's the truth."

"This is *The Hotel Midnight*. Surely you are aware of that, Mr Jakeman!"

"Where in London are we? The Strand? Mayfair? Canary Wharf? I know every hotel in the country. I've played in all of them. I've never heard of *The Hotel Midnight!*"

"And I've never heard of Canary Wharf! This is not a river boat or a floating seaside pier, Mr Jakeman!"

He was playing me for a fool.

"You suddenly appear from nowhere. You have no

ticket. Nobody knows who you are. And you don't play the saxophone."

There was a knock on the door.

"My dear, Melody!" said the fat man as the lady let herself into his office.

The fat man couldn't stand up fast enough for her.

"We will finish our conversation later," he said to me. "Don't go anywhere. I am not through with you just yet."

It was the lady in gold. She looked more beautiful than I had imagined. The colour and light from beyond the doorway where she stood was intoxicating as if it had a rhythm all its own. I remained in my chair.

She walked over to me and handed me an envelope.

"This is for you, Myles."

Her voice was soft and sweet, almost hypnotising.

"How do you know my name?"

"I heard you tell someone."

I opened the envelope. It was a ticket for tonight's performance. It had my name on it.

She put her hand on my shoulder. Her long pearl necklace grazed my ear.

"Myles is my special guest this evening," she told the fat man.

I was transfixed by her presence.

"Can I get you anything, Myles?" she asked.

"I hesitated, then said: "Yes, a cup of strong black coffee, please. I'm afraid I didn't catch your name."

"Call me Melody. Everyone else does."

Before I could thank her properly, she took my hand – her grip was commanding – and escorted me from the office, back to the bandstand.

The fat man was stunned and did not say a word as we left his office.

I sat down at the same table as before. There was a 'reserved' plaque on it.

A waiter suddenly appeared carrying a tray. On it were a cup of black coffee, a bottle of champagne and one glass – gold-trimmed, fluted stemware – identical to that in the painting.

Melody's last set of the night lasted forty minutes. I couldn't take my eyes off her. Question after question formed on my lips while she sang. I was shaking with anticipation.

When the music stopped and the applause faded, everyone, save for the waiters and the musicians, left the ballroom. In a matter of minutes, they had gone. The waiters cleared the tables quickly and quietly and in no time, the room looked as if no one had been in it.

As the lights dimmed, the ballroom was doused in tiers of impenetrable shadows and an eery silence.

Melody took my hand once again and we left the ballroom.

"Where are we going?" I asked.

"To meet my friends."

"Do you happen to have the time? I left my watch at home."

She paused before answering.

"The time signature is all that matters. Counting beats to the bar."

I followed Melody downstairs to another room. Its low ceiling and subdued lighting were in stark contrast with the rest of the hotel. With a capacity for about fifty people, it was quiet and empty.

"This is *The Crescendo*," said Melody.

Her voice resonated.

"It's a jazz club in the hotel basement. People come here to play their own kind of jazz and often jam until breakfast. Except for tonight. Everybody is entitled to one night off. At least we won't be disturbed."

She introduced her fellow musicians: Mr Keys on piano, Mr Strings on double bass and Mr Sticks on drums.

"And this is our resident trumpet player, Mr Bell."

Although their names were curious and more likely invented to amuse me, these musicians were as real to me as the taste of champagne on my breath and the music resonating in my ears.

I shook everyone's hand and was immediately lost for words when I caught sight of Mr Bell's trumpet as he placed it on the table in front of me.

"Do you mind if I have a look at it?" I asked.

I was shaking with excitement.

"Myles is a trumpet player, too," said Melody.

"Is that so? We don't get many opportunities to meet other trumpet players," said Mr Bell.

"I've brought my trumpet with me. You're welcome to play it if I can find it. I've put it down somewhere. I can't remember," I said."

"We'll help you locate it, Myles," said Mr Keys.

Melody shook her head and smiled.

"I must say that your horn is remarkable, Mr Bell. I've never seen this model before."

"It's the *Louis Armstrong Special*," he said.

He handed it to me.

"Here, take it. Entertain us."

I held it as if it were a delicate piece of sculpture. As I played a handful of jazz riffs, the notes seemed to float on air, lingering well after they had left the horn.

The other musicians applauded my efforts.

"This is a rare musical instrument," I said as I handed it back to Mr Bell.

"Not where I come from, Myles. I acquired this fine horn in thirty-three, about three years ago as I recall. It's comfortable to hold and it plays like a charm! You ought to take one home with you."

I was dumbfounded.

"Excuse me for asking. I'm terribly confused. And I am aware that this will sound crazy . . . exactly what year is it?"

They laughed.

Mr Keys handed me a bottle of champagne.

"Read the label." Said Mr Strings. "It may help to answer your question."

They laughed again.

### 1936 Veuve A Devaux Black Neck

"Time passes according to the label," said Mr Sticks. "We can always tell what year it is by the champagne we drink. It's quite simple when you get used to it."

"Is this really 1936?" I asked.

"Yes, and yes," replied Mr Bell. "The champagne *and* the year! You don't get out much, do you?"

"I think you've had too much to drink," said Mr Keys. "I know how you feel. Sometimes, the notes on the piano move every which way right in front of my own eyes!"

"We all live and work in *The Hotel Midnight*, so you can see how easy it is to lose track of time – days, months, years," said Melody. "Time passes by without much notice."

She put her hand on my shoulder.

"A change can be more valuable than you thought possible."

Her voice trailed off. There was a hint of sadness in her words.

Whether it was 1936 or not, according to the label on the champagne bottle, I had to focus on finding a way out of this time warp – this painting.

"I have been accused of trespassing," I said with a firm voice. "And I'm certainly not a spy!"

"So we've heard," said Mr Strings.

"It's a bad situation," said Mr Keys.

"I don't think you will be punished," said Mr Sticks.

"Can anyone help me?"

"Yes, of course," said Melody. "You will be free to go, I am sure. It make take some time unless of course you already know the way out."

The circumstances leading up to my unforeseen arrival were inexplicable, yet here I was *inside* an oil painting at *The Hotel Midnight* in 1936.

It was madness!

Although I was eager to get home and back to normality – a black cab would surely take me there – I couldn't simply leave now even if I knew where the exit was.

I wanted to learn more about my fellow musicians, how they lived and played jazz in such a wonderful time and place. There was also Melody to think of. There was so much more I craved to know about her.

\* \* \*

Mr Keys, Mr Strings, Mr Sticks and Mr Bell announced that they were retiring for the evening. One by one they left *The Crescendo*, kissed Melody on the cheek and wished her a happy future.

Their quirky behaviour was soon forgotten, for I was more concerned about my own welfare and where I would be spending the next several hours, preferably with my head on a pillow.

When the others had gone and were nowhere to be seen, Melody smiled.

I looked into her silky, chocolate brown eyes. They told a story of enduring unhappiness, not unlike the melancholic lyrics of the blues she no doubt sang every night.

"Come with me. You are tired. You need to sleep."

"Where are you taking me?"

"The hotel has guest rooms where musicians are permitted to stay for a night, a week, a month . . . whatever suits them. Your room is across the hall from mine. A wonderful saxophone player and a dear friend of mine lived there. He was the best friend anyone could ever hope to have. I miss him more than I can

159

say."

"Where is he now?"

"He found a way out."

"What do you mean?"

"He broke his contract and simply left the hotel."

"When?"

"In thirty-two. He's been gone four years. He was looking for a new life. He was lucky. When I heard that someone from the outside had arrived, I thought it might be him."

"Where *is* the outside? Which way is out?"

"We are musicians. For us, there is no outside. We entertain the those who want to hear us perform. This is what we do. Our work – our life – is here at *The Hotel Midnight*."

"Where in London is *The Hotel Midnight?* Where is the nearest tube station? I'd like to come back again and hear you sing. We could have dinner one night in Soho, in the heart of London."

She ignored my questions.

"This is your room, Myles."

She pointed to the door.

Instinctively, I turned round, and expected to see the fat man standing behind me, smoking a *Nat Sherman* cigar. I had no intention of returning to the room that had no windows.

"Am I in serious trouble? I don't think the fat man likes me. Does he have a name?"

"We call him *The Boss*. He knows more about *The Hotel Midnight* than anyone else."

"Does he know where my trumpet is? Have you seen

my trumpet? I can't make a living without it."

"We will talk later, Myles. First, you need to rest."

\* \* \*

My room was clean and spacious. It had a rose-pink, shuttered window that could not be opened from the inside for there was no visible latch. Nor was I able to see beyond the glass itself even with the lights turned off.

I nearly clapped when I saw a plate of cucumber sandwiches and a carafe of water with a slice of lemon floating at the top waiting for me on the bedside table. I tucked in and devoured the lot.

Then it struck me.

It's funny how often you fail to see what's right in front of your eyes.

Neat rows of pictures hung on the walls.

Paintings!

Oil paintings!

Each one signed 'M M'.

Each one, a snapshot of life at *The Hotel Midnight*.

The music, the musicians, the joy of life itself!

The style, the brush strokes, the texture.

All identical to the picture hanging on the wall of my own music room, given to me a month ago.

My painting was signed 'M M' as well.

Who was this person, this artist?

Another musician I had yet to meet?

I was drugged with confusion and beyond weary to think straight.

Tomorrow was another day.

I would ask Melody then.

I was roused from my slumber by a woman's voice. She was singing.

It was soft and gentle, yet it stirred my senses. When I opened my eyes, I could see a faint glow of light seeping through my bedroom window.

*How long had I slept?*

I shuffled over to the window, hoping . . . expecting to see a familiar London landmark. Inexplicably, my room overlooked the hotel's ballroom, not the outside world!

Melody was singing.

She was alone on the bandstand, wearing her silk and gold lamé gown and a long strand of cream-coloured pearls.

No one was there to watch or applaud.

I retraced my steps as best I could, turning right when I should have veered left, down one hall and up another. Eventually I found the ballroom, and not a single clock or telephone in sight.

Melody carried on singing as I sat down at the same table within arm's reach of the piano. She turned her head and smiled, stopped singing, then left the bandstand and sat down beside me.

My eyes played across her face in slow motion. I would have paid anything for her thoughts and wished they could be written down on paper and given to me as a gift.

"Why do they call this place *The Hotel Midnight?*" I asked. "There are no clocks or any other means of telling the time, let alone day from night."

"Midnight is not a question of time – the passing of seconds, minutes or hours. It is a place of opportunity. Midnight is where old and new encounters cross a line and go their separate ways, where inspiration and dreams mingle, and where music is all that matters. Midnight is about possibilities. *The Hotel Midnight* makes all these things possible, Myles."

"Melody is a beautiful name for a beautiful woman," I said without thinking.

"My full name is *Midnight Melody*, but Melody will do just fine.

My blood ran cold. I was stunned into silence . . . thinking . . . wondering . . . desperately trying to join up the dots.

I took her hand and kissed it as if I were playing the romantic lead in an old Hollywood movie.

"The paintings – here at the hotel! Are those your initials on each one of them – 'M M'?

She nodded and smiled.

How much more should I tell her? The facts were outlandish if not well beyond the realm of logic.

"You are the most beautiful woman I have every met."

We rose to our feet, wrapped our arms around each other and kissed.

"It is your own painting that has brought me here. I have a picture of this very place and of you performing on the bandstand with the others. My picture also bears your initials: 'M M'. It hangs on the wall in my own music room. I was looking at the painting as I played. I remember closing my eyes. I heard your voice. You were singing. Then, this room, this place, the hotel and everyone in it, engulfed me at once. So much has already happened since I've been here –"

Her eyes lit up.

"Then you must have seen him!"

"Who?"

"Aldo Reed, the musician whose room you've been sleeping in!"

The irony of her story was like a slap in the face. I sat down, trying to make sense of it. I quickly forgot about the fat man – aka *The Boss* – and his instant dislike for me.

As I looked into her eyes, she touched the side of my face.

"Aldo and I were lovers. He wanted to leave *The Hotel Midnight* for ever, to make a fresh start in life. He begged me to go with him, but I did not have the courage. This place is all I have known for as long as I can remember. After he had gone, I put all my paintings in his room. It made me happy. He promised he would come back for me. I fear he has lost his way. I have been waiting four long years. That is why I thought it was him when I saw you.

"Why did you kiss me if you love someone else?"

"A woman may kiss whomever she chooses."

Her body trembled. She began to cry.

"What's wrong? What have I said?"

"You must know him then! How else would you have my painting? I gave it to Aldo and now you have it! Why did he give it to you? When did you see him?

Is he well? Did he talk about me? When is he coming back for me?"

"Yes, I did see him – only last month, now that you mention it!"

I told her what she craved to hear, not what little I had been told about his young life and premature death. I ad-libbed my fictional encounter and brief friendship with Aldo as quickly as I could think of the words.

"Your friend is an excellent jazz musician, well liked by everyone. I played alongside him. He's fine and well, and in the best of spirits."

"And the painting?"

I was struggling for an explanation and could only come up with this . . .

"Aldo was having financial problems. Property taxes, I believe. The one thing of value he had was a painting. He said he could never part with it because it was given to him by the woman he loved. It could only have been you! *'As soon as I save enough money, I am going to bring her to London'*, he told me. I wanted to help him, so I paid his property taxes in exchange for the painting. It was Aldo's idea. The money was a loan. I never intended to keep the painting for myself. It was collateral. The painting belongs to Aldo, and he'll have it back soon enough. Then, he'll come back for you. He told me he would."

It was such a compelling story that even I believed every word of it.

"He said that? Did he truly say that he loves me?"

"Yes. He loves you very much. More than he thought possible."

"Is he coming back for me?"

"Yes. He told me."

"Did he promise?"

"Yes, he did. He promised that he would come back for you."

"Did he say when?"

"Soon, I imagine. You do believe him, don't you?"

She nodded.

I had neither the heart nor the courage to tell her the truth. The price for doing so was not worth paying. A dream shattered never heals.

My mouth was parched. I knocked back a glass of champagne as if it were tap water.

When I put the glass on the table, I was surprised to see Melody back on the bandstand.

Beside her was a small Gladstone bag with the initials 'M M' in gold letters.

She began to sing *Isn't It Romantic?*

I had another glass of champagne.

At the end of the song, she lifted the hinged piano seat and withdrew my trumpet. She cradled it against her body like an infant in need of human protection from the harsh world around it.

"I found your trumpet, Myles!"

Her words were filled with joy.

I stood up quickly.

My head was spinning. My knees buckled for a second until I found my balance.

"Will you take me with you, Myles?"

"Take you with me? Where?"

"Away from this place. Aldo found a way out and

you found a way in. Tell *The Boss* that you must leave straight away. You cannot stay here like the rest of us. You don't belong here. It will be easy for you to return home. Take me with you, Myles. Please! Take me to see Aldo."

She pointed to the Gladstone bag.

"I have already packed my belongings."

We didn't say anything for a while: she, standing on the bandstand embracing my trumpet and me, sitting at the table with yet another glass of champagne to my lips.

I had no idea how I came to be here or understood the mechanism by which I was taking part in a story hidden away in an oil painting! Reversing my direction and getting home was no clearer.

My feelings were true enough, yet I knew that such a promise might be impossible to keep. At least, she would always have Aldo to think about. Eternal hope for his return to *The Hotel Midnight* would be my gift to the lady in gold. I could do no less.

As she left the bandstand to sit with me at the table, I could feel the happiness radiate from her body. She returned the trumpet to me, and we drank to our future wherever that might lead.

"Yes, of course, Melody. I will take you with me. We will try to find a way out together. I don't think I could bear *not* seeing you again."

She reached into her bag and gave me a small painting. It was a self-portrait.

"Please, take this! I want you to have it. I want you to remember me always."

167

She began to sing. Quietly. Softly.

Just for me.

I was too tired to accompany her on my trumpet, so I closed my eyes and listened. For those precious minutes, I had never been happier and held the painting she had given to me against my chest.

Melody never finished the song.

There was a disturbance, an intrusion.

It was sudden, shrill and annoying.

I couldn't adjust to the incursion.

I was dizzy from too much champagne.

The noise was repetitive, relentless.

Then I understood.

It was the sound of the telephone.

I let it ring until it stopped.

I was sitting on my bar stool with my trumpet resting across my knees and Melody's self-portrait cradled in my arms.

Something fell from the bell of my trumpet.

I picked it up and unravelled it.

It was a letter. I was stupefied.

I shook as I read it.

Dear Myles

If you are reading my letter, then sadly, I have not been able to come with you. I am glad you found your way home. Maybe one day, I will find you, or you will come back to The Hotel Midnight to see me!

I apologise for hiding your trumpet and for not telling you the truth. I had hope that you might take me with you. Please do not think unkindly of me. I am truly sorry if I have been selfish in my behaviour.

Tell Aldo that I miss him. He promised to come back for me. You told me so. I will be waiting. Tell him I still love him. Perhaps Aldo and I will see you again and we can celebrate together, away from this place, with a glass of champagne!

I shall look forward to it with all my heart. Look after yourself. I shall never forget you. Until we meet again . . .

Love to Aldo and to you, my dear Myles! Midnight Melody . . . 'M M'

" . . . there is something else, something
far more important than just rows of books
waiting patiently to be touched and admired.
This library has a purpose. It's as clear to me
as my reflection in the mirror."

# The Obsession of Alfred Paige

Alfred Paige was a wealthy man. His affluence was of no importance other than what it enabled him to do. He adored books and he loved to read.

Every week, he bought dozens of books whenever and wherever he came across them: book shops, market stalls or boot fairs.

He spent considerable time ordering unwanted or surplus books from university libraries and museums and sought out private collectors and auction houses the world over to purchase the finest English translations that money could buy. It didn't matter whether they were pricey first editions or water-stained, second-hand copies – paperback or hardcover – with torn pages or crumpled spines. He spent as much time as possible reading his books.

He travelled to other worlds, other ages, from ancient

times to future civilizations, immersing himself in the culture and lives of others through the printed word, craving to know what made humanity tick.

His selections spanned every genre of literature and human endeavour: astronomy and earth sciences; world histories; philosophy and theology; political biography; folklore and mythology; novels and short stories – classic to contemporary.

For Alf, it was fiction in above all else that painted a picture of the truth – pure, simple and enlightening. Alfred was bewitched by people: how and why they behaved as they did. There was no better way to see ourselves, he reasoned, than through the eyes of a novelist – the characters and the storylines he or she had crafted.

For Alfred Paige, collecting and reading books was an obsession for which there was no cure. It was a way of life that nearly drove him mad. Married for more than forty years, his wife Sarah, loved her husband and supported him in this passionate and time-consuming endeavour.

At the back of their house was Alfred's ground-floor office. There were shelves of books at every turn. In the centre of the room was an old oak desk that overlooked a pond and meadow of enormous beauty. Beside the large rectangular window was a leather chair where Alfred would sit to read his books and marvel at nature's splendour.

Alfred was an accomplished painter – water colours exclusively – and enjoyed the challenge of capturing the natural world on canvas. More than a dozen paintings hung neatly in his office on the only wall space available to him. Every year Alf would submit one of his paintings in the annual *Village Art Show*, and for the past five years, he had won first prize for his 'pond and meadow' landscapes.

Alf also enjoyed writing 'Letters to the Editor' to the major newspapers, presenting his personal views on declining social attitudes and disrespectful behaviour. He often spent hours at his desk drafting his words of wisdom on a ten-year-old computer.

The more books Alfred collected, the smaller his office had become. He removed his cherished water colours from the wall to make room for another full-length bookshelf. In a matter of weeks, there was no space left in his office to display his new purchases.

Books were stacked in high, neat rows on his desk, then systematically arranged on the floor. The hoard of books grew higher and higher like plants nurtured from seeds, now in full bloom, swelling in every direction. Soon, Alf's desk was hidden and forgotten behind precarious towers of tightly packed books that literally touched the ceiling.

Alfred's wife, always knocked before entering. They often discussed their favourite books. Alfred liked to talk as much about the life of the author as he did about the contents of a specific story. He sat awkwardly on the floor while his wife reclined in the chair next to the window, now hidden behind a morass of books arranged in columns along the floor, blocking the light from entering. Only when the sun skipped off the glossy cover of a book at an obtuse angle or squeezed through a timely gap did the light from the outside world creep into Alfred's office. Even then, it was a weak and half-hearted cleft of brightness where dust particles careened in all directions like pulverised soot.

The room was without ventilation and smelled stale. It was gloomy even during the day, where distorted, geometric shadows played across the spines of a thousand books, orchestrated by a three-tiered, ceiling pendant light shade.

"What shall I do, Sarah?" Alfred asked his wife.

"What do you mean, dear?"

"My collection! I have no space left to display my books. I have no desk on which to write and I have no time to read!"

"Surely, you can read any time you like."

"My collection has grown too quickly. It has no order. I am lost. The light is bad, and I cannot see the pond and meadow. My mind is elsewhere. I cannot read without orderliness, and I cannot stop buying books. Knowledge is far too precious to me."

"Is there anything I can do to help, dear?"

"I need a proper room. I want to build a grand library with structure and symmetry where I can find the title of any book, a proper section for history and one for science, space for biographies and shelves boasting novels in every genre arranged by author and title as they do in public libraries and bookshops.

"I'll have two chairs and a new desk and two large picture windows – and a table as well where you and I can take afternoon tea and look out over the pond and meadow. I simply can't go on like this."

"Don't forget your paintings, too, dear?"

"My paintings?"

"Yes, you must display them as you did before. It will add dignity to your library."

"Then I must appoint an architect. I'll do it first thing in the morning, unless you object?"

"Why would I object? You must do what you love and what makes you happy!"

* * *

Alfred's plan was straightforward. He would simply enlarge the existing room and create a grand, single rear extension. To facilitate this, Afred had to clear out his office – remove everything! His wife helped to relocate his books to other rooms of the house.

During the four months it took to build and decorate his new library, Alfred and his wife had catalogued every book: title, subject, classification. Details were printed on index cards and filed in a bespoke oak cabinet. When he wasn't filing index cards, Alfred was out and about buying more books.

Alfred couldn't have been happier with the result. The new library was three times the size of his old office and extended much closer to the verge of his beloved pond and meadow.

As promised, there were two large picture windows set into the far side of the room. A table and two chairs occupied the space between the two windows. This area of the library was Alfred's pride of place, reserved for fiction and built on a platform three stairs high.

"Excuse me, dear," said Sarah. She took two steps inside the library. "George Willis has come to see you."

"George – George Willis? He's here? To see me?"

"I gave him a sherry. He's waiting in the lounge. He says it's quite important. I know how busy you are, dear. Shall I ask him to come back another time?"

"No, no. Please, tell him to come in!"

Alfred was rocking back and forth on his heels in anticipation.

"Alf! I hope I haven't come at a bad time."

"Not at all. It's wonderful to see you, George. You're looking well, I must say."

"And you, Alf."

George took his time inspecting the room.

"I see you've been busy! People have been talking about your book collection and wondered if you were well. We haven't seen you recently in the village."

"I must apologise for being such a recluse. I've been so busy these past few months that I haven't had any time to socialise. I've just finished building my new library. What do you think of it?"

"Very impressive, indeed. How many books do you have here?"

"I haven't had a chance to count them yet . . . a few thousand at least, I should think."

"Have you read them all?"

Alf laughed.

"Not yet! I haven't had much reading time of late. My library has become a full-time job."

"That's what I wanted to talk to you about Alf."

Alf was perplexed.

"Sorry, George, I don't understand."

Sarah suddenly appeared. She was holding a large silver tray.

"Sorry to interrupt, dear. I thought you and George would like s cup of tea and homemade chocolate cake."

"How wonderful, Sarah. You are a treasure," said Alf.

"I'll put it down on the table so you can both enjoy the view."

"You are most considerate, Mrs Paige, said George."

"My pleasure."

George and Alf sat in silence as they enjoyed their afternoon tea. George was eager to get to the point.

"The *Village Art Show*, Alf."

"Yes? What about it?"

"That's why I've come to see you. We haven't received your entry. It's one of the highlights of the year, you know. Everyone is looking forward to this year's painting. We love seeing your pond and meadow on canvas."

"Oh, I see. Well, I've been so busy with the library, George, that I haven't had the time to do much painting of anything. I might just decide to take a year off . . . take a break from the competition this year. Let others take the spotlight."

George narrowed his eyes and frowned. He thought carefully before answering.

"It shouldn't come as any surprise, Alf, but you do know that you are the best painter in the village?"

Alf's smile failed to hide his embarrassment.

"Please reconsider, Alf. It means a lot to us. It would

177

be a severe blow if you weren't there."

"I don't know, George. This library project of mine has worn me down."

"Please, Alf. Paint *something* for us."

Alf took a deep breath.

"When is the deadline?"

"Tomorrow."

"*Tomorrow!* I can't possibly finish –"

"Paint something different and smaller," advocated George with encouraging confidence. "What about a work in progress? You will still have time to read your books."

"One day is hardly enough –"

"Why don't you paint the library or a part of it? That should be easy for you, and it will take less time than a landscape of the pond and meadow. I know you can do it. What do you say, Alf?"

"Well . . . I don't know if I can George. A completed painting in only one day, I mean –"

"Can you at least try, Alf?"

Alf looked around at his completed library, his pride and joy, thinking and wondering if such a painting were possible. He started pointing, mumbling and nodding his head, up and down and from side to side like a snooker player weighing up the possible options before taking the next shot.

"I might be able to paint something for you. I can't promise a finished canvas, though. I'll do my best."

"I know you can do it, Alf. I'm certain it will be a masterpiece."

"Well then, I'd better get started right away. Come

by tomorrow at the same time, George."

"You'll make a lot of people very happy. I'll leave you now. Happy painting!"

\* \* \*

The warm sunshine of a new day eased its way into the library. Alf's head is slumped. His chin touched his chest. When he opened his eyes, he looked at his hand. It was still clinging to a paint brush, now dry and crusty.

Alf had painted throughout the night and well into the morning. He never left the library and went without food and drink.

He looked at his watch – noon.

He opened his eyes wider than he thought possible and saw what he had done. He was startled at what prevailed in front of him: a finished painting of the library showing the full width and breadth of the interior in all its colourful glory.

He stood up and walked around the easel, then placed it by the window, allowing the light to cast its verdict on Alf's brush strokes, the use of colour and the shape and perspective of the books he had painted!

Alf sat down and gawked at his handiwork. His gaze was relentless. He rubbed his chin and squinted as if trying to make sense of a puzzle. A profound idea was taking shape. He walked up to the painting and touched the canvas with his fingers as if trying to see the words of the very books he had just painted.

There was a knock on the library door.

"Yes, who is it?" asked Alf without shifting position.

His voice was groggy.

"Are you OK, dear?"

"Yes, indeed. Come in! I have something to show you. Look, Sarah – I've finished the painting for the *Village Art Show*. What do you think?"

"This is wonderful, dear! I think it's your best work! You've been up all-night painting, haven't you?"

"Please don't make a fuss."

"I'll make you a hot lunch, then you must sleep."

"Yes, I promise. If I have time!"

"What do you mean?"

"I have more important work to do."

She looked at Alf for an explanation.

He took his wife's hand. They strolled amongst the vast collection of books like two sightseers on holiday studying the architecture of a new city and straining their necks to see the titles on the top shelves along every row.

"What do you see?" he asked.

"More books than anyone can ever read."

"True enough, yet there is something else, something far more important than just rows of books waiting patiently to be touched and admired. It occurred to me soon after I had finished my painting and seen in detail what I had produced. This library has a purpose. It's as clear to me as my reflection in the mirror."

"Why don't you have lunch first, then a rest. We can talk about this later when you're more relaxed."

"I am too excited to relax, much less sleep!"

He stopped, held his wife lovingly by the shoulders and looked into her eyes.

"Writers have studied human behaviour – life itself – for hundreds, thousands of years through their writing. Their observations and conclusions are within easy reach, here in these books – my books."

"Are you sure you don't want to have a rest first?"

"Think about it, Sarah. There could be a pearl of wisdom right here in this room waiting to be discovered by *me*."

"What kind of pearl?"

"I don't know. It could be a *question* that we have never asked of ourselves, or it could be an *answer* that we have not imagined. Every book in this room has one thing in common – people. Is there something *new* or *forgotten* about people that we can discover from the words and wisdom of others, those who have written these books? It could be a simple truth about ourselves. Their ideas and opinions are part of a much larger puzzle. No individual writer can know everything, but I am certain there are clues from every writer in this room. Put them together and –"

"Clues to what, dear?"

"I don't know," he said smiling. "That's what I must find out."

\* \* \*

It was of no importance to Alfred Paige that his library painting had won first prize. He never collected his award or saw George Willis for the following eighteen months! He didn't care how he looked and had grown a long grey beard that covered much of his face. Alf saw no visitors either, except for the family doctor, who came by frequently at the behest of Alf's wife.

Distraught with her husband's intransigent state of mind and fearing for his physical and mental well-being, she felt powerless to change his compulsive behaviour. She hated the library and everything it represented and vowed that she would never touch or read another book again!

"Don't worry, Mrs Paige, your husband is fine," the doctor told her, and authorised a repeat prescription for supplementary vitamins and minerals for Alf.

"My husband has an addiction, doctor. Surely you can see that! He needs to see a different kind of doctor. You know, one for his mind."

"We shouldn't jump to conclusions, Mrs Paige. I've known Alf for a long time. He is a compulsive man. He has a one-track mind and never gives up until he finds what he's looking for. I shouldn't worry. I've examined him and I can tell you that he is in good health given his age."

"He lives by himself in his library, doctor! He's shunned by the neighbours and has no friends. No one comes to visit him! He eats and sleeps in his library! I am afraid to set foot inside. He doesn't even talk to me unless it has something to do with his blasted books! Sorry doctor."

"He could be going through a 'late-life' crisis."

"Oh dear! Is that serious?"

"It can be. Dissatisfaction with one's life and a loss of identity are two of the classic symptoms. I must say, though, the library seems to have given him a real purpose in his life, whatever that may be. You can't argue that he's dedicated to whatever he's doing. Has he told you what might be?"

"Something about a puzzle. He's looking for an unknown or forgotten truth about people . . . a question or an answer. I'm not sure I understand. He says there are clues in his books."

"That sounds thought-provoking, I must say." The doctor's words lacked any air of sympathy, much less interest.

"Make sure he eats well, stays hydrated and please insist that he gets a proper dose of fresh air. Remind him to go for a walk. Every day would be helpful. He looks tired and pale, but that can soon change. And tell him not to work so hard. I hope he finds what he's looking for. Then you can both take a long holiday!"

\* \* \*

Alfred Paige was a stubborn man, who ignored the well-meaning advice of both his wife and doctor. Nothing either of them said could dissuade Alf from his single-minded quest.

In order to make more time for his research and without consulting anyone, a small cloakroom with integral shower cubicle was built in the library. He demanded that his meals be served there as well and that the bed in the spare room be moved into the book-filled room along with his clothing and his computer. He devised a weekly schedule for his food and laundry requirements and insisted that it be followed to the letter.

Sarah cried herself to sleep every night, afraid to imagine where this madness would lead.

Every day, every week and every month for more than a year, books would arrive at the Paige residence. A coded tap on the library door told Alf his order had arrived.

Mrs Paige grew more distressed every time she peered into the room – a stuffy, unventilated and dusty space where billions of words waited to be read and understood.

* * *

Repetitive bursts of laughter – loud and grating – shook the Paige house to its core. Sarah shot out of bed, fearing for her life. It was 3am.

The boisterous voice was familiar. She was shaking as she rushed down the stairs.

"Alf! Is that you?" she called out.

There was no reply.

"Do have any idea what time it is? Is something wrong? Are you ill?"

The laughter stopped.

She tried turning the library door. It was unlocked. She opened it slowly and scanned the murky interior.

Along the far wall, she could see a pale light virtually hidden by a jungle of books. She took a few steps forward and saw Alf. He was sitting in a chair staring out of the window and into the blackness of the night towards his much-loved pond and meadow. He turned his head and smiled.

"Are you all right, Alf?"

"Come, sit with me."

"You scared me."

"I am so sorry, Sarah. It was not my intention. I have a great deal to tell you."

"Shall I call the doctor? I do worry about you. I always worry about you."

"I'm fine. It's over, now."

"What do you mean, dear? What is?"

"I found what I was looking for!"

"Oh, Alf, that's wonderful news! I'm so proud of you. Somehow, I never doubted that you would find what you were looking for. Is it what you expected?"

Alf stood up and sucked in a room-full of air, filling his lungs to capacity. He held his breath for an eternity, then exhaled with such liberating force that Mrs Paige gasped, fearing that her husband was having a fit and was about to die.

He extended his spine as if trying to grow taller in the process and paced back and forth with purpose – hands on hips – unexpectedly energised with a spirit not seen for a long time.

"I am content with what I have learned or should have known all along! I have been such a damned fool not to have understood it in the first place.

I have been looking for clues to a puzzle, something fresh and different about us. It's not a puzzle at all that I have solved, but confirmation of our own weakness."

The blank expression on her face was disheartening. Alf clasped Sarah's hands with loving tenderness.

"Come – sit down with me. Let me explain. Don't get me wrong, I found plenty of reminders about how we think and act towards each other. They are obvious and familiar. No treasure hunt is required to find them. They are out in the open for everyone to experience. We have both love and hate in our hearts; we're generous and greedy; kind and cruel; peaceful and violent; arrogant and wise; ingenious and ignorant; inventive and destructive – the list, I'm afraid, is long and varied. This tragic duplicity of human nature is woeful. But there is a more dangerous and sinister human frailty that is wired into every human brain. It is as old as time and impossible to reprogramme. There are no replacement parts or psychoanalytic treatment that can change the way we behave, and it is this imperfection, this weakness, this *flaw* in our brains that has come to my attention. We all know what it is. It has never been a secret. Yet, we have either forgotten about it or ignored it. That's what I have learned."

Alf looked into his wife's eyes.

"We LIE! It's as simple as that! It's vile and despicable, but that's what people do everyday. Our brain has a special talent for deceit and dishonesty. Lying comes easily and naturally to us like opening our mouth to breathe. Some of us do it better than others. People believe what they are told. Our brain excels at changing facts, creating a false reality and misleading others . . . and yet . . . as clever as it is, our brain cannot determine what is truthful on its own. It is helpless to do so. Our own brain is just too damn stupid to work out the truth for itself. Our brain is woefully inadequate to deal with the truth. It requires help from other, much smarter, brains to unravel this treacherous, double-dealing behaviour to find the truth. We must collect new facts to reveal the lies. We have to call in the specialists: lawyers, judges, juries and witnesses. It's imperative we have investigations, enquiries, evidence, testimony – and a great deal of time and money to unravel our vile behaviour. And even then – *even then* – we can never be certain of anything."

"What will you do now, Alf?"

"Let's take a long holiday, Sarah. Let's go on a cruise. Then we'll donate every single book to charity. Clear out the room, redecorate, open the windows and let in the light. And that's the truth!"

"Oh, Alf, that would be wonderful. Do you really mean it?"

"Would I lie to you, Sarah?"

The build was completed on a hot and sunny Saturday in July. Had it been twenty-four hours earlier, Finnegan Harper and Julian Wood would not have appeared on the evening news or been featured in all the Sunday papers. It was the fire that sold the story . . . and the much-anticipated Adriana – Miss Landscape Gardener of the Year – clad in an alluring, iridescent Kelly-green sequinned bikini.

# Adriana and the Hot Air Balloon

Strictly speaking, this was Finn's idea, so it seemed only right that he should take charge.

Finnegan Harper and Julian Wood had known each other most of their adult lives. They lived on the same street, grew up together and were partners in their own business: *Harper Wood Landscape Gardeners*.

It was nothing fancy or out of the ordinary, but they did provide a quality, professional and friendly service. It paid the bills and that was about all.

"We're going to need a thousand nails," said Finn as he took the first bite of his lunchtime sandwich. "Is there any coffee left?"

"A thousand! You've got to be kidding."

Jules wasn't arguing, he was voicing his opinion. He unscrewed the flask and filled Finn's mug with coffee.

"Call it an educated guess," said Finn. "It's difficult

to know the exact number of nails we're gong to need. Come to think of it, let's make it five hundred, 3-inch nails and five hundred, 2-inch nails. We have a lot of hammering to do."

"How much will a thousand nails cost?"

"I have no idea. Fifty quid . . . maybe seventy-five – a hundred. I don't know to be honest."

"I still think a thousand sounds over the top if you ask me."

"We can afford it," said Finn with a hint of sarcasm. "I've come up with a brilliant idea to make some easy cash so we can buy what we need. It's time to expand the business, make a bold statement about what we do, showcase our skills, enhance our reputation. We can't keep working from the garden shed. We need our own building, a proper corporate address – '*Harper Wood HQ*' – and we can build it entirely from wooden pallets! For free!"

"I know. You've been talking about it every day for the past month."

"I got the idea from the internet. People are building all kinds of things from pallets, even full-size houses. And you know what the best part is, Jules?"

"You've mentioned that as well, more than once: '*wooden pallets are free, they're everywhere, hundreds of them just waiting for a new home*'. Why bother building it when you can buy a prefab in steel, aluminium, timber or plastic? Or another shed, only a much bigger one, for that matter? It's hassle-free and quicker."

"That's what everybody else does, mate. We need to

be different, original. Besides, prefabs are common, boring and, more importantly, too expensive for our pockets. Let's be creative and save money. It will attract attention and that means more customers."

Jules thought for a moment.

"You're probably right."

"I know I am."

"Why don't we use screws instead of nails?"

"Far too labour-intensive, I'm afraid. We'd have to buy two cordless screwdrivers and wait for them to re-charge. There are no electrical outlets on our building site so you can forget about using power tools.

"What building site? I didn't know we had one yet. Why didn't you tell me about this before?"

"I didn't know until yesterday. I had to act quickly before someone else grabbed the land. I'll tell you all about it later."

"That was a bit urgent."

"There's no risk for either of us. Leave it to me, Jules. I have a clever plan! All we're going to need are two claw hammers and a couple of heavy-duty saws that can rip through anything, a shovel or two, strong cord and another ladder as well. Oh yes, I think we should paint our work of art British racing green!"

"I'm just letting you know in advance, Finn. I am not going up and down ladders with a pallet strapped to my back. Besides, I've got a dodgy knee from playing rugby. You know that!"

"Be honest, you're afraid of heights, aren't you?"

"Well, that too."

"Your disapproval of ladders is noted. Anyway, I've

191

got it all worked out."

"Yeah? Have you thought about the overall design? How many rooms do we need and on how many floors? What about the plumbing and electrics? Don't forget the roof! Have you got that worked out as well? Do you know anything about building off-grid?"

"You worry too much, Jules. How hard can it be? It shouldn't take us that long to build, and the sooner the better so we can expand the business and start making real money. Think of it as a model kit, only much bigger. We'll have to work evenings and weekends to get the job done. With any luck, we can finish it in two weeks, then move all our gear in! You have to look to the future and be positive. *'He, who dares'* . . ."

"Yeah, yeah, I've heard that one before, too."

"We've been trimming and pruning hedges, cutting and laying grass, digging up weeds and the rest of it for – how long now?"

"I make it about ten years, Finn."

"You're right. And yet, we don't seem to be getting anywhere. We can't get ahead of ourselves and save for the future. We've got a good reputation. Our customers seem to like us, but we need to do more. I want to take the family on a decent holiday for a change, move into a bigger house. That's why we need to build this place. It's a great opportunity for both of us, especially after that storm on Monday. Have you seen the damage done by the wind?"

"Tell me about it! I've lost three fence panels and a shed door!"

"That's where I got the idea from."

"What do you mean?

"Making money to build our new office. Look, the last thing people want right now is their grass cut and their hedges trimmed. To be honest with you, I have no desire to get involved with any major clean-up operations after the storm. It's backbreaking work and I can do without the hassle. We can still make money from this storm and pay for what we need."

"How?" asked Jules.

"It's simple. Hundreds of fence panels have already come crashing down. Damaged, broken, split in half. Certainly not fit for purpose. All we have to do is knock on people's doors and charge a fiver for each panel we take away – let's say three quid for smaller ones. It saves them a trip to the dump. We'll do the job for them. We can decide on the exact price when we see the kind of fencing people want to get rid of. Clever, isn't it? Money for old rope. We can use the dosh to buy the nails and tools we need and use the fence panels for other things. Don't forget, there's no point throwing anything away."

"Where's the building site you were talking about?"

"A couple of miles from home!"

"Are you serious?"

"How's that for a break?"

"Where'd you get the money to buy it and why didn't you talk to me first? We *are* partners!"

"I haven't actually bought it. I've acquired it – it's listed in both of our names. It was a bargain any day of the week. Money from the fence panels will more than cover our costs. You know *Wild Rose Common*?"

"That small plot of land with the old bench between Windmill Lane and Highfield Road? Yeah, I know where it is. We drive past it almost every day. It's a public park or communal area owned by the Council, isn't it?"

"That's what I thought. We're both wrong."

"Who owns it, then?"

"According to the Land Registry office, *Wild Rose Common* has never been officially registered, legal or otherwise. Nobody knows who owns it! The County Records Office and the local Council have no official documents, deeds or planning applications for the land. My son's girlfriend has just graduated from law school. I'm paying her to sort out the paperwork. She needs the work, and we need a plot of land to build on. It's worked out incredibly well for all of us. Better than I expected. I claimed it – *we've* claimed it as unattended land. *Wild Rose Common* is basically ours now, Jules, officially registered with the Council in both of our names."

"What about planning permission?"

"We don't need that either as long as whatever we build is a reasonable size – I think they said no higher than four metres. Let's say twelve feet in old money to be on the safe side. I think that's adequate for what we need. My son's friend – the newbie lawyer I was telling you about – is on top of things. I've left all the details to her. Oh yes, there's something else. You'll like this."

"I can't wait to hear it."

"The Council has recommended that we put up a fence around the property and landscape the site –

make everything look neat and tidy like it belongs to someone. They said it shows intention of ownership or something like that. By the time we're finished, our HQ will be a village landmark. We'll paint the fence the same colour – British racing green. We'll plant all kinds of plants and flowers. We'll turn it into a showpiece. It will be part of the landscape, you know, blend in with nature."

"Don't you need a permit or a licence to run a business from what is essentially a public park?"

"It's not public land anymore, mate. We own it. We're landscape gardeners. We offer a specialised service to the public. If we need a licence to make people's gardens look beautiful, then I'm sure our lawyer friend will sort it out.

* * *

Finn was well pleased with himself for having thought of this plan in the first place: from fence panels and pallets to claiming unregistered land for a posh, new commercial headquarters. He was always looking for new ideas to better himself and the business. The recent storm that sparked his imagination was the icing on the cake.

Jules, on the other hand, wasn't as ingenious as Finn. Nor was he proactive by nature. He was an ordinary bloke who relied on others to turn dreams into reality and would be the first to admit it.

For the next two weeks, Jules and Finn drove far and wide in their pickup truck looking for the building blocks of their new 'Head Office'.

They collected pallets from everywhere: department stores, supermarkets, food wholesalers, garden centres DIY merchants, industrial areas, construction sites, and recycling centres. They were only too pleased to get rid of them.

They stockpiled more than two hundred pallets – close-boarded and opened-boarded made of pine and oak. On average, they measured 120cm by 100 cm, or about four feet by three feet.

Closed-boarded pallets, with their solid, snug-fitting planks, would be used for the main structural walls and flooring while open-boarded pallets with see-through gaps between planks would comprise interior partition walls. Other pallets would be dismantled completely with a crowbar and the planks used as crude, yet effective, joining plates to connect the pallets together from the inside to create a firm, reliable structure.

They selected the best pallets – nearly 150 in total – and laid them in sections on the ground: first the floor, then the front, back and the sides. They settled on a structure that was about thirty-two feet long by twenty feet wide. It had a sloping roof made of waterproof viny-coated polyester tarpaulin with grommets every two feet, stretched taut, and tied to the supporting structure.

To help speed-up the build, Finn and Jules invited their friends and neighbours to lend a hand. More than a dozen people arrived on site with their hammers, their ladders and their paint brushes.

In short order, *Harper Wood Landscape Gardeners*

HQ was nearing completion. Openings were cut to exacting shape using nothing more glamorous than basic handsaws, then fitted with doors and windows salvaged from a local architectural reclamation yard. The installation was impressive by anyone's standard.

Finn and Jules were humbled by the generosity of their helpers, for they also brought with them an eye-catching assortment of useful equipment, fittings and fixtures: from portable toilets, hand-washing sinks, air coolers and gas cookers to water coolers, wood-burning stoves and even solar panels, although the exact location of the latter was a constant point of discussion given their size and weight on a roof comprising nothing more rigid than polyester tarpaulin.

"We're going to have internet connection as well," said Finn. "Apparently, my son's lawyer friend is also a computer genius. We're not exactly as off-grid as you may think. She said it wouldn't be difficult to set up."

The build was completed on a hot and sunny Saturday in July. Had it been twenty-four hours earlier, Finnegan Harper and Julian Wood would not have appeared on the evening news or been featured in all the Sunday papers. It was the fire that sold the story!

\* \* \*

Topping out day was an event to remember. The village had not experienced a time like it in decades. There was sufficient food and drink for everyone who happened to come by and say hello. Even Finn's son performed with his rock band.

A celebration of another kind also took place on that hot and sunny Saturday in July.

It was the twenty-fifth anniversary of *Celebrity Homes and Gardens* magazine.

This noteworthy milestone was commemorated in the air from a hot air balloon. Emblazoned around the circumference of the bulging nylon envelope was the name of the magazine and the fact it was their twenty-fifth anniversary.

Apart from the balloon's pilot, passengers included the magazine's publisher, the managing editor, head of the design studio, the advertising manager, the director of social media, a distinguished cinematographer who recorded the entire flight, and the much-anticipated Adriana – *Miss Landscape Gardener of the Year* – clad in an alluring, iridescent Kelly-green sequinned bikini.

Kelly green was the magazine's corporate colour. The annual competition was promoted nationally and eagerly awaited by the male subscribers.

The basket carried two more people than the permitted maximum of six, but the magazine owned the hot air balloon outright and could do what it wanted. The pilot was awarded a bonus for keeping his mouth shut.

Even though it was Adriana's first flight in a hot air balloon, she loved every minute of it. She wasn't the least bit nervous of heights, especially leaning out and over the square basket so everyone on the ground could see as much of her as possible.

Her sequinned bikini shimmered and sparkled in the dazzling sunshine like a battery-powered Christmas tree ornament.

She waved to her would-be, adoring fans who fumbled with their mobile phones, desperate to capture the moment in all its Kelly-green glory.

All necks craned towards the cloudless sky as the balloon approached from the southeast, directly in line with the new headquarters of *Harper Wood Landscape Gardeners*.

Voices rang out, one after the other.

"It looks awfully big from here!"

"And low."

"Shouldn't it be much higher?"

"That's what I was wondering."

"The pilot knows what he's doing."

"I hope you're right."

"He just needs to put his foot on the gas. You know, pump more heat into the balloon so it can rise."

"They're going to land here."

"Wouldn't that be amazing?"

"I've never seen a hot air balloon up close."

"Looks like you're going to get your chance."

"I'd love to get a selfie with Adriana! Don't tell my wife."

The rock band stopped playing.

No one spoke a word.

The faces of those on board came into sharp focus.

Their eyes glossed over with terror,

The pilot tried to gain altitude.

His attempt was futile.

Propane-fuelled flames spewed onto the balloon's inner skin. The excess weight in the basket had taken its toll. The balloon failed to gain height.

The only person smiling was Adriana, for she had no idea what was about to happen.

The balloon was coming down.

Its approach was fast and uncontrolled.

The envelope deflated, losing its recognisable shape.

People shouted and screamed, running in all directions to avoid being caught in the balloon's path as it descended rapidly.

The peaceful afternoon was ruined.

Finn and Jules kept their cool. They remained at ground zero, leading people away from their building to safety.

The basket slapped into the centre of the roof. The tarpaulin sagged with a fierce jolt, yet didn't rip or collapse in a heap as expected. It held its shape and remained securely rigged to the perimeter of the structure where it had been tied and secured. Even the grommets remained intact.

All eight passengers tumbled out of their nest, unable to gain a foot hold on the slippery slopes of the viny-coated polyester roof.

Jules grabbed a ladder and was the first to reach the scene. Finn was stunned by the quick-witted response of his partner and the dexterity that Jules demonstrated as he scrambled to the roof to aid in the rescue.

*'Bad knees! Afraid of heights, my arse!'*

In turn, Jules carried each passenger down the ladder to safety. Adriana, by her own insistence, was the last to leave the crash site. Miraculously, no one was killed or injured.

The cinematographer's camera was undamaged, and its operator continued to record the proceedings in real time.

As Jules placed both feet firmly on the ground – Adriana cradled in his arms, her hands wrapped around his neck – the most talked about picture in the history of *Celebrity Homes and Gardens* magazine was captured on everyone's mobile phone.

For Adriana, it was simply another adventure in her colourful life. She lapped up the attention and public concern for her wellbeing.

Unfortunately, a fuel leak, a spark, a burst of flames: Fuel hose? Blast valve? O-ring seal? Propane tanks? No one knew what had transpired. Everything was ablaze before Jules reluctantly released his hold on Adriana.

It didn't take long for *Harper Wood HQ* to morph into a heap of ash, mangled plastic and metal, for everything on, around and inside the building had been consumed by the fire,

The clamorous arrival of the fire brigade provided the perfect soundtrack as the cinematographer panned three-hundred and sixty degrees.

This was followed by filmed interviews with the leading players of this little tragedy. Finn, Jules and Adriana went first, followed by the pilot and the rest of the passengers.

The show must go on.

Once the chaos and confusion of the crash had run its course, Finn and Jules fell to their knees in disbelief.

Their tattered dream smouldered before them.

The smell of ash and cinders was noxious.

\* \* \*

Traumatic events, be they accidents or otherwise, have a way of surprising those directly affected. In the end, virtuous things can, and often do, prevail.

The crash of the hot air balloon and subsequent fire, the rescue and survival of all those on board, and the destruction of *Harper Wood HQ* was recorded exactly as it happened by the cinematographer.

The footage was edited later that afternoon like a movie trailer for the latest Hollywood blockbuster, with voice-over narration and music for additional dramatic effect.

Finnegan Harper and Julian Wood had become household names, literally overnight. *Celebrity Homes and Gardens* fared equally well. New subscriptions and advertising revenue increased by ninety-two per cent. That wasn't the end of the story. Not by a long shot.

Not only did the magazine retain Finn and Jules as regular, paid contributors, they also financed the design and construction of a new *Harper Wood HQ*, and on the same site.

As for the cover story for the magazine's August issue, well, you can imagine. Adriana photographed extremely well, it must be said.

She too profited from the events of the day and was immediately hired by Finn and Jules as their new, full-time office manager.

"Hey Finn! I was thinking. Why don't we buy our

*own* hot air balloon next year? You know, promote the business."

"That's the best idea you've ever had, Jules!"

"What's our corporate colour?" asked Adriana.

"You choose," replied Jules.

The printed word – the writing system of language itself – had vanished as if systematically removed from Melanie's apartment by some outrageous trickery.

# The
# Dictionary

"Mia, it's Melanie."

"Hey, girl. I just spoke to you an hour ago. What's wrong? You don't sound well.

"Something's happened, Mia."

"Are you all right? Are you hurt? Are you sick?"

"No. Nothing like that. I'm fine – sort of. It's just that, well, something peculiar has happened. I can't explain it. You need to come over here right now and see for yourself. I'm scared."

"Oh my God, what's going on?"

"Please, don't ask any questions. You'll think I've lost my mind."

"Not any more than usual!"

"Don't make fun of me. I'm not joking, Mia. This is serious."

"Have you called the police?"

"The *police!* That's the *last* thing I need to do!"

"I can't help you if you won't tell me, Melanie."

"Not over the phone."

"Has Kevin been hassling you again? Are you being followed? Is someone trying to break in?"

"No. Nothing like that."

"If you're that worried, you ought to call the police."

"I can't. Not yet. Never."

"Are you in trouble?"

"I don't know."

"You don't know? What do you mean? How can you not know if you're in trouble? If it's an emergency, call 999!"

"It is and it isn't. I can't tell you over the phone. You won't believe me. You'll tell me I'm crazy. Listen Mia, you need to come over right away. Something spooky has just happened."

"I'm leaving now."

"Oh, Mia?"

"Yeah?"

"Bring a newspaper. Any date is fine. And a book as well."

"You're not making any sense, Melanie. Don't you get your Sunday paper delivered?"

"Yes, but I can't read it – or anything else! That's the problem."

"Oh my God, it's your eyesight. Are you going blind? Pack a small suitcase, if you can, and we'll go to the hospital straight away."

"NO! Put the phone down, Mia, and get over here. I don't need to go to the hospital – well, maybe the funny farm. This is not the time to be asking dumb questions. I need your help. Please!"

\* \* \*

Melanie and Mia met when they were both five years old. More than twenty years on, they were still the best of friends – in a word, inseparable.

Mia was the regional manager for a high-end, branded clothing chain and Melanie worked for an international banking group as a financial analyst.

She hated being called 'Mel'.

In business, they had become decidedly successful. When it came to love, however, they had yet to find lasting happiness. After seven years of a childless marriage to Kevin, Melanie was newly divorced and living on her own, while Mia had endured life as a single woman, on the never-ending quest to find that perfect partner.

Like her short name, Mia was petite, yet graceful with an eye-catching figure. Why she had remained unattached was still a mystery. Melanie, on the other hand, was the complete opposite: sturdy, thickset and portly – all six feet of her.

On this particular Sunday, Melanie had other things to worry about besides her incessant weight problem and new-found freedom.

Something bizarre and inexplicable had taken place the previous evening in Melanie's luxurious penthouse apartment.

\* \* \*

When Mia arrived – she had her own key – Melanie was sitting quietly and comfortably in her antique *bergère* upholstered French armchair with a glass of white wine in hand.

Mia handed Melanie a paper bag.

"As requested . . . a newspaper – sorry, it's three days old . . . and a novel you might enjoy about romance and love in pre-war France. What's going on. Melanie? You don't look ill."

"Thanks, Mia. Sit down and pour yourself a glass of wine. I've already had three. This is my fourth."

"Oh dear, you are serious. OK, start talking."

Melanie got up and turned on the TV.

"I have a television, too, you know, Melanie."

"Here's the remote. Watch whatever you want, but pay close attention and tell me what you see."

Mia flicked the remote, moving from programme to programme. She took her time, fixated on every station and picture including the adverts, intrigued to find something of concern.

"There's something wrong with your TV. It could be the signal, Melanie. There's no text anywhere."

"Bingo! The picture and the sound are both perfect. Right?"

"Correct."

"There's no text, Mia It's disappeared, gone! That's the problem."

"You're right. How strange. Then you need to buy a new TV, right? Problem solved. I could have told you that over the phone. Well, at least I've had a glass of wine for my trouble."

"It gets worse, believe me. Now take the newspaper out of the bag and examine it," said Melanie.

Mia was dumfounded.

"What the –! The ink has disappeared. I mean, all the pages are blank. Look, there's nothing there!"

"Tell me about it. It's the same on every page. Now look at the book."

When Mia took the book out of the bag, she was astonished. She examined the front and back covers, then leafed through all the pages, back and forth, and over again.

"WHAT!? There's no text here either. Every page is blank, just like the newspaper. It looks like a school notebook. How the hell did that happen?"

"If you really want to freak out, Mia, come with me and open all the cupboards in the kitchen. You won't believe it."

Every tin, packet and box were blank. The coloured labels and their branded icons were as sharp and clear as they had always been, yet the names of the products, their promotional slogans, cooking instructions and lists of ingredients had been expunged from every surface.

The printed word – the writing system of language itself – had vanished as if systematically removed from Melanie's apartment by some outrageous trickery.

"What about your neighbours? Have you mentioned anything to them?"

"NO! And don't you go knocking on any doors, either. I'm the only one who's been affected."

"What makes you believe that?"

"Come with me, Mia."

Melanie handed the newspaper, book and a box of cereal to Mia. They left the apartment, closed the door behind them and stood in the corridor.

Slowly and in an orderly fashion, words, sentences and columns started to reappear in the newspaper, book and on the box of cereal, one after the other as if they had been programmed to do so.

Mia screamed. It was short and sharp as she dropped everything and ran back into Melanie's apartment.

Melanie apologised to her inquisitive neighbours for the sudden and unexpected outburst, picked up the three items from the floor, and retreated to her well-stocked bar where she brandished a large bottle of gin.

"You're scaring me, Melanie – and you know it takes a lot to rattle me!"

"Now you know why I can't go to the police. What exactly are they supposed to do? Look at the newspaper and book – the cereal box too. There are no words again. Something has happened to this apartment. Here, this should help. Do you want ice and tonic water with that?"

Mia drained her glass in one gulp before she could reply. Melanie refilled her glass.

"At least no crime has been committed –"

"Wait a minute! That's just it, Melanie. A crime may well have been committed. Don't you get it? Think about it."

"About what?"

Mia steadied her nerves.

"Listen to me, girl. This is important. I know this is

going to sound daft, but where's your dictionary?"

"MMMmmm, I had a feeling you were going to get round to that. To be honest with you, Mia, I threw it out. I did a bit of spring-cleaning last night. I had a lot of clutter around the place and well, you know, I never used the dictionary, so why keep it? I never thought this was going to happen."

"Look Melanie, you know perfectly well that everyone is issued with an official dictionary from the *Ministry of Meaning*. It's compiled and published by four universities, and is the only one there is and you threw it out?"

"What about, sort of losing it? Surely, there's no harm in accidentally misplacing it," enquired Melanie.

"No, not unless you want to pay a £5,000 fine and not be able to read anything. Remember? Every word in this apartment has disappeared because you threw out your dictionary."

"Oh dear!" said Melanie.

"You know perfectly well that each dictionary has an exclusive barcode registered to your home address or place of business. Every year, the dictionary is updated. The new edition is delivered to you directly and the old version is taken away to be destroyed. You don't have to do anything. It's automatic. You have to keep up with these things, Melanie. You aren't allowed to give your personal dictionary away to anybody, and you are not authorised to throw it out! When you move, you have to leave the dictionary behind for the next person who moves into your property. What are you going tell the RIP if they come knocking on your door?"

"The what?"

"The *Random Inspection Patrol* – the RIP."

"I forgot about them. I thought we left 1984 behind us for good."

"We still have the freedom to write, reason and express ourselves as long as we stop making things up as we go along to suit our own selfish needs. We ought to agree on what things mean, don't you agree? The world can't carry on like this."

"You are in a philosophical mood today, Mia."

"I know. I'm sorry."

"OK, I get it, but what about me? I haven't got a dictionary now and I don't want to pay £5,000 to get a new one! I'll have a black mark against my name. More importantly, I need to see words and sentences again. Can't I replace the one that I threw out with another one, Mia?"

"Bookshops are not permitted to sell dictionaries, and certainly not *this* one. There is only source of meaning you are allowed to use becomes it comes from the *Ministry of Meaning*."

"We could break into the *Ministry*, hack into their computer system and steal another copy so it looks legal."

"This isn't a movie, Melanie."

"I can't remember the last time I used a dictionary for anything! If I need to check the meaning of something or other, I just use the internet. It's fast and easy."

"We all do that now," said Mia. "And look where it got us. Everyone's got their own definitions for words."

\* \* \*

As predictable as darkness follows light, people started to change the meaning of words. It was habitual. The printed word was shunned and disrespected

Nobody had any idea what was right, wrong, true or accurate. People simply stopped using dictionaries, to check the meaning of language.

Instead, they have put their trust in the wisdom and sanctity of cyberspace, controlled and manipulated by digitally deranged lunatics, who didn't – and don't – care about the meaning of anything.

When that happens we get brainwashed, confused, and mistaken. They accuse each other of ignorance and stupidity. That's usually the time when confrontation and accusations usually begin.

People are always fighting over land, money and religion, why not language? It's all about the meaning of words.

Who said what to whom? What did they mean? If we can't agree on the meaning of things, we are in big trouble.

Never underestimate the power of language.

\* \* \*

"How was I supposed to know that something like this was going to happen, Mia?"

You do understand the rules and regulations, don't you? We *are* talking about the *Ministry of Meaning*, you know: *MoM's the Word* and all of that? It is 2029, Melanie!"

"The government has gone too far, Mia."

"I know life is crazy. Personally, I think we're all better off with a proper 'in-your-hands' dictionary – good, old-fashioned ink on paper. One official source of meaning for everyone. There has to be agreement on what it is we mean to say. We need discipline when it comes to language and meaning."

"What about the TV, the newspaper and the book, and the stuff in my kitchen – the tins and packets? How do you explain that?"

"Digital technology, capability that we know nothing about. That would be my educated guess. We don't know a fraction of the things that are going on behind closed doors these days."

"So, what should I do? Is someone going to arrest me? Am I going to jail? Do I have to pay a fine? I can't afford a black mark on my record. I'll lose my job for sure. You've got to help me, Mia. Tell me what to do. I can't leave my apartment every time I want, or need, to read something. That would be stupid."

Mia and Melanie sat quietly. Pondering. Drinking. Sighing. Muttering. Wondering what to do.

"Wait a minute!" shrieked Melanie. "I've got it. It's so simple. We're both as dumb as each other."

"Enlighten me, my dear."

"Don't you see, Mia? Don't you get it? I threw out the dictionary yesterday – Saturday. That means it's still here, more or less. Then I haven't lost it!"

"Well done! Of course, you haven't. Why didn't we

realise that before?"

"Only, I sort of left it outside. I threw it out of the window, as one does. I did look first before I chucked it out. Nobody got hit over the head."

"Ahhhhhh. MMMmmm."

"OK. Let me consider all the facts. Then it's not missing at all!" rejoiced Melanie at the prospect of saving £5,000 and, more importantly, not falling foul of the *Ministry of Meaning*. "It's somewhere outside. I just have to find it. Then I can read again."

In chorus, Mia and Melanie turned their heads slowly towards the window. They hadn't been aware of it, but it was raining hard.

"Right!" said Melanie. "I'll be back in a minute. Open another bottle. Anything you like. You choose We'll celebrate when I get back."

Melanie returned ten in minutes with the dictionary. It was truly and utterly soaked. She wrapped it in a towel and handed it to Mia with marked care, as if it were an explosive device in need of defusing.

"Well, at least I still have it," said Melanie. "I haven't given it away and I haven't thrown it out. Look! Everything's returned to normal: the television, the newspaper, the book and the stuff in the kitchen. Aren't words beautiful?"

"That's fine, but you'll never be able to use this dictionary again even if the pages dry. Unfortunately, it's seriously warped as well. They'll be stuck together like a lump of concrete. I think your precious dictionary is well and truly knackered beyond use. This is not a good thing, girl!"

"Can't I replace it?" asked Melanie.

"I'm afraid you'll have to. It's your only choice, especially if the RIP comes knocking. But you'll have to pay a hefty fine, no doubt, and appear before a committee at the *Ministry* so you can explain in written detail how it is that your dictionary ended up in this unusable state. What are you going to tell them? *'Sorry MoM, I never use a dictionary, so I threw it out the window. It got soaked in the rain and now it's completely ruined.'* I don't think that excuse will go down too well, do you? Your dictionary might dry out. I doubt it."

"There is, of course, another solution, Mia."

"Yes, I know. The thought did occur to me. We'll be taking a big risk."

"We're too clever to fail!"

Mia and Melanie had arranged to meet at the sales office of a prestigious housing development first thing on Monday morning.

They were in luck. Only one property was still available.

"I love it," said Mia to the sales agent, then turned to Melanie and said: "It has everything the two of us could ever want. We should have thought of this years ago. What do you think? Should we take this one and move in together?"

"We'll take it!" Melanie said to the sales executive. "The sooner we can finalise the deal, the better for everyone. We have two properties on the market, so naturally, you'll get a bigger commission."

Melanie leaned forward and stared long and hard at

the sales executive. Their faces nearly touched as she whispered . . .

   *"Does it come with a dictionary?"*

He is muzzled with indecision, unable to know where the road of love will lead. He is afraid to say yes and be wrong . . . scared to say no and lose.

# A Memory of Love

A man, old and tempered by time, strolls through a landscape of lush trees bathed under a blue sky in June when all is right with the world. The old man's skin is soft and his complexion healthy.

He stops and fidgets with his pipe. A gentle finger prods a knob of tobacco into the chamber. He strikes a match, draws on the stem, and enjoys the soothing aroma.

His mind wanders back to another time as he thinks about a girl he once knew and focuses on a memory of love, knowing only too well that love punctures the spirit of a man. It withers a man's mettle beyond repair when it has abated, when it has been lost.

The old man strolls silently onward past trees of gilded memories. He recognises one such tree and one such memory etched into its bark, now worn and corroded by time. It is a tree amongst four cradled by a modest grassy knoll where picnics are enjoyed.

He stops to remember.

A heart-shaped figure, unfinished, encircles two initials near the base of the tree. It is a mark of lost lovers, carved into the bark with a penknife a long time ago.

So sees the old man.

He turns from the tree towards a wooden bench. It is a log sawn in half propped up by two stumps at either end. The old man sits down and leans forward, looking through smudged, dusty glasses.

His elbows rest upon his knees as he stares at the carving he knows so well.

As the old man watches a dog play happily with a stick, he dwells on a moment in time, unchangeable, irreversible, yet hoping – as much as any human being could – to relive that time, act differently, utter new words and, ultimately, find happiness.

Silky strands of the old man's silvery hair flutter like long blades of uncut grass caught by the afternoon wind.

He grows weary from thought and strays from reality, thinking about a memory of love.

\* \* \*

Two people, both in their twentieth year of life, enjoy this day for a picnic. Imagine a long and narrow path inscribed with flowers that speak of every colour of the rainbow, for this is where the lovers come into focus.

220

They reach the pinnacle of a modest grassy knoll set within the romantic enclosure marked by the four trees of experience.

The girl is full-bosomed and round-shouldered with smooth white skin and a touch of pink in the cheeks. She lives by the name of Anne and carries a flapper hat, ribbon trimmed.

The boy is lean, yet fit-looking and strong. He lives by the name of Robert and carries a picnic basket and soft blanket. His hair is short and his upper lip is hidden by a thick, well-shaped handlebar moustache.

Arm in arm, the lovers laugh, but their words are distant and trivial as they settle on the perfect spot for a picnic. Robert's dog enters the scene, captivated by the sights, and smells on this summer's day.

Anne twirls about like a dancer. She curves her lips in perfect symmetry, sculpting a gentle smile upon her innocently looking face.

Robert stops, unmoved by the environs of country bliss and is unable to enjoy the moment. He twists a corner of his moustache and studies his companion, hoping to hide the uncertainty he feels.

Anne can see contentment only in Robert's eyes this day for she loves him beyond any imaginable doubt, unaware of the conflict simmering in his heart.

Robert loves Anne, yet is unable to tell her, to reveal his feelings in words or in deeds. He is reluctant to give of himself, to show what he truly feels, to say: *'I love you, Anne'*.

The very seed of love's tragic tale is in the silence between these two lovers.

221

\* \* \*

Dejected in spirt, Robert sits down upon the stump of a fallen tree, while Anne collects a bouquet of flowers to garnish the centre of their picnic blanket. The dog barks, then jumps up and down around the girl's faded pastel yellow dress.

Anne giggles and taunts the animal's wet nose with a sweet-smelling flower that she had just picked.

She acknowledges Robert with a shy tilting of her head as if embarrassed by her own grace and charm.

Robert quarrels with his emotions – silently and poisonously – waiting for the day to end.

The young couple reach a clearing where the sun is bright in the noonday azure sky. Off to the right is a shallow brook, clear and inviting.

"Let's go this way," says Anne.

The dog scampers past the two lovers and runs into the brook, splashing freely and tries to catch the spray of water droplets with his tongue.

Anne removes her white suede pumps, places them by the brook's edge inside the shadowy umbrella of a tree, and feels the cool, soft sand beneath her feet.

Robert kneels in the sand. He picks up a handful of pebbles and tosses them half-heartedly into the water causing the surface to splash and bubble. He sees his reflection undulating in quick tempo and pushes his cap further back upon his troubled thoughts.

Anne tickles the brook with her toes and regards Robert with a questioning glance. She lifts her dress daintily by the hem as she places both feet firmly in the water. She looks up, frowning at her beau, for she fully expects him to show a bolt of spirit and join her.

Robert meets her inviting glance, nods accordingly and pulls himself up, wishing for only a moment that he were as free and simple-minded as his dog who dances in the water.

"Come on in," says Anne as if opening a door to a friendly neighbour who just happened to drop by for afternoon tea.

Robert's face is carved with a false sense of contentment – a mask recurring endlessly without warrant. The swift passage of a smile curves his drying lips as he reaches the water's edge.

"Don't be shy, Robert," says Anne as she takes hold of his hand. "It's only water."

"I still have my shoes on," he replies like a child as he stops short of the water.

Anne giggles.

Robert retreats to a grassy ledge to remove his shoes. He sits in suspended animation contemplating Anne's being. His shoes and socks sit neatly to one side. His jacket lies on the ground, neatly folded and his cap on top.

He slips the silk ascot from his neck and takes his time to fold and place it under his cap. Anne turns round, waiting patiently.

Robert moves awkwardly. He flinches as his feet touch the cool water. He takes Anne's hand firmly and is desperate to reveal his feelings, but he cannot.

Words are the tools of love. They can protect it. They

can sway its return. They can render it viable, and they can prevent it from being lost.

Actions alone are not enough. Without words, love – any love – will be lost.

The two lovers wade out into the brook until the water covers their ankles. They exchange laughter of the moment.

The dog watches the scene with uncanny interest.

\* \* \*

Anne places the leftover food and drink in the picnic basket. She teases the food crumbs off the blanket with her nimble fingers and straightens the creases made by the weight of their two bodies.

Robert sits hunched in front of a tree. His shirt is opened wide from the neck. His cap now dangles from an overhanging branch.

He changes position. One leg is outstretched, the other tucked under him. His left hand is spread wide upon the lower trunk for support. The other hand holds a penknife and exerts pressure against the bark with measured, accurate strokes.

Anne is intrigued.

Playfully, she rips a handful of grass and holds it tightly to keep it hidden from sight. Robert shifts his body as he continues his artistic endeavour.

Anne sneaks up on him. She crouches low in her bare feet, ready for a playful thrust of grass while Robert continues his handicraft, ignorant of the approaching lover.

As Robert rises to his knees to take stock of his effort, he is met head on with a shower of grass that lands squarely in his face.

He tumbles to the ground and lands awkwardly on his backside. Anne rubs up against him as she kneels close, trying to see past Robert towards the tree, now a point of marked interest.

"What . . . what's behind you, Robert? What are you hiding? What have you been doing? Show me!"

She tugs on his sleeve and pushes him to one side.

"Oh . . . nothing."

Embarrassed, he leans sturdily against the scarred trunk, protecting it from her gaze.

"Come on, Robert. Robert!" There is a subtle rise to her voice. "Move over! Let me see!"

As they jostle, Anne topples onto him. She looks up, excited by the mystery of the tree and its hidden secret. Near the tree's base, a heart-shaped figure, unfinished, encircles two initials – *their* initials.

Robert remains motionless, his body warmed by hers, still unable to say or do anything.

"How wonderful!" says Anne. "That's really sweet, Robert. And so romantic."

Without hesitation, she kisses Robert on the lips. He is surprised, yet returns the kiss.

\* \* \*

Spikes of light collide on the grassy knoll where the two lovers enjoy a rest. Anne's eyes show contentment, Robert's – an air of lassitude.

225

"I love you," says Anne with full reverence. She looks to Robert for his reply – the words of love.

He is muzzled with indecision, unable to know where the road of love will lead. He is afraid to say yes and be *wrong* . . . scared to say no and *lose*.

He looks away, thus cementing the last brick in place, walling himself off from his lover. He speaks shallow words to fill the wind-creaked silence of a dying summer's afternoon. He looks towards the sky to avoid Anne's piercing eyes, now moist and hurt.

"I think we'd better be going now." His voice is shaky, his body language awkward.

"But Robert, it's still early."

Her arms extend outward for an explanation.

"No . . . it will be dark soon," utters Robert with no sense to the thought as the sun continues to shine.

Anne is wounded, dishonoured, by Robert's words. For his part, Robert wears a mask of shame. He scoops up a handful of grass and tosses it back to the ground in defeat as if trying to grab onto a moment already lost.

\* \* \*

The sun's yellowy glow touches the back of Robert's neck. He sits squarely on the grassy knoll, staring into the distance at nothing special.

Anne lies on the blanket and faces in the opposite direction. Her eyes are heavy, weighed down by unexpected sadness.

Summer afternoons in the month of June are said to be lazy, even maudlin, when human beings dream of pleasure, love, perfection, and their past, drawing upon memories from another day, another time.

The shadows of afternoon crawl along the ground and up the knoll. Robert stares at the ground glumly, as detached and isolated as ever.

An alien shadow appears.

An old man towers above, peering down upon the young couple. He smiles kindly and holds a petite bouquet of flowers. With a distrusting side glance, Robert scans the old man quickly focusing on his glassy eyes and is unnerved by this sudden intrusion.

"Who are you?" Robert mutters from his sitting position. "What do you want?"

The old man looks at the flowers and replies in a soft, yet rising voice: "I thought you might like some flowers for your girl."

He extends the brightly coloured foliage as a gesture for Robert, but he is tongue-tied. He looks at the flowers, at Anne, then back up at the old man. As Robert starts to speak, he is held in check by the old man who holds a finger of silence to his lips and starts to walk away.

Robert follows yet is hesitant in complying. With his growing annoyance at the old man, the situation and himself, Robert hurries along trying to catch up, and finds himself falling awkwardly into step with the old man. Robert reaches out, yet not quite touching the stranger.

The old man radiates a sense of dominance. He looks coolly at Robert, at his flowers, then walks on, drawing on his pipe.

Again, Robert finds himself following, matching step for step with the old man, wanting to know, more urgently than ever, the identity of the stranger.

The old man reaches a wooden bench. It is a half-sawn log propped up by two stumps. He leans forward, rests his elbows upon his knees and looks through dusty glasses up at Robert.

Hands on hips, Robert tries to assert himself.

"Do you live around here?"

The old man nods.

"Not far," he says. "Beyond the next ridge."

He hides a smile and looks up at Robert who gazes off in the other direction.

"She's a nice girl."

"What?" snaps Robert.

"She's a nice girl."

With an unpretentious shrug, Robert glances back over his shoulder towards Anne.

"She seems to like you a lot," says the old man. "You can tell by the way she looks at you."

"She's all right," says Robert, who sits down next to the stranger.

The old man leans forward, confronted with a golden moment, the hope of every man and woman. Whether by dream or invention, an old man on this summer's day sits beside a younger man who lives by the same name.

The old man begins again.

"I bet you like her too, Robert."

"I suppose so," says Robert casually.

He becomes aware of the old man's wary appraisal.

"I mean, I do like her a lot. She's all right."

The old man takes off his glasses and is almost unwilling to ask his next question. He speaks softly.

"Do you love her?"

Robert looks up at him with surprise, but the old man stares at the flowers he clutches tightly in his hand. Robert looks off towards Anne, who sleeps peacefully on the blanket a short distance away.

"I don't know, I suppose so. Yes. Sort of . . . I don't know."

The old man relaxes, confident that the verdict of love will be changed, that a moment in time can be reclaimed and altered.

He tries to sway Robert's opinion, his thoughts and decision.

"You're going to lose her, Robert, if you don't tell her how you feel."

Robert turns to look back at Anne, struggles with this truth and its implications.

The old man tries to penetrate the young man's skin of indecision, trying to change a moment in time.

"Follow your instincts. Be willing to love her as she wants to be loved. Take her in your arms. Tell her how you feel."

He watches the young man's struggle and strains to tip the balance. He lifts a hand to touch Robert's arm.

"You'll lose her, Robert, believe me."

Robert jerks away from the old man's grasp.

Robert snaps back.

"What's it to you? It's none of your – how do you know my name?"

"I heard her calling you."

Robert springs to his feet.

"Listen. Nobody asked you. You have no business here. This is private property."

"This land belongs to me, don't you know," said the old man as a matter of fact.

His voice was soft and soothing.

"I have been living here all my life, remember?"

"Remember what?" I have never seen you before."

The old man is losing the battle.

"You and your dog come here every weekend to play and to think, and sometimes to swim. He likes to chase sticks in the water. How could you forget such happy days?"

"Have you been spying on me? If you don't leave me alone, I'll report you to the police."

"You remember the big brick house on the hill, the one with the white picket fence. You paint it every summer."

"The James family owns that house and I have never taken a brush to that fence."

"But I own the house. I live there. It is your house too, Robert!" says the old man.

"You are talking in riddles. I have no money to buy a house. The James family lives there. I've already told you so."

"I'll show you the property if you like. Bring your girl. Come for afternoon tea. We can talk about it. Once you're married, the two of you can live there. It will be your house. It was meant for you."

"You're a crazy old man that needs to be locked up."

The old man is completely played out as he tries to alter time itself. The young man begins to walk away.

"Wait! Listen! Don't go!" implores the old man.

Robert ignores the stranger's pleas.

The old man looks down at the flowers, and his sadness weighs heavily upon him.

"You'll lose her, Bob. Believe me," he says, scarcely resonating a sound.

No one is there to hear the words of an old man.

His eyes are smeared with the unmistakable gloss of melancholy. He is fatigued, dejected in spirit. His body is bent and alone.

\* \* \*

Robert stands over the sleeping figure of Anne. His shoulders are hunched. He kneels beside her and regards her with compassion in his moment of solitude and indecision.

Anne opens her eyes and smiles sheepishly at him. She is partially blinded by the backdrop of the fading light of day as Robert reaches for his pocket watch – a simple cue that announces the end of their day.

Arm in arm, the two lovers walk down the grassy knoll, leaving no vestige of their presence. Robert's dog follows, and he too is lost from sight.

\* \* \*

The sun is low in the sky, now a deep apricot. On the bench sits an old man. His head is bowed, extended to its limit as if his mind had been hypnotised into a false reality.

As the golden glow of sunset sweeps slowly across his eyelids, he is prodded into consciousness ever so gently.

The old man lifts his head up and looks off into the distance. He sighs heavily, looking listless and wan. He wanders over to a carved tree. A heart-shaped figure, unfinished, encircles two initials near the base of the tree.

He releases his grasp of the flowers, now tired and wilted, and leaves them on the ground.

He puts his pipe into his mouth and walks up and over the knoll, unaccompanied, leaving no vestige of his presence.

The light of dusk smothers all.

* * *

The young man who lived by the name of Robert was the old man himself. And the girl who lived by the name of Anne was his lover, lost and not a part of him anymore.

The old man had been unable to change his life during this rare and unscheduled encounter in time. He had been unable to influence the laws of the universe. He had lost his first and only love and hoped, as much as any person could, to change the course of events that had already taken place, vanished forever.

Moments in time are irreversible. Words are the tools of love – without them, love is lost.

So learned one man on this day, wishing to have grown older with his first love, now only a memory of love.

Misjudgement, ignorance and confusion dictate
the course of events and how they play out.
Second guessing and recriminations come later.
That Dom was victorious in the inaugural
Night Drone Endurance Challenge is also true.
That's when things got messy.

# Stolen

"I've been burgled!"

"Can I help you?" responded Cheryl Smith.

Her name was displayed in a brass nameplate holder screwed into the wall next to the information window.

"Are you *Sharell*?"

"It's pronounced Cheryl, as in *Cherry*. What can I do for you?"

"Are you a police lady like a Constable or Sergeant?"

"No, I'm a civilian – Mrs Smith will do.

Oh . . . well, like I said, I've been burgled!"

"Do you need a doctor or an ambulance?" she asked in the same casual tone.

"I haven't been shot or stabbed if that's what you're getting at. You need to arrest the thieves. I need my stuff back as soon as possible."

Cheryl placed a form on a clipboard and grabbed a pen.

"Name?"

"Tristan Teller. My friends call me Tel. And not Tris either."

"Address?"

"*The Oval Avenue* – Number 1a."

He tapped his fingers on the counter. They were cold and jittery. He watched Cheryl print his name. She was forty-something – that was his guess – and had long brown hair pulled back from her face in a tortoiseshell banana clip, dull burgundy nail polish and too much make-up, principally around her eyes. A darker shade of lipstick would have improved her overall image, Tristan mused. He also believed that Smith was not her real surname.

After all, this was the local police station.

Teller liked to study people, examine their physical appearance, and how they moved and reacted to the world around them. It was habitual, second nature to him. He was a serious writer, always on the prowl for fictional characters.

"When can you get my stuff back? I can't do without it. It's terribly important and worth a great deal of money."

"Someone will be with you in a few minutes to take your statement."

"I've already given you, my details. My name is on the form. Tristan Teller – *The Oval Avenue, Number 1a*. I've been robbed. Can't you help me?"

"I am trying to help you, Mr Teller. We do have an efficient system for crimes of this nature. Theft is a nasty business. Take a seat and one of my colleagues will be with you shortly."

"How long do I have to wait?"

"Someone will be with you soon, I promise."

"Cheers, Mrs Smith," he said begrudgingly.

Teller looked at his watch and sighed louder than necessary with a raspy grunt for punctuation.

The shock of unforeseen events can often push you over the edge, making it easy to slip outside of your comfort zone. Thinking straight becomes a struggle. Rude and arrogant things are often said, only to be regretted later.

Call it bad behaviour.

Teller was a quiet, easy-going young man of thirty. He had the patience of a saint and could wait as long as the next person. As the innocent victim, however, he had become grim-faced, lost and angry at the world.

"Excuse me, are you Mr Teller?"

"Yes," he answered abruptly.

"Hi. I'm Miss Sonia Smalley."

She was pretty and much shorter than Teller and seemed to appear from nowhere.

Teller was quick to stand up, eager to begin.

"How are you today?" she asked.

She carried a laptop under her arm.

"Could be better."

His voice was flat and lifeless.

"I understand you'd like to make a statement about a burglary."

"That's why I'm here!"

"I am sorry to hear that. I will try to help you."

Sonia led Teller to *Interview Room 1*.

"Take a seat and we'll get down to business."

"Are you a police officer?"

"Not yet. Still a civvy. One day, I hope. I'll see how it goes."

The room was just big enough for a desk, two chairs and a wastepaper basket. The walls were matt white and bare, except for a cheap, white plastic wall clock with black hands. It was eight minutes fast according to Teller's watch.

Teller angled his chair closer to the desk so he could see Sonia without being obstructed by her laptop. *She's still a teenager*, he thought.

"I think they've just decorated the room," said Sonia. "You can still smell the paint."

"How long will it take?" Teller asked.

"I'm sure the paint has dried. Don't worry if you accidentally touch the walls."

"No, I mean the interview, finding the person or gang that robbed me and returning my property?"

"We'll see how it goes. Thirty or forty minutes. I need to ask you some questions first. One thing at time, Mr Teller. We need to know all the details first. Now, let me see . . . I must find the right form – there are quite a number of them. Bear with me. Awesome . . . found it. There it is. Let me copy this onto the desktop, so I don't lose it, and we'll be ready to start."

"Have you worked here long?" Teller asked, visibly agitated with Cheryl's choice and doubtful that Sonia had the experience.

"Quite a while. Six months now. It's my first full-time job. It's quite exciting."

Teller sighed again. He couldn't help himself. This time it was quieter without any accompanying sound effects.

"Now let's see, we know your name and where you

live. You said you were burgled –"

"Yes, several times," interrupted Teller sharply. "I mean I was robbed only once. I did mention it several times."

Sonia showed no signs of irritation at Teller's quip and remained fixated on her computer screen.

"Occupation?"

"What's that got to do with anything? The crooks are still out there!"

"Please be patient, Mr Teller. The questions are on the form. This is all standard, routine procedure, and just as important."

"OK, OK. I'm a writer. I write fiction . . . novels, that sort of thing."

"Oh, how fascinating. Anything I would know?"

"*Loose Chippings*."

"I'm sorry, what?"

"My first novel. It's called *Loose Chippings*. Takes place in a fictional village in the Costwolds. Murder mystery thriller. Stolen paintings, espionage, mistaken identity, aristocracy . . . that sort of thing."

"A famous writer. That's awesome! Married?"

"Me? No. I have a girlfriend."

"What's her name?"

"Why? Is it important?"

"It's one of the questions on the form."

"Christabelle Williams. We live together."

"I see. When did the burglary take place?"

"About two hours ago."

"What was stolen?"

She started to read from a list.

"Wallet or money, rings, watches, other jewellery, clothing, house keys, car keys, vehicles, paintings, silverware, motorcycles, musical instruments, hearing aids, cameras, other electrical items, mobile phones, garden furniture, cigarettes, food, liquor, computer equipment, documents –"

"Stop right there! I don't smoke and I don't drink. Documents – computer documents. That's what was stolen and right from under my nose."

"Were you in your property at the time?"

"Yes, of course. We're both working from home, though Christabelle is unemployed just now."

"Sorry to hear that."

"She's a talented actress. She'll find something."

"Awesome! I'll look out for her name. Two famous people in one day! Was there any damage to your property – doors, windows, or locks? Anything broken inside your property?"

"No, none of that. I was hacked!"

"Oh my God! Are you all right? Are you sure you don't require medical attention?"

"No, my computer has been hacked, not me! My intellectual property has been nicked!"

"Any witnesses? Did you see or recognise anyone?"

"Witnesses to what, a computer hacking?"

Sonia stared at Teller for a long time, thinking and wondering exactly what he was talking about. He knew that she was confused, if not unfamiliar with the nature of the crime.

"Nobody broke into my place, and nothing was smashed or damaged. My computer has been hacked.

240

Electronically, remotely, from somewhere else. All my files, emails, documents and intellectual property are missing. Wiped clean!"

"I see."

"I'm not convinced you do. Is there anyone else who can help me?"

"If you're not happy, Mr Teller, you'll need to speak to someone at the front desk and fill out a complaint form. It could take up to two weeks to process."

"OK, OK. I'm sorry if I sounded abrupt. I didn't mean it. I'm terribly upset, terribly nervous. I can't do any writing. This has never happened to me before and I need help. I'll tell you everything you need to know."

"Awesome! Let's begin with your stolen intellectual property. I'm not sure I know what you mean. Tell me what kind of information was taken? Can you do that?"

Teller forced a smile. He knew that he would have to be patient and polite if he was going to get any assistance from Sonia Smalley and the local police.

"I write for a living. Mostly fiction – novels and short stories. My first novel – *Loose Chippings* – sold remarkably well. It's being adapted for the stage. I'm still waiting for the production to open at *The Limelight Assembly Hall*. I'm working on a new project now. It's a bit complicated. I'll try to explain. To help pay the bills between books and maintain my cashflow, I started a new company. It's called *The Write Plot*. It's quite clever. I think it is, given the recent publicity I've been getting."

"Awesome! I will certainly buy a copy of your first book," added Sonia.

Teller talked quickly.

"Anyway, I have produced a list of fifteen different categories for novels and short stories: science fiction, mystery, western, fantasy, romance, horror, gothic, historical, supernatural – the list goes on. For each group, I have written ten detailed outlines: sample plots, characters, wardrobe suggestions, choice of time periods, settings, endings, even an explanation of special effects and how to use them – everything you would need to write the novel or short story of your choice. They're a collection of inspirational synopses for anyone who wants to write, needs help to get over the finish line, or is looking for a successful story idea. If you're counting, that's 150 synopses at £200 pounds each! A potential income of £30,000 – a year's wages! I've already sold six outlines and I haven't yet started to promote it on social media. Now the entire collection of work is gone, along with my business plan, income generation forecast, access to all my accounts and contact details! No doubt my computer is knackered by now and probably under the control of a rich teenager with the name of Cosmo lounging around in silk pyjamas in his thatched roof overwater bungalow in Bora Bora."

"That's terrible news. Do you have an address for this Cosmo person, and his last name?"

"What? No. I made him up. I was being facetious."

Sonia had no idea what the word meant.

"I was being flippant. It was an off-hand joke."

"I see. Sorry. I misunderstood what you meant. Can't your intellectual property be replaced, then? I mean, surely, you must keep copies of your work?"

"Of course, I do. I always keep digital copies of my stuff on a variety of separate devices. That's not the point. Whoever has stolen my work can now sell it on to someone else as their own work! I might be able to prove that I am the author . . . how am I supposed to sue a nameless hacker? It's not worth the hassle or cost, in or out of court! Too damn messy."

"Could you have deleted your files by accident and not remembered? I do it all the time. What about your girlfriend? Have you checked with her?"

"We each have our own computer and our own log-on password. She doesn't have access to my computer. if that's what you mean. No, it's not possible. Nothing has been deleted by accident. Besides, the thief sent me an email with his ransom demand."

"Awesome! That's excellent news, Mr Teller. I mean, that's clear evidence of the crime. You should have mentioned this at the beginning."

"Sorry, you didn't ask me."

"What did it say?"

"It's the only document left on my computer. He or she wants half of my annual earnings in advance from *The Write Plot* – a one-off payment of £15,000 pounds. Further instructions about paying the ransom are supposed to come later in another email. The message wasn't encrypted as far as I know, and my computer doesn't appear to have been infected with any kind of malware."

Sonia looked perplexed.

"There were no details about how and when the

money is to be paid. At least, not yet. I'm assuming the crook wants to be paid in cryptocurrency."

Sonia stopped typing.

"Was there a sender's name on the email?"

"I don't think so. I would have noticed if there was. I can't remember. It looked anonymous to me."

"What about a return email address?"

"Sorry. It never occurred to me. I believe that was missing as well. I didn't notice, to be honest. There may be another message waiting for me. I'll check for a name and return address when I get home."

"Awesome! Were there any threats made to you in the email?"

"No . . . no threats."

"Did you bring the email with you?"

"I ran out of printing paper. Christabelle says she's going out to buy a new pack. What happens next? What am I supposed to do now?"

"Nothing for the moment. Go home and try to relax. I will pass this information over to CID –"

"Sorry – what's that?"

"The Criminal Investigation Department. You might be asked to come in again for another interview –"

"You've got to be joking. What good is that going to do? I've told you everything I know."

"Please don't worry, Mr Teller. There will be a full investigation, I promise. The Cyber Crimes Regional Task Force may also want to have a word with you. Remember, you have been the victim of extortion. One of our detectives will contact you within the next forty-eight hours."

"Can't you make it sooner, like in the next twenty-four hours or this afternoon?"

"The detective will need to see the ransom email. Make sure you print a copy and don't delete it from your computer."

Teller nodded.

"By the way, this cryptocurrency you mentioned –"

"Yes?"

"What country are we talking about?"

\* \* \*

Had it not been for Dominic Williams's passion for international competitive drone racing, none of this would have happened.

Dom was a computer genius. Instead of working for a leading player in the industry as a key innovator, he preferred to spend all his time, and money, travelling around the world racing his collection of drones in big-money competitions.

*'It's my brother's shameful obsession'* Christabelle would often say.

The more he talked about it, the more she listened to her brother's future schemes, specially when he had revealed months earlier, his plan to design and build a customised racing drone for the inaugural *Night Drone Endurance Challenge* over Loch Ness in the Scottish Highlands: first prize, £50,000!

"Will you help me build it, Chrissy?" he asked her time and time again. "We can work together. I'll teach you everything I know. It'll be fun and it will keep you occupied. Let's do it."

"Tel is much smarter than I am," she told him more than once. "Why not ask him?"

"He doesn't approve of my lifestyle. He thinks I'm an idiot. Besides, all he ever does is write. Now that you have the time – what have you got to lose?"

"As long as Tel doesn't mind. I don't want him to be angry with both of us."

"He won't, Chrissy, you know that. Besides, you'll be helping your baby brother."

"Yeah. What a *baby*. I'm only two years older."

"Come on. Work with me, just this once. It's the biggest race I've ever entered. I'll be competing against the best drone pilots from all over the world. Fifty-thousand pounds for the winner! I can do it. I can win, Chrissy. Please? I'll even pay you for your time. Consider it wages. Tel can't argue with that."

Neither did Christabelle at the time.

So, the two of them worked seven days a week. They finished building the drone with only three days to spare before the big race over Loch Ness.

Dom's creation was a masterpiece of drone aviation and cutting-edge technology that included a Global Navigational Satellite System, an infrared camera with a telescopic lens; three-dimensional aerial coverage; Bluetooth; digital megaphone box; carbon propellers – eight in all – flight control software; a propulsion system, radio receiver, automatic collision control and long-range searchlights. Dom called it 'a flying laptop' with bells and whistles.

The only task remaining was to practice. For this,

Dom took enormous pleasure piloting his airship along *The Oval Avenue*, back and forth at low level and often hovering outside the window of *Number 1a* – Teller's study – where Dom would always wait for Teller and Christabelle to gaze out of the open window to applaud his piloting skills.

Dom had underestimated the capability of what he and Christabelle had designed and built. Unwittingly, he had hacked into Teller's computer remotely and swiped everything onto the drone's hard drive during fly-past practice sorties, leaving Tel's computer wiped clean.

The facts of the story are true. Teller's computer had indeed been hacked. His files had been stolen and the ransom note was genuine.

Ultimately, Dominic Williams was to blame for what happened, but he was not guilty of extortion, definitely not against Tristan Teller and his partner, Christabelle Williams – Dom's own sister – for he had no idea what he had done.

Misjudgement, ignorance and confusion dictate the course of events and how they play out. Second guessing and recriminations come later. That Dom was victorious in the inaugural *Night Drone Endurance Challenge* is also true.

That's when things got messy.

\* \* \*

"Hello. I'm Detective Inspector, Charles Cody from the Criminal Investigation Department. I'm looking for

Tristan Teller. I understand he's expecting me."

"Tel's not here, I'm afraid. He'll be back later this afternoon. Is there anything I can help you with? I'm Christabelle Williams, his partner."

"Ahhhh . . . yes . . . your name is in my notes. May I come in? I won't take up much of your time. I do have a list of questions for Mr Teller. He reported a burglary, a computer hack, I believe it was. He's already given a detailed statement. Are you able to provide additional details and whether or not you've had any further contact with the hacker?"

"I don't think there's much to report. You see, the missing documents have now been returned! Would you like coffee or tea?"

"No thanks, I'm fine. You say the documents have been returned? Did you pay the ransom?"

"It's quite funny when you stop and think about it and totally harmless. The missing documents are back on Tel's computer. We never did receive any further ransom demands, so nothing has been stolen at the end of the day, no money has been paid and there's no one to blame or even arrest."

"That's odd."

"I agree Detective Inspector –?"

"Cody, Charles Cody. Your partner, Mr Teller, was visibly shaken when he gave his statement at the station."

"I think there must have been some confusion. Are you sure you wouldn't like a drink?"

"No, thank you."

"Everything is fine. Back to normal. Computers have

a mind of their own sometimes, don't you think? A case of mistaken identity if you ask me. I'm sure it happens all the time. You must see this sort of thing every day."

"When did this unusual turn of events happen?"

"Oh, about an hour ago. Tel had to go out. His first novel, *Loose Chippings* – have you heard of it? – is being adapted for the stage at *The Limelight Assembly Hall*. He's meeting with the director as we speak. It might open before Christmas. I'm sure he'll stop by the station later and confirm that nothing more needs to be done or investigated."

"Even so, it would help if I might see the original email you received from the hacker?"

"I don't have access to Tel's computer. He's a hard rock about that sort of thing and rightly so. You can never be too careful. Computer security is a big thing these days. I think he's deleted it, though. It might have been a practical joke. No reason to keep it. There's not been any real crime as such."

"I see. So, neither of you have had any further communication from the hacker, then?"

"Nothing, I'm afraid. Everything's been resolved. Here one day, gone the next and back again. It's a funny old world."

"Thank you for your time, Ms Williams. Please tell Mr Teller that he must report to the station to confirm that his case has been resolved, and that no further action by the police is required. And please, try not to waste police time in future."

"I certainly will. If there's anything we can do to help the police, please let us know. I do apologise for any

249

inconvenience. Have a lovely day."

Christabelle was pleased with her performance, for that's exactly what it was. There were a few threads of truth. Teller *did* meet with the director of his play, *Loose Chippings* that morning. No ransom had been paid – *yet* – and according to Christabelle, the police were no longer required.

She made that decision herself.

Everything she told the Detective Inspector was a lie. Teller's computer documents were, in fact, still missing and the first ransom email had not been deleted.

More revealing was what she didn't tell the Inspector Cody: the receipt of a *second* ransom email and two telephone calls from Dom: the first to announce his victory in the *Night Drone Challenge* and the second to report that his drone and radio transmitter had been stolen.

It didn't take long for Christabelle to work out what had gone wrong and what she and Tel would have to do to make things right. There was also no reason to say anything to Dom about all of this, just yet.

She had more important things to do first.

The safe return of Teller's data while protecting her brother from a police investigation and possible retaliation from the thief topped her list of priorities. That and the ransom money – Christabelle and Teller would split that fifty-fifty. She would break the news to Teller when he returned home.

* * *

## SECOND RANSOM EMAIL

Dear Mr Teller
Your computer appears to have been hacked. Not by me, I hasten to add, but by a drone. How and why this has happened to you is not my concern. I have examined the drone's hard drive carefully and found the contents to be of great interest.

I now own the data from your computer. I am sure you would like to have your original files and documents returned to you along with your friend's famous flying machine. Yes, I know all about that as well.

It will cost you £15,000 for your data and another £10,000 to get the drone back. It has suddenly become a race winner and a mighty valuable asset. People ought to take better care of their precious property.

I am a reasonable person and will give you three days to raise the cash. I will return your data including the drone for £25,000. CASH ONLY in £100 notes! We will meet at 3am this Friday in the ruins of Urquhart Castle, 21km southwest of Inverness and 2km east of Drumnadrochit on the west shore of Loch Ness. Make your way to the rooftop viewing platform of Grant Tower and wait there for further instructions.

DO NOT involve the police or any of your friends or family. If you do, I will know before you set foot inside the castle ruins, and I will keep everything for myself to do with as I please. These are my demands.

\* \* \*

"I do hope your plan works, Chrissy. Otherwise, I may be applying for Jobseeker's Allowance first thing on Monday morning. How much further is it?" Teller asked.

"We should be there in less than two hours. I've booked a small hotel not far from *Drumnadrochit*. We'll have a rest before heading off to the castle, and don't worry. We'll both get our money back."

"Tell me again why we're doing this and not the police?"

"If the police make a mess of it – and it has been known – Dom will never see his drone again and you'll lose all your data. By the way, I know how to transfer it back to your computer. Don't forget, I helped to build the drone! If the police did make an arrest, the thief will know it was you who was responsible. Then there's Dom. I'm sure the police would also like to know how he managed to hack your computer by accident. Flying along residential streets with a drone and hovering in front of people's windows for fun is not something one ought to boast about. Who knows what the police are likely to do? I can't risk finding out. That's why it's up to us."

"Got it!" said Teller. "But what about the ransom money that neither of us can afford?"

"Don't worry. I got that figured too. Dom won the race, and a £50,000 prize, didn't he?"

"Yeah."

"Well, that's it, isn't it? We'll simply ask Dom to pay us back from his winnings."

"And if he says no?" asked Teller.

"He can't. I know Dom, He won't. Trust me. Besides, I can always sell his drone. He won't like that! Is your mobile charged?"

* * *

They made their way on foot to the castle. Christabelle carried the bag of money. A full moon delivered all the light they would need to reach the top of *Grant Tower*.

"Well, here we are at the top of a thirteenth-century castle – I make it five storeys – at nearly three o'clock in the morning with a bag of readies in hundred-pound notes and a bird's eye view of Loch Ness," quipped Teller.

"Pay attention, Tel. Keep alert! We're not on a sightseeing coach trip."

"Who knows? We might see the monster in the moonlight. Now *that* would be worth the trip alone!"

"Don't forget why we're here, Tel! That reminds me. I need to go back down and hide somewhere. You were supposed to come alone, remember? Be careful."

At exactly 3:00am a drone appeared unexpectedly from the other side of the castle wall where Teller waited. Suspended from the centre of the vehicle's frame was a nylon bag. Teller had to shield his eyes from a stabbing beam of light as the drone hovered above his head.

In a calm and measured tone, a woman's voice told him what to do through a speaker box. She sounded American.

"Unzip the bag and put the money inside. If I am happy with the contents, I will return the drone to the castle tower. Do not move and do not call attention to yourself, Mr Teller, or you will lose everything. Do you understand?"

As Teller started to speak, the drone soared like a rocket and disappeared into the blackness.

"What's going on?" uttered Christabelle in a husky whisper.

"Shhhh! Keep your voice down and don't move. Stay where you are and keep out of sight. Nearly there. Waiting for Dom's drone to return."

*And if it doesn't? What happens then?* thought Teller. *Were we fools to trust a thief? Did we have a choice? Have we lost everything? Should we have told the police? How long do I have to wait? Damn!*

Teller wanted to punch a hole through the ten-foot-thick stone wall with his fist. His unanswered questions were choking him.

Then, from despair emerged hope. A sound. It was faint, yet recognisable. Surely, the drone was coming back!

This time, it approached from the far end of the tower and landed gently in the middle of the main viewing platform below where Christabelle wash hiding.

The nylon bag was still affixed to the drone's frame and the drone's power had been switched off. No voice spoke.

Teller looked down not knowing what to expect or what to do, while Christabelle approached the drone slowly from the spiral staircase.

As the stillness persisted, the safer Christabelle felt. She bent down and examined the drone. She unzipped the nylon bag and retrieved the drone's original controller. It was neatly wrapped in a cotton cloth and had two small initials – 'D W' – inscribed in the top left corner.

"Got it!" she said in a hearty voice. Watch your step coming down.

Teller joined her as fast as he could. They examined the drone in more detail under the glare of their torches.

"Looks like the micro-SD card is still intact. Can't see any damage to the hard drive. I think we're back in business, Tel."

After Christabelle had safely transferred all the data from Dominic's drone to Teller's computer, the three of them arranged to meet for a celebratory drink. Dominic was pumped-up about the return of his drone.

"So, when do I get my drone back, Chrissy? There's another race at the end of the month."

"Don't you want to hear about our little adventure first? We had a couple of problems along the way getting your drone back from the person who nicked it."

"Yes, of course. I can't believe you found it! Were you there? Did you see the race? You must have been. What an extraordinary coincidence! You should have told me. Any way, grand job. Both of you. Did you bring the drone with you? Is it still in one piece? How on earth did you manage to get it back, let alone find it? The local newspaper wants to do a story on me and the race. Fifty grand prize money! Can you believe it? What a perfect team we make, Chrissy. We built it together – you and me! Great memories."

"If you shut up for a minute, I'll tell you all about Tel's computer and how you managed to hack into it. Then there's Tel's interview with the local police, my meeting with the Criminal Investigation Department and our memorable cloak-and-dagger rendezvous at Scottish Castle at 3am on Friday. Did I mention the ransom we had to pay to get your precious machine back with all of Tel's data on it? More great memories, eh?"

"Oh my God. What are you talking about, Chrissy? What happened? Police? Ransom? I hacked into Tel's computer? What have I done?"

"I'll fill you in on the details later. Let's start with the ransom that Tel and I had to pay – £25,000 for the safe return of your drone and the rest of it! That would be £15,000 for Tel's data on the drone's hard drive plus another £10,000 for the drone itself!"

"You did the right thing, no question about it," said Dom. You should have told me. I would have helped!"

"Don't worry, you will now! We had to get it back, our own way, Dom. We couldn't risk making a mess of a bad situation and losing everything."

"At least no one was hurt," said Dom. "And please don't worry about the ransom money, Chrissy. I'll pay you and Tel back every penny from the prize money. I promise. First thing in the morning."

"That's what I was hoping you would say," said Chrissy.

"Who said crime doesn't pay?" said Teller more like a statement than a question.

"That's all right for you to say," said Dom, smiling. "What about me? I've lost half of my winnings."

"You still have our everlasting gratitude and love," said Christabelle. And that my dear *baby* brother, is priceless."

"This is a delicate matter and I do apologise
for writing a book about your life without
permission or fair warning. The book you hold
is a love story that has unfolded in a maze
of dreams – my dreams!"

# The Biography

The whole thing is outrageous! I am still reeling in utter disbelief!

*The Tringwood Summer Carnival* is a good place to start. A record heatwave certainly didn't discourage anyone from attending. Except for my wife. She said it was too hot and went swimming with the kids instead.

I had only been at the carnival for twenty minutes. It happened so quickly and unexpectedly. I bent down on one knee, as one does, to tie my shoelaces.

A hand appeared from nowhere and slapped a leaflet on the ground in front of my shoe. It was a woman's hand, of that I have no doubt. Men have an instinct for noticing this sort of thing. Besides, I could smell her alluring vanilla and ginger perfume.

By the time I craned my neck and looked up, she was gone – out of sight. Around me in every direction was a gaggle of arms and legs in perpetual motion.

I stood up and read the leaflet:

Carnival of Books
Today Only
Tringwood Memorial Park
July 23rd, 8pm-9pm
Something for Everyone!

That alone wasn't what caught my eye, it was the name of a book mentioned in the leaflet:

Jason Marvel
The Unauthorised Love Story
– Free Copy –

Everything around me became unexpectedly lifeless and distorted as I focused on a black and white ink drawing centred at the bottom of the page. I hadn't paid any attention to it at first. I couldn't believe what I was looking at. I was convinced that it was a drawing of Jason Marvel himself! The subject of the book.

What's more bizarre, it was an exact likeness of ME!

It was absurd that someone could have written a book about my life without me knowing, let alone without my permission.

*The Unauthorised Love Story?* You're damn right it was unauthorised!

A published book about me – Jason Marvel – a love story? Not bloody likely!

*Don't flatter yourself. Don't jump to conclusions. It can't be me! It's a book about somebody else with the same name*, or an elaborate hoax, I kept thinking.

260

Yet, the resemblance of the drawing . . .

Anger and resentment and a tally of other knee-jerk emotions were swirling around in my calculating brain as the sun baked my hatless head.

I walked quickly in all directions, showing the leaflet to dozens of people: paying customers, stall holders and carnival stewards.

"Have you heard of this book?"

"Have you seen a woman handing out leaflets like this one?

"Is there a book fair today?"

"Do you have the correct time?"

"Where is the *Tringwood Memorial Park?*"

Bastards! I'll sue the agent, the author, the publisher and anybody else involved. The artist too!

Wait a minute. Who wrote this deplorable book? I checked the leaflet, front and back. There was no mention of the author's name.

I must have gone back and forth, circling every trade stand, at least a dozen times in pursuit of the *leaflet lady*. My nervous energy was wheeling out of control.

Then it occurred to me.

Who's going to read a book about Jason Marvel in the first place?

Whose love story are we talking about?

Who cares?

It's not like I'm a TV reality star or a rich and famous movie actor with a dozen homes and a yacht on the French Riviera.

I don't get it. Nobody even knows who I am, apart from my wife, friends and colleagues.

261

I am a chartered accountant.

That's no reason for anyone to write a book about me!

And a love story?

How dare anyone do that!

I am so pissed off, I can't speak!

Never mind. It won't be long now. I'll have all the answers.

At least the book is free!

\* \* \*

"Hi, it's me. How was your swim?"

Pause.

"Did the kids have enjoy it?"

Pause.

"Sounds wonderful."

Pause.

"The carnival is great. Crowded and very hot. You would have hated it."

Pause.

"Probably a little bit later than planned."

Pause.

"Somebody told me about a book sale or something. It doesn't start until later."

Pause.

"Eight o'clock, I think. I'd like to have a look, then come straight home."

Pause.

"I'll find a restaurant with air conditioning."

Pause.

"Don't worry, I won't be late."

Did I tell my wife about the leaflet? No, not over the phone. I had to think about it.

\* \* \*

After dinner, I walked to *Tringwood Memorial Park*. It took me twenty minutes.

It was 7:55pm.

The park was located at the far end of town, away from the majority of restaurants and shops. It was also odd that there only few people to be seen for a Saturday evening. I checked the leaflet. I was surely in the right place and at the right time.

The park was larger than I had expected.

Neat rows of brightly coloured flowers bordered the park on three sides. Two wide paths converged into one and disappeared into the back and beyond.

I stood at the entrance looking for books. People with books in their hands. Tables, stands, displays of books. Not a front cover in sight. I stood there staring at everything and nothing.

It was 8:10pm.

*Jason Marvel? The Unauthorised Love Story?* We'll see about that!

I clenched my fist, ready and waiting to lay it into the face of the author. I started walking down the path and into the heart of *Tringwood Memorial Park*. Thick-edged shadows underscored the eerily quiet landscape.

This was not what I had anticipated.

What's that? Looks like a small table. There was a

single book placed in the middle of it. *One book!*

Hang on a minute. There's someone standing beside the table. Who is it? Looks like a woman. Tall. Athletic build.

Not enough light to see clearly.

My steps turned into strides. Agitation welled up. My arms swung with confidence. I was beyond eager to get my hands on the book and, if my hunch was correct, the person who wrote it!

As I got closer, the stranger began to back away, then turned and ran. She was wearing a long, light and fluffy scarf wrapped over her head and shoulders.

"Hey! Wait a minute! Are you the book person? Are you the author of this book? I need to talk to you. It's important. STOP!"

I ran after her. Gone.

*A carnival of books?* Hardly!

*Something for everyone?* No, just me!

I returned to the table and picked up the book as if it were a trophy, a special award. I was reluctant to sully it with my fingers.

The book had weight to it: three-hundred and twenty-eight pages. It was hardback, as well, with a separate dust jacket. The cover design was simple, yet effective. The title of the book was printed at the top in raised, glossy white letters. In the centre was a detailed drawing of Jason Marvel – ME! Yes . . . ME! And at the bottom was the author's name: Cristal Rivers.

I had never heard of her.

I was nervy.

Flattered? Yes, that too. I won't deny it.

I sat on the table and was immediately drawn to the *Foreword*. I read it under the fading light!

Dear Jason

If you are reading the Foreword, then you have found my book. It is for you and you alone. Do not be angry with me. Please know that I wish you and your family no harm.

This is a delicate matter and I do apologise for writing a book about your life without permission or fair warning. The book you hold is a love story that has unfolded in a maze of dreams – my dreams!

You have been in my dreams for twenty years, by my side every day and every night as if I were your best friend, lover and wife. I know you better than you know yourself.

I have laughed and cried with your friends, been on holiday with your family, sat next to you in school and even played football alongside you, always on your team. We were always meant to be together.

By some unlikely means, I have been living a secret, disconnected life with you. We have

never met face-to-face unless you too have
been lucky enough to dream as I have.

I have seen your life – our life – unfold in
every detail, days and sometimes months after
it had been lived, like a video recording, to be
watched and shown again.

Now, after all these years, I have grown tired
of hiding from reality. This is why I have written
the book before my dreams come to an end . . .
and to see you at last! This book is my gift to
you. I ask for nothing in return.

* * *

I started reading the book.
What should I do when I've read the last sentence?
Throw the book away?
Burn it?
I hid the book in my office drawer under lock and
key. I read paragraphs, pages and chapters when no one
was looking, and time allowed. For the better part of a
week, I stayed late after everyone had left the office.
I was dumbfounded.
The book contained detailed accounts of my entire
life, exactly as the author had said: people I had known
and loved, places I had visited and special occasions –
as a child with my parents and as a husband and father

in unimaginable detail.

How could anyone have known?

This is an invasion of my privacy.

How could this have happened?

How was such a thing possible?

Who exactly is Cristal Rivers?

Is she human?

Is she a spy?

Is she a witch?

Is she an alien?

A stalker?

She could be dangerous.

She wants to see me . . .

She said as much in her letter.

Should I contact the police?

My solicitor?

My wife? Absolutely not!

I decided to tell no one.

I checked the title on the internet. Nothing.

I searched the author's name. Nothing.

The only other piece of information was the name of the publisher. It was printed on one of the inside pages:

> *The Private Printing Press*
> *99 Four Mile Walk*
> *Old Sanborngate*

I drove there during my lunch hour. It was the last commercial premises on *Four Mile Walk*.

*The Private Printing Press* was nothing more than a local printing house. A wooden sign across the width of its façade was cracked in various places. All but a handful of painted letters had long since weathered away. The window frame was mouldy and rotten, and the exterior brickwork needed repointing.

"Excuse me. I'm looking for a woman named Cristal Rivers."

"There's nobody here by that name, sir. Only me. Is there something I can help you with?"

He was exceptionally tall and threadlike and had a clunky hearing aid draped over each ear.

"Well, I'm looking for the author of one of your books. Her name is Cristal Rivers. Do you know where I can find her? It's important that I speak to her."

"You say it's one of *my* books?"

I reached inside attaché my case and showed him the book. I held it in such a way so that the drawing of me was hidden by the palm of my hand.

"Ah, yes. It was printed only last week if I'm not mistaken. I'm afraid this is not a book shop, sir. We don't sell other people's books."

"I'm looking for the person who wrote it! Can you tell me the name of the author?"

"It says right there on the cover, sir – Cristal Rivers."

"Is that her real name?"

"I'm afraid that's confidential."

"Can you tell me where she lives?"

The man laughed in my face.

"No, no. I can't tell you that either. I have no idea who you are, sir."

"A friend of the author."

"Then you should already know the answers to your

two questions, sir. I am a printer."

"How many copies did you print? Can you at least tell me that?"

"Two, sir. I told the customer it would have been much cheaper to print fifty copies than two! Still, that was what she requested. I never turn away business no matter how small the request."

I was perspiring.

"Has she brought you other books to print?"

"I am not aware of any, sir. You never know. Writers are a funny lot."

"One last question, if you don't mind."

"Not at all, sir."

"The author has kindly sent me one of her two copies in the post. You see, I am a freelance journalist and will be writing a review of her book for one of the major weekend newspapers. Usually, in such cases, I like to interview the author. So, you can see my problem. If I don't know how to reach her . . ."

"Reviewing such a small print run is odd I must admit, but still . . . yes, I see your dilemma. Can I suggest, sir, that you write to her."

"That would be a splendid idea. Does she have an email address? That would be easier and quicker."

As soon as the words fell out of my mouth, I realised the fatal flaw in my reasoning. Sending and receiving emails from a woman who claims to be in love with me – *she's written a book about the last twenty years of my life for God's sake* – is asking for trouble. How would I explain the trail of digital correspondence?

"She may well have an email address, sir. I am old-fashion and prefer the old ways. I'm afraid I don't own a computer. I have lived well enough without one in the printing business for nearly sixty years, sir. I would be happy to post the letter on to her. Drop it off to me here whenever you like."

"That's a very kind offer. I shall write to the author immediately and return with my letter. I will even provide the required postage."

He smiled, I smiled. And that was that. It was the best, if not my only choice. I was ready to contact Cristal Rivers.

I drove back to my office with a sense of triumph. I had now the read book, found the publisher – such that it was – and was now going to write to the author, the woman who claims to have been in love with me for twenty years!

I wondered what she looked like. How tall was she? Was her hair long or short? Blonde, black, red or brunette? What would it be like to meet a stranger and look into her eyes, knowing that she had been, and still is, in love with me? I was percolating with excitement on the one hand and anxiety on the other.

I was also wading in uncharted territory. What did Cristal Rivers want from me? Was her book a fake? Was this whole thing a con? Was she a blackmailer? They were all possibilities, yet how could I tell?

I ought to tell my wife, share this far-fetched drama with her. Meet the woman. Invite her to dinner. Have a drink or two. Talk it through. Discuss the book like adults. Get it over quickly and forget all about it.

She said the book was a gift and didn't want anything

in return. But I did!

I wanted the *second* copy!

* * *

Dear Ms Rivers

Thank you very much for a copy of your book.

(I decided to play it casual, relaxed. Miss? Ms? Mrs? I couldn't make up my mind what to do, so I picked one at random. There was no point in worrying about it.)

It was a privilege to read your story. Or should I say 'my' story.

(I wanted to remain humble. I was tempted to say, 'our story', but that would be moving in the wrong direction, leading her on.)

You have a remarkable talent for sharing your dreams. I am both flattered and impressed with your work. You write very well.

(Was I overdoing it? Yes, without doubt, but I was well aware of my intent.)

I would be delighted to meet with you. Shall we arrange it for this Friday, the twenty-second, at

271

The Feathered Duck? It's in Kuridge High Street. I'll be there at 2pm.

(I allowed three full days for the letter to reach her. I also gave her my office address in the event she preferred to write to me. On reflection, this was a bad idea. What was I thinking?)

May I buy you a drink? We can talk about your marvellous book and share our wonderful memories. Besides, you haven't signed my copy!

(There! I made the first move. I felt like I was cheating on my wife and kids. I was sick to my stomach. 'Our wonderful memories' stuck in my throat. I had no such intention of sharing anything with Cristal Rivers. There was another objective that I simply couldn't – wouldn't – pass up. I wanted ANSWERS! Who the hell was this woman and what was she after?)

I wanted to ask her about the print run – I already knew the answer – and whether she intended to print more than just two copies and sell it commercially. I returned to *99 Four Mile Walk* and gave my first-class-stamped letter to the printer for posting.

There was nothing more to do, except wait for a reply. *That*, and rehearsing a believable explanation for my wife.

The truth doesn't always play out well.

* * *

Friday came round soon enough. It was 1:30pm. Had I not sat down to tidy my desk and check the diary for the rest of the week, I would already have left the office and would not have heard the phone ring. It's funny how trivial things like that can alter the course of your life and affect the lives of others.

"Hello?"

Ten seconds of silence.

"Hello? This is Jason Marvel. Can I help you? Is anyone there?"

More wordless static.

*Then* . . .

"This is Cristal Rivers."

My head was spinning. I sat down.

What was she . . .? How did she . . .? I was slow to react shaking.

"Hello. This is a surprise."

I tried to remain calm. I was doing well, I thought.

"How did you find my telephone number?"

"You gave me your office address, remember?"

"Yes, so I did."

Her voice was light, soft . . . I don't know. The word *wispy* came to mind. In that moment and during those awkward seconds, I imagined a face of soft, pale skin and tired, searching eyes – the kind of appearance often reserved for writers, who sit far too long in dim, unkind artificial lighting while trying to put words on a page that meant something to others.

The word *vulnerable* also came to mind.

"Cristal? Are you there?"

"Yes, I'm here."

She sounded subdued, dispirited.

"Is something troubling you?

She paused before replying.

"I have changed my mind."

"What do you mean?"

"I need more time to think about it. I'm not sure it's the right time to meet you. I thought it was, now I'm not so sure."

I had mixed emotions. I didn't know whether to be disappointed or relieved.

"What about your book? You've gone to a all this trouble to publish it. I've read it, from cover to cover. And now that you've found me . . . well, I thought you wanted –"

"Yes . . . I know . . . I do . . ."

Her voice trailed off again.

I had no idea what to say or do next. I picked up the base of the phone, turned round with it in my hand and looked out the window. Fate had decided otherwise.

"Are you still there?" I asked.

"Yes."

Across the road, opposite my window, a woman was standing on the pavement talking on her mobile phone. She was wearing what looked like the same long, light and fluffy scarf wrapped over her head and shoulders that I had seen before in *Tringwood Memorial Park*.

It was Cristal Rivers! I was sure of it.

I opened the window and called out her name. My voice was surprisingly loud and distinct.

She looked up and saw me at once. She put a hand across her mouth as if trying to hide her identity, then started running.

She took two steps off the pavement and was knocked down by a cyclist at speed.

She fell at an awkward angle.

The phone flew out of her hand.

She was lying on her side.

"NO!" I shouted.

People on the street gasped, screamed and looked up at me as I peered out of my office window.

"Call an ambulance!" someone cried.

I threw the phone to the floor and rushed down two flights of stairs, thinking it was all my fault.

I fought my way through a knot of people.

I could see the ambulance approaching.

Someone had put a cushion under Cristal's head.

Her eyes were closed.

"Is she OK? Did anybody see what happened?" I asked impatiently, trying to catch my breath.

"I think she bumped her head on the handlebars," I heard someone say.

She looked almost serene in a strange sort of way, prettier than I had imagined, and about my age.

"Where are they taking her?" I asked of no one in particular.

"*Westview General Hospital*, I should imagine. It's the closest," someone replied.

"Do you know this woman?" someone asked.

"No. Yes. No. I've never seen her before."

\* \* \*

The phone was still on the floor when I returned to the office. I kicked it as hard as I could. It flew across the room, struck a wall and broke into a dozen pieces.

I sat down and rubbed the back of my neck. It was stiff and ached along its entire length. I found a bottle of aspirin in my desk drawer – I had nothing stronger – and swallowed two tablets with a mouthful of coffee.

I stared at the walls of my office for an hour. I should *never* have opened the window and called out her name.

I grabbed my mobile phone, found a number for *Westview General Hospital* and made the call.

"Yes, hello . . . I wonder if you can help me. A cyclist collided with a woman this afternoon on *Kuridge High Street*. It happened around two o'clock. I saw what happened and – my name? Oh, well . . . there were a lot of other people standing on the pavement. I'm sure they would be happy to give you a statement – well, I was across the street in an office building . . . second floor – yes, I did see the accident – I was looking out of my window. As I've said, I wasn't that close to it, not as close as other people. It was a terrible thing and well, I thought I'd call to find out, you know . . . I was wondering how she – I see . . . well, thanks for letting me know."

\* \* \*

I was in a dreadful state when I got home. Queasy, light-headed and low on adrenalin. There was no hiding it. I felt awful.

"Are you all right, dear? You don't look well."

"I need a drink – a large brandy. Do you mind?"

"Yes, of course. What's wrong? Tell me."

"There was a traffic accident this afternoon."

"Are you OK?"

"Me? Oh yes, I'm fine. Nothing to do with me. I was in the office at the time. I was looking out the window – it was around two o'clock. I saw the whole thing."

"What happened? Was anyone hurt?"

"This woman was talking on her mobile phone. She was standing in front of the bakery across the street. You know, the one that's opposite my building. She was suddenly distracted. I couldn't tell what it was. She seemed terribly agitated, frightened. Then she started to run –"

"Run?"

"It looked that way. I don't know why, she stepped into the road. I don't think it was deliberate. She didn't appear to know where she was. Then, a cyclist rode straight into her!"

Telling the truth didn't sound like a good idea.

"Oh my God!"

They took her to *Westview General*, apparently. Somebody told me. I wanted to know how she was – you know . . ."

"That was thoughtful, dear."

"So, I called to find out –"

"And?"

I steadied myself.

"She died."

A woman – a stranger – who said she loved me died today. I never knew her! I never met her! She wrote a biography of my life.

Our life!

Made of her dreams.

Her dreams!

I have a copy of her book in my office desk drawer. I have read her words and yet, I mustn't tell anyone about it! Certainly not my wife!

"How awful!"

"I sat in the office all afternoon, doing nothing, just thinking about it. I couldn't do any work."

"You'd better have an early night after dinner. I'm sure you'll feel better in the morning. At least you didn't know her."

"What do you mean?"

"Think how awful you'd feel if it had been a friend of yours or someone who worked with you in the office. That would be unbearable."

It was nine o'clock. I had turned off the bedroom light when I heard the doorbell. I got out of bed and put my ear to the door to listen.

"Good evening. Mrs Marvel?"

"Yes. Is there a problem, officer?"

"I'm sorry to bother you so late. Is Jason Marvel at home. I'd like to speak with him."

"Yes, he's my husband. He's gone to bed, I'm afraid. He's had a frightful day. Please, do come in. Is there anything I can help you with?"

I opened the door slowly and quietly, and through the narrow gap I saw my wife talking to a police officer. He was holding a copy of the book – the *second copy*!

"It's about Cristal Rivers."

"Who?"

He showed her the book! She took it from him and leafed through the pages. Even from a distance, I could see the reddish glow of embarrassment on her cheeks.

"She was killed this afternoon in a traffic accident on *Kuridge High Street*. A cyclist hit her. I understand your husband works across the street from where the accident happened. He might know how to contact the victim's family. Someone found the woman's phone on the pavement. The victim called your husband earlier today at his office around the time of the accident. It was the last call she made. There's also this book."

I thought the silence would crack the walls.

"I can explain everything," I said with a distinct measure of confidence as I appeared at the top of the stairs in my pyjamas and dressing gown.

I wouldn't be going back to bed any time soon.

"Tell me, Sir Lowen . . . what crime was committed? What happened at Druid's Fell Manor on New Year's Eve? You have not said as much. Was it, in fact, suicide as reported? Is that what you believe?"

# The Oxymoron Murders

The case of *The Oxymoron Murders*, as it became widely known at the time, was my last official case before retiring. My illustrious career has been well documented across this island nation and throughout the great countries of Europe, so I need not take up your valuable time with my colourful exploits, with the exception of this unique and sensational crime, the details of which I humbly divulge to my reading public.

Scotland Yard has its own methods of solving crimes, yet it is Detective Roule, your storyteller, who alone possesses the resolve and clarity of mind to comprehend puzzles of unmatched complexity, if I may be so forthright in asserting my remarkable talent.

As the incredibly famous and successful detective in all of England – the British Empire to be factually correct – it should come as no surprise to learn that I was contacted by Sir Lowen Bittersman to clear his family name and reputation following the tragic loss of his two sons in a twisted tale of love and revenge.

Sir Lowen Bittersman was a giant amongst men in British society. His longstanding investment in British industry, from coal and steam power to iron, steel, textiles and ship building, was legendary as was his sustained philanthropy for which he was knighted.

According to a story in *The Illustrated London News* published on 7 January 1911, Sir Lowen's two sons, Edmund and Victor, died on New Year's Day during the annual fox hunt at *Druid's Fell Manor*, the Wiltshire estate of the Bittersman family.

The reporter's surprisingly sketchy narrative, which received modest attention from the public, said the two brothers perished instantly when they were thrown from their horses – Edmund striking his head on a rock and Victor breaking his neck when he collided with a fence. The official cause of death was 'misadventure'. The funeral was a low-key affair, attended by a small circle of family and friends.

Six months later, however, new and contradictory details appeared in *The Daily Telegraph*. Startling testimony from an eyewitness claimed that Edmund and Victor Bittersman died *not* from some freakish mishap, but as the result of a brazen and reckless deed.

It was described as a cold-blooded, double-suicide-murder pact between two brothers on New Year's Eve during the spectacular masquerade ball held at *Druid's Fell Manor*.

Accompanying this shocking story in *The Telegraph*

was a bewildering cryptic verse, reproduced below. It was a lyrical *oxymoron*, to be precise, composed by the same unidentified eyewitness. The rhyme was utterly contradictory, illogical and absurd in every detail.

On a dark and stormy night,
When the sun was shining bright,
Two dead boys stood up to fight.

Back-to-back they faced each other,
Drew their swords and shot each other.

A deaf policeman heard the noise,
And came to save the two dead boys.

If you don't believe the tale I've told,
Ask the blind man who saw it unfold.

Nonetheless, it was not without meaning to *me*, for it proved to be more enlightening than I could possibly have imagined. As the main antagonist, Lord Henry Wotton, said in *The Picture of Dorian Gray* by Oscar Wilde: "I am quite sure I shall understand it, and as for believing things, I can believe anything provided that it is quite incredible."

My well-deserved, and may I say, much-anticipated summer holiday at Glencoe in the Scottish Highlands, had scarcely commenced when I received word that my services were urgently required closer to home. As an individual of some repute, it is public knowledge where and when I spend my holiday. It is, therefore, not uncommon for me to receive dozens of requests of one sort or another which, I must confide, I wholeheartedly ignore at the best of times.

Having announced my retirement a fortnight earlier, I had deliberately avoided the press – reporters *and* their papers – during my annual retreat away from the formalities of publicity, preferring the peace and quiet of the Scottish countryside. Thus, I had not been made aware of such misfortune and had no idea what I could do to help.

In a hand-delivered letter, Sir Lowen Bittersman expressed his heartbroken distress about the death of his two sons and the devastating effect these new allegations in the British press were beginning to have on his life and financial standing.

Detective Roule . . .

A great tragedy has befallen our family.

My wife, Lady Celia, and I have endeavoured to keep the facts of this scandalous crime hidden from public scrutiny to protect our own reputation. We have lied to all those who have put their trust in our family name and paid others for their silence. We are on the edge of despair. I implore you to help us at your earliest hour to find the truth of our unwavering grief.

I will pay handsomely for your service. I have enclosed a first-class train ticket for your journey to London where my chauffeur will collect you in the Silver Ghost. Please join us at Druid's Fell as our guest. We will tell you everything we know. Your reply – indeed, your promise to accept my plea – is eagerly anticipated.

Faithfully
Sir Lowen Bittersman

Retired or not, I accepted Sir Lowen's urgent request at once, packed my bags and caught the next available train to London, though I delayed my visit to *Druid's Fell* by three days. I had a few enquiries of my own about the case to undertake before meeting Sir Lowen and Lady Celia in person.

* * *

Following a sumptuous lunch set for three in the Grand Hall, I accompanied my hosts to the library where we relaxed for a further thirty minutes savouring the divine taste of *Constantino Colheita Port – 1900* – served in glittering Baccarat crystal glasses. Sir Lowen also offered me a fine-looking, hand-rolled *Juan Lopez* Cuban cigar, which I enjoyed to the last draw, enjoying the creamy aromatic smoke of cedar and spice as it swirled gently in the back of my mouth.

"This is a splendid house, Sir Lowen. I make it . . . what . . . sixty acres?"

"Sixty-seven," said Lady Celia.

"You have a sharp eye, Detective," said Sir Lowen.

"My view was partially obstructed by the front entrance of the house, which would account for the discrepancy, although I do have a keen sense for detail. This is how I have made my living."

"Indeed!" said Sir Lowen.

"Built in the mid-eighteenth century. I'd say1739. Georgian, naturally," I said more as a statement of fact than a question.

"The exact year, Detective. Well done."

Sir Lowen bowed his head in agreement and would have tipped his hat if he had one.

"What do you think of the port?" asked Sir Lowen.

"The best I have ever had."

Lady Celia smiled.

"And the ride up from London in the *Silver Ghost?* Was it comfortable, Detective Roule?"

"The finest ride I have experienced. Have you had the Rolls long?"

"I bought four of them – delivered to my door in the Spring of 1907!"

I too, would have tipped my hat.

"You are a gracious man, Sir Lowen. It is a shame that you and I, and Lady Celia, had not crossed paths before during happier occasions."

Lady Celia nodded in accord.

"Yes, I do agree," said Sir Lowen.

"I am here, nonetheless, at your invitation and will

help you in any way I can."

"You are most kind, Detective Roule."

"Now to business," I said. "I must confess, I am at a loss on this occasion as I do not have all the facts before me. I do have several questions first if I may."

"By all means, Detective," said Lady Celia. "Ask us whatever you like."

I removed a small notebook from my jacket pocket and put pencil to paper.

"In your letter . . . here, I have it with me in my jacket pocket . . . you wrote: *'My wife, Lady Celia, and I have endeavoured to keep the facts of this scandalous crime hidden . . .'*

"If I am to be of any service, I must know the exact nature of this 'scandalous crime', as you have referred to it, however brief or painful it must be to recall such a tragedy. I am of the opinion that your two sons died on New Year's Day – an accident – while out riding during a fox hunt. How unfortunate for you and Lady Celia! I understand that *The Daily Telegraph* seems to have had a different view, describing it as a double-suicide-murder. It cannot be both. You must agree on that."

It did not go unnoticed that Sir Lowen cradled his wife's hand with the utmost tenderness.

"Edmund and Victor are – *were* – identical twins, in every way –"

"Yes, of course. This is a well documented fact."

"They were also born on New Year's Eve. For their twenty-first birthday party, Lady Celia and I decided to put on a lavish masquerade ball – what better way to celebrate your children's twenty-first birthday and see in a new decade, eh Detective?"

"Yes, I do agree. So, there was no fox hunt on New Year's Day, then, as originally reported?"

"None, sir."

"Do you have a guest list – names and addresses – of everyone who attended and those who did not?" I asked.

"Why would you want to know who was not there?"

"They are often the most interesting! I must examine every detail of this case however insignificant it might seem to you and Lady Celia.

"Yes, of course."

"Tell me, Sir Lowen . . . what crime was committed? What happened at *Druid's Fell Manor* on New Year's Eve? You have not said as much. Was it, in fact, suicide as reported? Is that what you believe?"

Sir Lowen stood up and started to pace around the library as he recounted the events on the night his two sons died.

"It was an hour before midnight. The masquerade ball was a huge triumph – better than we could have ever expected. The costumes were sumptuous . . . the pomp and circumstance truly of another world, another age . . . the colours of the ball were magnificent – a feast for the eyes, Detective. It was the irrepressible spirit of the Carnival of Venice itself!"

As he recounted the scene his eyes widened. They seemed to sparkle as he recalled that evening.

"There were nearly fifty guests, mostly friends of Edmund and Victor. Of course, there were also notable acquaintances of our own for most of the evening: Thomas Hardy, the English novelist – have you read *Time's Laughing Stocks and Other Verses*? Wonderful writer; the Spanish painter, Pablo Picasso – his painting *Les Demoiselles d'Avignon* is magnificent; the adorable British socialite and actress, Lillie Langtry – still a beautiful woman, I must say; and the incomparable English composer, Ralph Vaughn Williams – his glorious *Sea Symphony* was performed for the first time only a couple of months ago as I recall. They had other engagements to honour before midnight and left before the tragedy ensued."

Sir Lowen's eye's drifted away from my gaze as he thought about the day in question.

"It is no secret, Detective Roule, that my sons were disposed to excessive drinking. On their birthday, they commenced to stage a mock sword fight to entertain their guests. Their charade began along the perimeter, then they slowly made their way to the centre of the ballroom floor. You should have seen it. Everyone gathered round and applauded. Louder and louder. The guests cheered and shouted and sang songs to the limit of their voices. The string quartet carried on playing with rousing zest and exuberance. Edmund and Victor loved the attention – every minute of it. They pretended to be stabbed and die, falling to the floor, only to stand up again as quickly to begin their theatrical performance all over again. Then they counted – no, they shouted – to ten, pointed their swords at each other – they were not more than ten feet apart – and called out TAKE THAT! That's when the shots rang out just before the stroke of midnight."

Sir Lowen was affected by his own words and could not continue.

"I'm sorry, Detective. Please forgive me. It is more painful than you know to recall these terrible images."

"I beg you, if you could just spare me a few more minutes."

"Yes, yes . . . of course. I will try."

Sir Lowen wiped his eyes.

"WHAT SHOTS?" I asked.

"The swords, Detective," said Lady Celia first. She tapped Sir Lowen on the shoulder for comfort.

"Ahhhh . . . yes, a pistol sword, I take it?"

"Yes! How did you know, Detective Roule?" Sir Lowen asked.

"I *am* familiar with such a weapon. A German-style silver-hilt hunting sword crafted by *Vandebaize of London* I would say? A twenty-inch, double edged blade with a three-inch pistol barrel mounted on the left side? Flintlock pistol mechanism? Circa 1700?"

"Why yes. How –?"

Sir Lowen and Lady Celia looked like they had been struck by lightning for they remained transfixed and did not blink.

"Detective Roule . . ." Lady Celia began to ask. Her hands were shaking. "Were you there, masked and in disguise? I don't remember seeing your name on the guest list. I scarcely know how you would know such things if –"

"Had I been in attendance, Lady Celia, the crime would already have been solved before the morning

290

sun. However, I do know of the reported theft from your widely acclaimed collection of arms and armour, specifically two pistol swords fitting the precise description I have just given to you."

"This is remarkable. How did you know this too?"

"I am not without friends and influence at Scotland Yard, Sir Lowen. I make it my business to know things that other detectives pass over with the blink of an eye. I understand you filled out a police report three days prior to the death of your sons, yet you withdrew your statement on the same day, shortly thereafter. This is somewhat erratic, if not puzzling. Do you have an explanation, may I ask?"

Sir Lowen wore a half-hearted smile and answered my question after a protracted sigh.

"You are quite right. I do possess a much-admired collection of arms and armour. It is a mere hobby of mine. I travel the world and purchase pieces that are of interest to me: samurai armour, ornamental helmets, shields, Indian chainmail, Ottoman plate, broadswords, rapiers, crossbows and of course my two pistol swords, of which I am very fond. What you have said is perfectly true. I did file a report with the police. I thought someone had stolen my two pistol swords. They are quite rare, you know. I believed the thief to be a member of our staff, although I dismissed that idea outright."

"And the reason for doing so," Sir Lowen?"

"I simply assumed – believed – that Edmund and Victor had borrowed them."

"For what purpose, may I ask?"

"For practice: fencing lessons, three times a week."

"Surely not with real swords, Sir Lowen . . . and pistol swords at that!"

"They were always looking for adventure. They wanted to experience life from all angles and often borrowed various pieces from my collection without informing me. They had removed the pistol swords without permission, so naturally I thought at once that they had been stolen."

"Why did you allow this behaviour to go on?"

"Edmund and Victor took a keen interest in my hobby, the things I treasured most of all. They liked to touch them, to wear them . . . use them as people had done throughout our history. They would never hurt each other. As their father, I promised my sons that I would never hide anything from their grasp provided they had respect for the artefacts I treasured. And now they are dead because of it."

"These shots, Sir Lowen. It is most important that you remember."

Sir Lowen nodded.

"Did both pistol swords fire?"

Reluctantly, Sir Lowen nodded *yes*.

"Edmund was hit in the stomach and Victor in the chest. Both of them fell to the ground instantly. I was standing not more than a few feet from them. What does it mean, Detective?"

"Quite simply, it means that both pistol barrels were primed with black gunpowder and lead balls. That is an undeniable fact. Tell me, Sir Lowen, do you keep lead shot and suchlike in the house?"

"NO SIR, I DO NOT!" Sir Lowen's facial muscles stiffened. "Furthermore, I had no idea that my pistol swords *could* be fired! You must believe me, Detective. I had never fired them at any time! They are more than two hundred years old! What are you suggesting?

"Nothing for the moment, Sir Lowen, except for one thing . . ."

Lady Celia stared into my eyes.

"Your sons meant no physical harm to each other. Of this I am certain. And I do not believe for one moment they killed each other as part of a suicide-murder pact – call it what you will – between brothers – or even knew that their pistol swords were at the ready to fire. Your sons' fatal mistake in this case was to amuse themselves with such dangerous weapons in the first place to show off – entertain their family and friends – during the masquerade ball held in their honour."

"If I had only been a better father –"

"You mustn't blame yourself, Sir Lowen. You had no way of knowing how the evening would end."

"He's right, dear," said Lady Celia.

"What punishable crime do you think was committed here in this house that you would *'keep the facts hidden from public scrutiny to protect your own reputation and pay others for their silence'*? Those are your words, Sir Lowen, paraphrased, of course. You have employed me to find the truth. What truth are you looking for?"

"Come, Detective, I think it is time to open the doors of the ballroom. They have remained closed all these months. We will talk there."

As I followed Sir Lowen down a long, narrow

293

corridor, I looked over my shoulder and saw Lady Celia walking in the other direction. Her head was held high. She was a proud woman.

\* \* \*

Sir Lowen closed the ornamental doors to the ballroom once we had set foot inside. He had not returned here since the tragedy of New Year's Eve and only the police had come to this place since then.

Electric lights illuminated the imposing room with its exquisite silk tapestries adorning each wall, a domed ceiling of gold leaf and peacock-blue carvings, and lush ivory-coloured, *peau de soie* curtains with matching ballroom chairs. Glass vases were filled with white feathers and black beads.

Gold and red sequins lay scattered on every table, and strewn on the scuffed, mahogany parquet floor were party masks of flamboyant colour and design: *Pierrot* the clown; *Harlequin*, the mischievous and amusing trickster; Harlequin's mistress and comic servant *Columbina*; the unscrupulous and villainous *Scaramouche*; boaster and braggart *Il Capitano*; and the greedy *Pantelone*.

The hint of sour champagne and stale smoke – a ripe blend of cigarettes and cigars – still hung in the air and nestled uncomfortably at the back of my throat as I surveyed the crime scene. I walked slowly around the room and was acutely aware of my own footsteps. I tried to imagine the scene.

I could almost hear the singing and shouting from

that shameful New Year's Eve and, for a moment in my mind's eye, I thought I saw a puff of smoke from one of the spent pistol swords. I sat down at one of the tables at the far end of the room and bellowed across the empty space to make a leading point.

"What did the police say, Sir Lowen? I assume they made a thorough investigation, examined the weapons, interviewed your guests . . . those who attended and those who did not? Surely, the police came to their own conclusion. You have not spoken of this."

Sir Lowen remained standing.

"The police came by the following morning. We came to an understanding. We agreed that Edmund and Victor's death was accidental, exactly as reported in *The Illustrated London News* the following week. Unknown to the police, I also agreed to pay each guest attending the masquerade ball £5,000 for their co-operation and loyalty."

"You mean their silence. That is bribery!"

"Call it what you will. I'm not proud of it. It had to be done."

"Five thousand pounds is a great deal of money, Sir Lowen."

"I would have paid anything to protect my family name and the reputation of my sons from such a loathsome end. The death of my two sons, Detective, is hard enough to endure, not to mention the ruination of my reputation, perhaps my career and, above all else, the well-being of my wife. All of these things weighed heavily upon me. I dared not risk any of it. My decision had to be quick, forceful and effective. Whether their deaths were an accident or intentional – and I know not which – the events of New Year's Eve had to remain here, in this room. I had to avoid the public shame and humiliation at all costs."

"Your sons are dead. Neither of us can change that. What happened in this room, Sir Lowen?"

Sir Lowen's face was animated and his voice bold as if he were making an announcement to an attentive audience.

"Edmund was going to announce his engagement during the masquerade ball on the eve of his twenty-first birthday My son was going to wed!"

"To whom?"

"Henrietta Worthing. She had just turned nineteen. My wife and I adored her. Such a sweet, loving child. Henrietta and Edmund were inseparable and loved each other more than I can say. She comes from a well-respected family – not short of a penny or two, either. Have you heard of the Worthings? They own a great deal of property in London. Her father is a keen sportsman, hunting mainly. He also has an excellent antique gun collection."

Sir Lowen sat down. I walked across the room to join him.

"On the afternoon of the party. I heard Edmund and Victor quarrelling over something. Their voices were muffled. A short while later, a package was delivered to the house.

"A package?"

"Yes, from Henrietta. I assumed it was a birthday present for Edmund. It was wrapped in Henrietta's red

Paisley silk scarf that Edmund had given to her for Christmas. I do not know why she used the scarf or why she did not come into the house. She left straight away before Kingsley had a chance to deliver the gift."

"Kingsley?"

"The Butler."

"Yes, of course. And the package, Sir Lowen? Surely you must have known the contents. Edmund and Victor lived under your roof. You are your sons' father. I will wager it was two pistol swords that was Henrietta's gift to Edmund's was it not?"

"Why would Henrietta have possession of my pistol swords, Detective? I do not understand the logic?"

"This will become clear as my theory builds on the facts. In the meantime, I wish to know Henerietta's state of mind."

"She looked pale and tired. She had been crying."

"One woman loved by two brothers? Was that it, Sir Lowen? Was Victor jealous of his brother, Edmund? His bride? His forthcoming marriage? Or was it Edmund, who became suspicious of his own brother's feelings towards Henrietta?"

There was a knock on the ballroom door. I turned my head as the doors opened and saw Lady Celia with her hand planted squarely on the shoulder of a tall, slender young lady.

"Please forgive me Lady Celia and Sir Lowen. I took the liberty of inviting Miss Henrietta to the house. I thought it best that I meet with her at once."

Henrietta bowed her head and smiled courteously.

Sir Lowen and I stood up as Lady Celia prompted

Henrietta to enter the ballroom and join us. Lady Celia closed the ballroom doors behind her and left the three of us alone.

"It is lovely to see you again, Henrietta," said Sir Lowen. "It has been much too long. You look well. I am so pleased to see you. May I introduce you to Detective Roule? I am sure you have heard his name before."

"It is indeed a most pleasant surprise to meet you in person, Henrietta," I replied. "Thank you for accepting my invitation."

"You are most welcome, Detective Roule, I have heard your name spoken in our household on many occasions. I have been looking forward to answering your questions, for I have been suffocating with guilt for far too long."

I nodded my appreciation. Her voice was soft and gentle and reminded me of a spring flower. Although I had not met Edmund, I understood in a heartbeat his attraction for such a charming young woman.

"Please, shall we sit?"

Henrietta was visibly affected by the atmosphere and tried to hide her emotions from Sir Lowen's enquiring eyes.

"Henrietta . . . with your permission," I began, "I have a raft of questions circling around in my busy mind. Although I am certain I know where the answers will lead, I do not know why. It is a fact that Edmund and Victor died here in this room on their twenty-first birthday during the masquerade ball."

Henrietta nodded in accordance with my statement.

"Was it an accident or was it suicide, or something else? This is what we must know. Sir Lowen will not find peace until the truth is told and my work in this matter will be incomplete. And I fear that you too will not find peace until this matter is put to rest."

Henrietta clutched her face, trying to disguise her sadness, her fear, her remorse! Sir Lowen and I waited patiently until she was ready to speak.

"Edmund loved me. He told me so every time we were together. And I loved him. I made no secret of that either. That is the simple truth, Detective. Victor loved his brother very much too and the three of us spent considerable time together. I did not object. I would soon be Edmund's wife and that was all that mattered to me. Edmund and Victor often played practical jokes on each other. Victor's pranks were often crude and reckless. I was not amused by their behaviour. Then, things began to change."

"What things and when?" I asked.

"During the past six months. Their manners . . . "

Henrietta's voice cracked as her emotions surged. Her eyes filled with tears.

"Are you all right, my dear?" asked Sir Lowen.

"Yes, I am sorry. Please let me continue."

"Yes, of course," I added. "As long as you wish to carry on."

"Yes Detective, I must tell you everything. I will be fine. Mr Bittersman – Sir Lowen – must know what I have done. I cannot bear it any longer."

I could not hide my anticipation as I quickly regarded Sir Lowen. My own theory of events, before, during and after the masquerade ball on that New Year's Eve was quickly taking shape and I was self-assured that Henrietta would provide the missing facts to prove me correct.

"Edmund and Victor appeared to be the same person. They had the same expressions, the same way of speaking and the same habits, and often dressed the same. They were identical twins . . . impossible to tell apart. They had their own quirks and mannerism of course and could fool you if they wanted to do so. And often, they did. To them it was a game of trickery and deceit – for the fun it. They did it because they could. They even managed to baffle and confuse their friends at their own time and choosing. It was Victor's idea. Then Edmund joined in the deception. Soon, I became their victim, their source of diversion and ridicule. Victor pretended to be Edmund and Edmund became Victor. I could not tell them apart, one from the other! They took me dancing, to parties, to dinner, to shows . . . and to *bed*, sharing me like a common dockyard whore when all the time I thought I was with Edmund – my future husband. And they bragged about their exploits to their friends, and how they could manipulate me like a puppet on a string, for that is how I came to learn what they had done to me for so long. I was afraid of hearing the truth. I didn't want to know. I pretended it wasn't so and could not accept my own ignorance."

Henrietta was inconsolable. She could not resist the natural urge to cry her heart out. Sir Lowen took her hands, bidding her to stand by his side so he could wrap his arms around her as the father he would never become. His tenderness was most touching.

I waited for nearly a minute before diving in to cross-examine the star witness. The finish line was close at hand.

"My dear child, I was unaware of your torment," said Sir Lowen. "I was unable to see the truth for what it was and for that alone I have failed as a father to my own children. I can never forgive myself."

"It is not your fault, Sir Lowen," I said. "Parents are usually, if not always, the last to know. You must not blame yourself for your sons' deceit. Things happen in this life over which we have no control."

"Dear Henrietta, my heart is with you," I said. "You are a brave girl for being here and talking to us. All I ask of you is a few more minutes of your time."

Henrietta wiped her eyes and forced a smile.

"You took the two pistol swords home, didn't you?"

"Yes."

"You took a measured amount of gunpowder and lead shot for each of the two pistol swords from your father's gun collection, didn't you?"

"Yes. I had seen my father do it on various occasions. He enjoyed the ritual of loading and firing his antique pistols. But how could I have known that the pistol swords would discharge as they did? It was pure chance and bad luck."

"Was that your birthday gift to Edmund – the two boxed pistol swords you had taken in secret – wrapped in a red Paisley silk scarf that Edmund had given to you for Christmas?"

"Yes."

"What did you hope to achieve, my dear?"

"They hurt me more than my words could ever explain. I could not love Edmund anymore for what he had done, and I could never marry him. I made up my mind to teach them both a lesson. To frighten them and maybe hurt them – each with their own injury and pain – but not to kill them – oh my God, please believe me! Not that! I should have known they would bring those silly pistol swords to the ball and show off in front of everyone."

"Including yourself? For you were there as well!"

"Only to undo what I had already done. I thought it over – realised it was a mistake. I couldn't go through with it. I was afraid for them. When I arrived, Edmund and Victor were already playacting, swinging their pistol swords at each other. I screamed and struggled to reach them through the crowded room. Nobody took any notice of me. I was helpless to stop their stupid game by any means and prayed it would end before anything bad –"

She covered her mouth with both hands and gasped for breath. Nonetheless, I continued with my interview.

"Months after the incident, you contacted *The Daily Telegraph*, didn't you?"

She nodded.

"And the poem? A fine piece of writing. A secret confession of sorts, or at least an attempt to tell the world what really happened. And yet, my dear Henrietta, you told the *Telegraph* that it was *'a cold-blooded, double-suicide-murder pact between two brothers'* when you knew otherwise. Why?"

302

"*Anger – hatred – revenge* for what they had done to me! It was my way of getting even. It was time for them to be ridiculed. It was foolish, I know."

"This is terribly confusing, Detective Roule," said Sir Lowen. "I cannot say that I understand one word you are saying. Am I, once again, the last to know?"

"Please sit, both of you. First, let me say to Sir Lowen, that I am overcome with deep sorrow for the misfortune that has beset your family and hope that you might find it in your heart to forgive Henrietta. To you, my dear Henrietta, I wholeheartedly understand the motive and full import of your actions, driven by the deeds of others. Edmund and Victor accidentally and unknowingly killed each other. Was it murder and if so, by whom? That question is for others to decide. Let us not forget, there was malice on both sides to be sure. Tell me, who bears the greater guilt: the man who knowingly degrades and humiliates a woman, or a woman who attempts to exact revenge upon the man? And as to the verse you have penned, Henrietta –"

"Yes, Detective," said Sir Lowen, "I am more than eager to know what it means!"

"It is an oxymoron. Call it a literary paradox if you have a mind to. Henrietta's account of the crime is a contradiction of events. Meaning is muddled, confused – simply absurd. And yet . . . I shall prove otherwise! Let us take the first three lines, shall we?"

> On a dark and stormy night,
> When the sun was shining bright,
> Two dead boys stood up to fight.

303

I will dispense with the *night*. It is always *dark* by nature, is it not? And it was New Year's Eve!"

"Yes, continue," said Sir Lowen.

"*Stormy*, however, is another matter. It is true to say – correct me if I am wrong – that in recent months Henrietta's relationship with your sons, and not just with Edmund alone, was anything except idyllic."

"Sir Lowen nodded in agreement.

"Based on Henrietta's version of events, the affair was volatile and tempestuous. Passionate and wild, one might add without objection. In other words, her relationship with Edmund – and with Victor posing as Edmund – was *stormy* to say the least!"

"I see now where you are heading, Detective," said Sir Lowen.

Henrietta sat upright. She looked composed, almost serene as her eyes never left my face.

"Sir Lowen, am I correct in assuming that Lady Celia wore a Venetian sun mask to the ball?"

"Why, yes! How did you know – ?"

"An educated guess . . . call it the *Roule of Logic*."

"Bravo Detective!" replied Sir Lowen.

"Even I will agree that it is impossible for the *sun* to shine at night, unless we are talking about something completely different – in this case, the masquerade ball, the scene of the crime. Lady Celia was no doubt, shall I say, glittering in her costume and glowing with pride – *shining bright* – on this wonderful New Year's Eve celebration in her sun mask."

"You are an inspiration, Detective."

Henrietta did not stir or speak.

"According to your own words, Sir Lowen, Edmund and Victor *'pretended to be stabbed and die . . . falling to the floor, only to stand up again as quickly to begin their theatrical performance over and over again'*.

"That would account for the *'two dead boys'* who *'stood up to fight'*. Is it not obvious?"

Sir Lowen simply nodded.

"It is also true, I put to you, that in keeping with the flamboyant and obviously extravagant nature of their personalities, Edmund and Victor wore not *one* costume, but *two* costumes of the same character! Call it a simple illusion and a clever one at that."

Back-to-back they faced each other,
Drew their swords and shot each other.

Henrietta was captivated by my interpretation as I continued to unravel the oxymoron she had set to verse.

"Your narrative, Detective, is uncanny . . . accurate in every detail," said Sir Lowen.

"As for the swords, it has been well established that Edmund and Victor handled pistol swords from your own collection. The logic of drawing their swords and shooting each other requires no further clarification. It is obvious, is it not?"

"And now, I come to the ending of the verse and the most important pieces of this puzzle."

A deaf policeman heard the noise,
And came to save the two dead boys.

"I put it to you that the part of the deaf policeman was played by Henrietta herself."

Henrietta's eyes alone confirmed my assumption.

"I don't understand," said Sir Lowen.

I looked directly at Henrietta.

"Your deafness stemmed not from your head, but from your heart, for you refused to hear what others had been saying about Victor's trickery and manipulation of his own brother's fiancée – you, my dear Henrietta. You were powerless to listen to your own confusing thoughts . . . *deaf* to all well-intentioned advice. You have also told us, here in this room only moments ago: *'I was afraid of hearing the truth. I didn't want to know. I pretended it wasn't so'*. That you came back to save Edmund and Victor from harm is not in question. *'I was helpless to stop their game by any means'* you admitted. I believe you. And so, my dear Henrietta, you came to the masquerade ball attired in a striking red and black costume of intricate design and fabrication. You also wore a finely crafted mask – your tacit lips painted a blood red no doubt. In addition, I am of the belief that you wore a resplendent headdress brimming with an array of grand embellishments in matching shades of red and black so that you would not be recognised as you tried to stop the chain of events from reaching its grisly climax."

"How did you know," asked Henrietta.

"For me it is obvious, my dear. *Red* is the colour of anger, passion and danger. *Black* is the colour of evil, darkness and despair. And what better symbol can there be for law and justice – a figure of authority to settle disputes – than a *policeman*? You wrapped yourself in these two colours of red and back to elevate your confidence and to embolden your actions."

"You are remarkable, Detective."

"You are most kind, Sir Lowen. Once again, the *Roule of logic*."

Henrietta wiped her tears.

"Finally, I come to the last two lines of the verse, and to *you*, Sir Lowen."

> If you don't believe the tale I've told,
> Ask the blind man who saw it unfold.

"Like Henrietta, you too, had an affliction of the heart. You too, were blind to your sons' games, blind to the reality under your own roof. And, to a degree, not even Edmund's own father – *you sir* – were able to see what was happening to this beautiful, young woman, whose love of your son ended in tragedy. By your own words, you have admitted: *'I was unable to see the truth for what it was and for that alone I have failed as a father to my own children'*. You were blind to the real truth that killed your two sons and feared it would destroy your name and reputation. You have implored me, Sir Lowen, to find the truth and now you have it."

Sir Lowen's solemnity was to be expected.

"I will of course tell Lady Celia exactly what we have discussed and I alone, take full responsibility for the tragic events that have stained this family's name. As for your fee, Detective Roule –"

I dismissed Sir Lowen's financial intention with a

307

wave of my hand.

"My fee is of no concern to me, personally. I would prefer that Henrietta receive what you think is fair for my services so that she may use it for her own legal defence, should you wish to bring charges against her. I am a mere detective, Sir Lowen, not the police or a courtroom judge."

Henrietta and Sir Lowen stared at me, unable to grasp that the case of *The Oxymoron Murders* had at last been solved.

It would be remiss of me to end the story here, without revealing Sir Lowen's decision. You will be pleased to hear that Henrietta retained the full amount of my fee, to use as she wished, as Sir Lowen had no intention of bringing charges of any nature against her for the *unintentional* death of his two sons.

Moreover, at the time of writing, he was planning to meet with the Editor of *The Daily Telegraph* to set the record straight, as he put it. He also made a solemn promise to Henrietta that her name would never be mentioned from this day forth to anyone in connection with the events at *Druid's Fell Manor* on New Year's Eve in 1910.

I look forward to reading Sir Lowen's account.

# Acknowledgements

*Front Cover*
Designed by Tim Jones

*Front Cover Image*
Helena Jankovičová Kováčová
(pexels.com)

*Author's Picture*
Elaine Myers

\* \* \*

*A special thank you to my dear friends*:
*Barry Freud* for his generous encouragement,
unflagging enthusiasm, and meticulous reading;
and *Ruth Rabin* for her time, her remarkable
attention to detail and for helping me stay on track.

I am also grateful to *Mary Jo Tomori* for her support
and being part of the journey; and *Rob Doe* for his
specialist knowledge for 'Stolen'.

# Story Notes

This collection of short stories is a work of fiction. Any similarity of characters and their names to individuals living or dead, is entirely coincidental. All characters and dialogue, events, towns, cities, places and street names are invented for dramatic style and effect. Additional notes are also provided for further clarification between fact and fiction.

### North of 58
*Bayport Plaza*, the *Duke of Marlborough School*, the *Churchill Volunteer Fire Department* and the *Iceberg Inn*, two miles southeast of the Churchill River, are real places. Other travel and geographical facts, including the comings and goings of wildlife in Northern Manitoba, are also accurate to the best of my knowledge in this whimsical encounter with a *snow woman*. Her name, *Nutaryuk*, is from the Inuit language, and means 'fresh snow'. *Hathaway's Hardware* in Winnipeg is fictitious,

### The Brewster Boy
The leading edge of the lightning bolt struck the top of Henry's head and emerged through his shoes, irradiating his entire body like a special effect in a macabre horror film. Unfinished business, no matter what it might be, can sometimes take on a supernatural life of its own. *The Crow's Nest* pub and *Returned to Life* recycling centre are both fictitious.

**The Competition**
Tourist attractions and pre-booked excursions elsewhere in our solar system, while fanciful to say the least, should not be discarded outright as impossible. The future has an uncanny way of revealing all manner of unfathomable surprises. While *The Daily Encounter* and *Martian Media* are fictitious, the opposite is true for the *Tower of Babel*; suggested locations for the *Nevis Rue* hotel; *Olympus Mons*; and previous space missions to Mars such as *Viking*, *Pathfinder*, *Spirit*, *Opportunity*, *Phoenix*, *Curiosity*, *InSight*, and *Perseverance*.

**The Allotment Business**
The *Coronovirus* (Covid-19) and the need to stockpile toilet paper will never be forgotten. Panic-stricken people and their obsessive demand for such household basics should not be underestimated. A mother and daughter take things into their own hands – *literally* – when the opportunity arises. *Shadow Glen*, the name of the local neighbourhood allotment, is fictitious.

**Mystery Weekend**
Four thousand years ago, there existed two legendary cities of ancient Palestine along the south-eastern coast of the Dead Sea: *Soddom* and *Gomorrah*. The story of a woman turned into a pillar of stone, according to the *Book of Genesis*, is revisited. As to its timely connection with the mystery weekend at *Chillgrave Castle*, you'll have to be the judge of that. The latter is fictitious, along with the castle's founder, *Lord Bonnie the Tranquil*; and *The Mystery Weekend Players*.

**It's About Time**
Who hasn't thought about staying young and turning the clock back? We dream about it most days, if not all the time. Two men experience both the pleasure and the pain of doing just that and come to realise that nothing is given away for free. Historical references to the *Battle of Paardeberg* during the *Boer War* are accurate to the best of my knowledge, while *Little Dewsford* and *The Barking Goats* pub are fictional.

**What's Your Complaint?**
We complain all the time – morning, noon and night. It's part of the human psyche and one of life's annoying habits. However, complaining can also affect our ability to learn and remember new things as part of our brain actually shrinks, according to medical studies. Not that I'm complaining about it. Tune into the *Jimmy Dreem Show* from *Times Square* in New York to learn more. The latter is fictitious, along with Nia-Rose Sale, her charity *Women Evolving*, and the website she founded, called *What's Your Complaint? University College London* is real.

**The Hotel Midnight**
Inexplicable things happen to us all the time. Imagine stumbling *into* an oil painting! It's 1936 at *The Hotel Midnight* where music and love prevail. Is there a way back from this time warp? *It Don't Mean a Thing (If It Ain't Got That Swing)* was composed by Duke Ellington in 1931, lyrics by Irving Mills. *Isn't It Romantic?* was composed by Richard Rodgers in 1932, lyrics by Lorenz Hart. Also genuine are *Nat Sherman* cigars; *1936 Veuve A Devaux Black Neck* champagne; and the *Louis Armstrong Special* (trumpet) designed by American jazz trumpeter and vocalist, Louis Armstrong in association with instrument designer/manufacturer, Henri Selmer, in Paris, circa 1933. Also real is *Canary Wharf. The Hotel Midnight* and *The Crescendo* jazz club are both fictitious.

**The Obsession of Alfred Paige**
For one man, collecting books takes on new meaning. A simple fact of human imperfection – frailty at its very core – comes to light. Ignored or forgotten, we are stuck with a unique fact of life and a vile capacity to alter the truth for our own selfish gain and preservation. We LIE!

**Adriana and the Hot Air Balloon**
Traumatic events have a way of surprising us. In the end, good things can often prevail. The crash of a hot air balloon and subsequent fire is a case in point. Details about wooden pallets in this short story are accurate to the best of my knowledge, while

*Harper Wood Landscape Gardeners*; and *Celebrity Homes and Gardens* magazine are both fictitious.

**The Dictionary**
The meaning of words – written *and* spoken –has reached a critical stage in society. Language in has lost its clarity, no thanks to mobile phones and the internet. To set things right, everyone is issued with an official dictionary from the fictional *Ministry of Meaning*. It's the only dictionary you are permitted to use. Lose it at your peril and hope the *Random Inspection Patrol* – also fictional – doesn't coming knocking on your door. After all, it is 2029.

**A Memory of Love**
If there's one flight of fancy that we can never relinquish, it is our yearning to influence the laws of the universe, change a moment in our life and, if we're lucky enough, alter the course of events that have already disappeared from our lives, never to return. We carry this failed, tragic endeavour in our hearts until the end.

**Stolen**
Time and time again, we rise to the occasion to get what we want. We are always clever and resourceful. Hacked computer files, unintentional consequence, a stolen drone, lies and extortion play out in the ruins of *Urquhart Castle*, southwest of Inverness on the west shore of Loch Ness. The latter is real. Tristan Teller's first novel, *Loose Chippings*; *The Limelight Assembly Hall*; *The Write Plot*; and the *Night Drone Endurance Challenge* over Loch Ness in the Scottish Highlands are all fictional.

**The Biography**
Would you read a biography about your life, especially if it had been written by someone you didn't know and had never met? How would you react? Who would you tell? *Jason Marvel: The Unauthorised Love Story* by Cristal Rivers – the book in question – is fictious, as are *Westview General Hospital*; *The Tringwood Summer Carnival*; and *Tringwood Memorial Park*.

313

**The Oxymoron Murders**

Nonsense poems, hymns and folksongs have been handed down from generation to generation, with more variations than you can imagine. I call them *oxymorons*, where meaning is contradictory or simply absurd. In this short story, I set out to prove otherwise. The oxymoron I have adapted represents a young girl's confession to a crime. Was it suicide, murder or an unavoidable accident? The scene is set at the fictional *Druid's Fell Manor*: a masquerade ball on New Year's Eve, 1910. Detective Roule unravels 'the impossible'. Making guest appearances in this fictional tale, and in name only, are: *Thomas Hardy*, the English novelist; Spanish painter, *Pablo Picasso*; British socialite and actress, *Lillie Langtry*; and English composer, *Ralph Vaughn Williams*. Also genuine are *Juan Lopez* Cuban cigars; *Constantino Colheita Port – 1900*; the Rolls Royce *Silver Ghost*, once known as 'the best car in the world'; and the flintlock pistol sword, circa 1700. In 1891, Irish poet and playwright, Oscar Wilde's first novel, *The Picture of Dorian Gray*, was published by Ward, Lock and Co. Although *The Illustrated London News* (1842-2003) existed at the time, the story alluded to on 7 January 1911 is a fabrication.

# Other Books
# By the Same Author

*Twenty Million Leagues Above the Sea*

The gravitational attraction between the Earth and the Moon suddenly stops. The breach lasts no longer than the time it takes to tie a shoelace, but there are dire consequences for anything caught inside this unpredictable corridor of invisible dark energy. On July 20, 1969, the day of the Apollo 11 Moon Landing, Milo Storm and his two teenage friends fall upon this supercharged void and are hurled into deep space where others are also marooned – twenty million leagues above the sea. Facing annihilation from a super comet and the gravitational pull of a black hole, life goes on. Friendships blossom and relationships evolve into everlasting love as the reluctant navigators attempt to find a way home against all odds. Secrets are guarded and exposed. None greater than the legendary treasure of the Incas lost four centuries earlier, and now one man's obsession to hoard and hide his priceless cache until he can get it back to Earth. An idea, a plan, but at what cost aboard an impossible saviour – the most infamous ghost ship that ever sailed the seas? Is there a way back from the brink of extinction? Milo Storm takes us back to that July day in 1969, capturing every twist and turn of this unpredictable epic adventure!

*e-book* October 2017
*Paperback* January 2018
*New Edition* January 2020 (340 Pages)
ASIN: 1973224437. ISBN: 9781973224433

## The Colour Conspiracy

Declan Wilder, a veteran reporter for *The Daily Capital* newspaper, falls victim to a plot of grand deception. Set up from day one, Declan is manipulated, bullied and blackmailed by MI7 – the purveyors of propaganda since World War I – to report global events. But are the stories true or simply fake news? People do whatever it takes to gain the advantage and profit by deceit. A black dye that absorbs the entire visible spectrum of light is stolen and its inventor murdered. Reflected light, and colour, are denied to your senses. Your brain is confused, unable to determine what rightly appears before your eyes. Objects are disfigured and unrecognisable. A deadly recipe that distorts reality is a must-have weapon for extremists, political adversaries and irrational individuals operating in the corridors of political power or lurking on the streets of our great cities. How will the dye's formula be used? And who are the Black Phantoms that terrify London? Driven to save his reputation and career, Declan Wilder embarks on a plan to unravel the chain of lies and trickery and discover the truth. Above all else, he must protect the woman he loves at all costs for she is at the heart of a conspiracy that is spiralling out of control.

*e-book* January 2020
*Paperback* January 2020 (280 Pages)
ASIN: 1655630482; ISBN: 9781655630484

## *I Shot the Sheriff*

Sheriff Smoker is no longer a lawman by title or deed. Just a man, bewailing the life he had lived and the woman he left behind more than twenty years earlier, trying to undo the one great mistake of his life. When he retires in 1899, aged sixty, Smoker makes the long journey from Amarillo to San Francisco to see Bella Watters, the most famous opera singer of her time – and the only woman Smoker had ever loved – give her farewell performance. Had it not been for A chance meeting in Deadwood and the cold-blooded murder of Wild Bill Hickok in '76, there would be no story to tell and no life-changing secrets to uncover. Old paths cross and new adventures begin as The Gambler, The Bounty Hunter, The Prostitute and the infamous Wilcox Train Robbery threaten to destroy everything. A frenzied chain of events accelerates at an alarming pace until the legendary shoot-out in Union Square throws everything into chaos and sends everyone scrambling for survival.

*e-book* February 2021
*Paperback* February 2021 (222 Pages)
ASIN: B08X63B789; ISBN: 9798701973242

Printed by Amazon Italia Logistica S.r.l.
Torrazza Piemonte (TO), Italy

37779195R00187